PRAY

For The

DEVIL

MAGGIE MAXFIELD

Also by Maggie Maxfield

STEPULI CHRONICLES DUET

Stepuli Chronicles: The Tracks We Leave
Stepuli Chronicles: The Souls of Men: Coming Soon

THE DEATH WITCH SERIES

Pray For the Devil
Devil In the Details: Coming Soon
Deal With the Devil: Coming Soon

To my Dad, whose favorite author is Stephen King. And to Ian, my wonderful husband, who has to do a lot more laundry and dishes when I'm writing. Love you, babe.

One

Eliza

The old woman's mouth curled cruelly. Her lank hair fell around her shoulders, and her eyes peered at me from their sunken sockets. Gooseflesh broke out across my skin, and it wasn't from the cold, wet New England day. I stared back grimly, and her smile widened.

In resignation, I broke off the path I had been walking to St. Peter's and wound my way through the graveyard, hundreds-of-years-old tombstones crumbling. I wondered what had made her choose this place.

I kept my eyes on the ground as I closed the distance between us, careful not to tread across any graves. I felt her presence in front of me and finally looked up, meeting her eyes. My gut clenched. I braced myself against the cruelty in them. Her mouth opened, and blackness enveloped me.

I woke up staring at the gray sky. My back was soaking wet, and a soft mist covered my face. I shivered, this time from the cold. As I sat up, I slicked back my dark hair, wiping my sleeves across my eyes to clear the wet blurriness. I had been right. She wasn't a nice woman. She had spent her life entrenched in gluttony so severe her toes had rotted off her feet. The diabetes had been so uncontrolled it had shut down her kidneys, and her body had refused to keep her alive.

In the end, the pain from her flesh rotting away had driven her mad. She struck out at anyone trying to give her care. She hadn't wanted dignity. She hadn't wanted solace. She had ached for her coming death. She had lunged for it. And she had hated anyone near her who had dared try to keep it from taking her. She had seen me as no less of an adversary. I had been her last step between this life and hopefully a better next.

I glanced at my watch as I rose to my feet. My stiff joints informed me I had been out longer than usual. My heart began to race when I saw how long. The convent had expected me back over an hour ago. Mother Superior would hear about this. The fear of her disappointment and others' questions was as sharp at twenty-five as it was as a child. I hastily exited the graveyard, heading down the small-town street to the spire breaking above the buildings and trees. A beacon of hope to some, of judgment to others, and a beckoning to me. To return to my life, my home, and my prison.

I drew glances from the early passersby heading to their breakfasts at our local café. As I turned onto the busier street the cathedral's entrance sat on, I imagined what I looked like, soaked through, dirt on my habit, and my face blotchy from cold and exertion. I kept my eyes down, not meeting anyone's curious glance, and pasted a tight-lipped smile on my face. The rusty iron gate sitting on the right side of the polished stone steps creaked as I opened it, and I rushed into the courtyard, where we could walk and say our prayers, down into the basement quarters where the nuns lived.

Sister Olivia walked toward me, and I put my head down, intending to rush past her to my room. I couldn't go to my class like this. It would be worse than not going at all. I would take a quick shower and change my clothes so I wasn't so tardy I missed the entire thing.

"Eliza, my God!" Olivia slapped a hand over her mouth at her slip. The corner of my mouth quirked, but I suppressed the smile. Olivia was so good, so pure. She looked like an angel with her blond hair haloing around her apple cheeks. A contrast to my brown hair and angular face. She would torture herself for taking the Lord's name for the next week.

I felt antsy but stopped and enveloped her warm hands with my chilled ones. Her wide eyes glanced down at them before looking back up at me. "It's okay, Olivia. I went to the local cemetery to pray, and I think I must have fallen asleep. I need to make myself presentable so I can get to my class."

She nodded as if my explanation made sense. At this point, most of the nuns were used to my oddity. Olivia, kind to everyone, was never derisive of it.

"I'm so sorry for my vulgarity. I was just so surprised. You look like death!"

I snorted, trying to turn it into a cough. Olivia, with her sinful curves perpetually hidden beneath the habit, *would* think her words were vulgar. I squeezed Olivia's hands a final time before turning away. Her words hit me, and I said over my shoulder as I walked away, "I suppose you're not wrong."

After a scalding shower to warm my bones and hopefully melt the frost off my soul, I dressed in a clean habit and rushed up the back stairs to the classrooms above. Having grown up in Catholic orphanages, I had tried to break free from the Church to live my own life. I had always been reckless though. After too many hard life lessons and no real idea of how to take care of myself, I had returned to take my vows.

I worried my lip. Anxiety about being late weighed on me. It was in my nature to want those around me to be happy with me. Their approval had meant my survival when I was young, and somehow this had saturated my adult psyche so much that it was second nature. I chafed from the walls built around me, wanting to explore the world, but after my first attempt at breaking away, it had always felt too big, too impossible. For better or worse, this was my family now. I tried to ignore the creeping feeling that it had always felt wrong.

The door creaked as I opened it. The old building, built in the 1800s, hindered sleuthing. I winced as every head in the class turned to me. Local parishioners used to receive their Sunday sermons in this large wooden room. The high ceilings made you feel like you were in a cathedral. The pews had been rebuilt as rows of student desks, ascending to allow as much room as possible and help the instructor's voice carry. Father Paul frowned at me, his thin face framed by short, cropped dark hair, and his hawkish nose stark in his disapproval.

I cleared my throat and continued to my seat without a word. Excuses would just make this worse, and I tended to ramble when nervous. You could hear a pin drop as I headed to my seat. I felt the father's eyes bore into me the entire way, sending a shiver down my spine.

He was a severe man. I would say bordering on cruel, but then I would have to say a Hail Mary for him, and I'd rather pee on his burning corpse. As one of the most lauded exorcists alive today, he was our natural instructor, but having encountered this man throughout my childhood due to my "oddity," I couldn't help but harbor a grudge.

"Now that we're all here, though some of us chose to arrive when they were supposed to and respect everyone's time," a few of the other postulants turned toward me, and I shifted, "we can continue."

I finally found the courage to look up from my lap, feeling the combined weight of everyone's glances. Father Paul pulled down the projector and retrieved his pointer from the podium. "I was waiting for our final peer to arrive to go into today's task. We have a new patient in the infirmary, and it may be the evilest possession the Church has ever encountered."

A collective murmur rose around me from a scattered group of men and women. The men tended to hold an archaic view of women, supported by the Old Testament's decree for women to serve, while the women maintained an almost guilty curiosity. In recent years, the attendance for male exorcists had dropped so low as to be deemed a crisis by the Church. As such, they had finally, officially, opened attendance to women.

Next to me, Sam whispered, "Finally, something more than just a wandering eye or an incurable urge for petty theft."

Michael, on his other side, whispered back, laughter barely contained, "I can't wait to see a head spin or someone crawl on the walls like in the movies."

I rolled my eyes when Father Paul answered them, their whispers not inconspicuous in the least.

"Yes, well, your excitement may be tempered when you meet the entity." As he finished, his eyes fell on me, and I fidgeted again, my brows coming together in consternation at the intensity of his stare. "We feel this class is uniquely qualified to handle this very special possession. A possession we believe has been active but somehow in stasis for…well, for centuries."

A cacophony of voices erupted as everyone began speaking at once. Dread pooled in my stomach. Father Paul maintained eye contact with me for a moment longer, a corner of his thin, cruel mouth lifting before he turned away and continued briefing us on our newest patient's circumstances.

When he was done speaking, the class filed out after him

toward the infirmary, their excitement palpable in the nervous chatter and the way people eagerly crowded into the hallway. Instead of excitement, a chill crept through me. Father Paul's keen interest in me on a day I was tardy, on a day I'd had a crossing, didn't bode well for me. Especially as I voluntarily descended into my worst nightmare with him.

As a child, I could see the dead. I had asked a sister why a civil war reenactment soldier always wandered the grounds. She rapped my hands so severely it hurt to write and told me never to tell my "stories" again. I made the mistake again when a sister I had been close to tragically died. I saw her that night while I lay down to sleep. Her eyes had been so sad and her spirit so careful as she had passed through me to what, at even a young age, I had understood to be the other side. I told Mother Superior about it the next day, eager to reassure the nuns who had been her friends and family that she was at peace. This time, the beating was across my back, and I never talked about what I saw again.

Because of my visions and my relationship with the dead, talk had been tossed around of me being possessed. They had spoken of sending me to the infirmary when it first opened in my teens. Legendary for being the first infirmary based in the United States, the Church was eager to show its value.

Mother Superior had stopped it, declaring, "She is a fanciful child, not a possessed one. After repenting for her lies, she has never pretended again." Having grown up in the Catholic Girls House, an orphanage dressed up as a school for unwanted children, I knew what a gift she was giving me and adamantly agreed my wicked imagination was tamed.

But I never stopped seeing the dead, never stopped feeling when those who came to me for passage to *somewhere* left this plane and went on to the next. I started calling them crossings. I was pretty sure Father Paul, one of the loudest voices calling for my exorcism, also never forgot. His constant attention always gave me goosebumps.

I bumped into Sam in front of me with a grunt. We had stopped at the doors. They required key card access, and even as practitioners, we weren't granted access yet. Our exorcisms were still performed only under supervision. Sam looked back at me, his light sandy hair tousled and his boyish features concerned. His brow quirked in question. I smiled back reassuringly. I knew he had a crush on me. He always went out of his way to be attentive. After my experience during my gap year, as I called it, I didn't encourage it. Never mind that we both had taken a vow of celibacy, one broken often these days, something about his earnestness, his devotion to the Church, kept me from ever trusting him or myself to get too close. Still, I saw him as an ally in the postulant class. And I didn't have a lot of those. His mouth pulled to the side in a frown, but he nodded before turning back.

Father Paul, at the head of the group, pulled all our attention when he began to speak. "We will go in four at a time, in working groups. The infirmary is not built for a large postulant class such as this. Afterward, we will go back to the classroom, and you will be given a research assignment. Whoever completes it to my satisfaction will be elected to be a part of the working group that will exorcise the demon from this…*being*." With that, he led the first group through the automatic doors.

I frowned at his pause and choice of words. A precept of exorcism school was that we treated people, victims of an affliction. We always humanized the person, no matter how far gone or how awful the powers the demon who possessed them exerted.

Our postulant class was made of eight students, and I had fallen to the back of the line of the second group, with one person behind me. There was a low hum of activity, everyone murmuring to each other, guessing who this person was that Father Paul claimed could be centuries old. The swish of habits and cassocks filled the air from all the shifting as we waited impatiently for the first group to come back.

Finally, the door hissed as it opened, and the first group filed past us, faces white as a sheet. Nobody made eye contact. Everyone seemed to look inward. Michael passed by me, his dark brown hair falling into his eyes, long past due for a haircut. His eyes darted to mine, wide like he'd just gotten off a rollercoaster or like the first time I'd seen a ghost and known what it was. Just as quickly, his eyes shifted back in front of him, and the person behind me pushed me forward, Sam already a few steps ahead.

I hurried to catch up, passing through the door that Father Paul held. I kept my eyes in front of me to avoid any other awkward exchanges today. We came into a familiar dark hallway lined with sliding glass doors that were frosted for privacy, I assumed. You could just see bodies moving beyond them, but we kept walking. The stone paver steps dampened the sounds of our shoes. The stone above always made me feel like we were in a cave, and my heart went out to the poor, scared souls who lived down in this damp prison until the Catholic Church deemed them cured enough.

I shook myself. *I'm part of the Catholic Church*, I reminded myself. It was a choice, though for much of my life, it hadn't felt like one. Pity turned to curiosity as we continued past any part of the infirmary we'd been in before. Father Paul led us into a narrow hall that brought us down a narrow winding staircase. I'd barely noticed the opening to it all the times I'd been to the infirmary before. It led us further down until all sounds from above were muted and then gone. Horror spread through me as we stepped onto a dirt floor.

This wasn't another room of frosted glass but iron bars.

Father Paul's hushed steps came up beside us. He stopped the line of students in front of one of these cells. My hand covered my mouth, and I heard a gasp from one of the other students. I couldn't look away, my eyes riveted to the scene before me. Straw covered the cell floor, empty except for a chamber pot and a few tattered blankets in the corner. Shrouded in those blankets were the odds and ends of skeletal limbs, with dark matted hair, long on the sides, covering what I assumed was this person's face. We all stared in horror, waiting for Father Paul to explain, when suddenly, the barely covered bones in the corner moved.

I wasn't alone in jerking back. The limbs extended and grew until they were a man whose torn pants barely covered his bottom half, with no shirt, stumbling toward the bars. The dark hair hung over olive skin, stretched across strong cheekbones, with full but dry, cracked lips. The man's blue eyes glowed against the rest of his emaciated form, every rib prominent as he gripped the bars. "Is this the last of your sheep that you brought to see me, devil?"

Father Paul's mouth twisted in his customary frown. He didn't address the man but turned to us. "We found this man with the name Lukman written on a broken stone beside him. He was found with a dead parishioner and a dead deacon. Blood painted his mouth, dripped there from the two men's fight onto his desiccated form, and that had seemingly brought him to life."

"A vampire." Martin scoffed beside me. Everyone's eyes were glued to the man, Lukman.

I cleared my throat. He couldn't have been dead. He didn't feel like the dead I encountered. But he didn't feel like the living either. "Who are you?" I asked, my voice annoyingly tentative.

Father Paul shot me a death glare, walking to me swiftly. I shrank back instinctively, memories of his demands to send me here as a patient, not as a postulant, urging caution. "You do not speak to the patients without my consent." He raised his hand, seemingly without even realizing it. He noticed it and shifted it behind his back, clasping his hands there, and, with his head thrown high, walked back along the line of students.

I swallowed, gathering my courage before I looked forward again. I wasn't a child anymore, and Father Paul couldn't hurt me. I repeated the mantra in my head, determined not to forever be the scared child I had been while at the girl's school. I met brilliant blue eyes in a sallow face, suddenly concentrated on only me. He spoke, and I felt my peers' glances again.

"You know me, Hecate's daughter. Our mothers are friends."

I frowned. Before I responded, Father Paul shouted, "Enough! Back to the classroom, where we will discuss!"

Agitated, he moved his arms in a shooing gesture. The others shifted, forcing me to move back toward the stairs that would take us to the frosted sliding glass doors. To the part of the infirmary that didn't look like a dungeon. The man's words echoed in my ears, stirring something in me. Like when you remembered you forgot something, but the thought was just out of reach. I looked back at Luk, holding the iron bars, his eyes intent on me the entire way, wondering what it was about his words I couldn't remember.

Two

Luk

I walked on weak and broken legs back to the corner of my cell, wrapping the tattered ends of the blanket around me. I fought between my repulsion of their stench, their soaps and perfumes much stronger than I was used to, and my need for warmth in this horrible place.

The current bars of my cage were the only thing I recognized since I woke. My initial surroundings had been so different. The short amount of daylight I had experienced when they had dragged me from the tomb I awoke in to this dungeon was nothing I recognized. Sand beaches had been exchanged for green fields, buildings like nothing I had seen before. Even with my supernatural ability to understand, their language and phrases foreign as to be indiscernible.

The Church though—that never changed. They were cruel in the Holy Land, a pretty face and a pretty promise, and they were the same now. I prayed again to the mother Sekhmet to help me find an opening, nourishment, anything to escape this cell and continue my purpose.

"Demon."

I scoffed, not looking up, refusing to give this tall, gangly man any recognition.

"Devil," I said to the ground.

His shoe scuffed the dirt. I recognized his annoyance. He

shifted whenever he wished to lash out, but appearances didn't allow him to.

"Back so soon?"

The blood in his veins sang to me, taunting my hunger as he got closer to the bars. I tensed, ready if he got just close enough. This man would fuel Sekhmet's purpose and could be just enough life force to help me regain my strength and get out of this hell.

"Do not talk to the girl again. She is to be a part of your care, but she is fragile. Do you understand me?"

I couldn't help but laugh. The sound rasped from my dry throat, and the motion of my face and mouth caused a crack in my lips to bleed. I licked it back, refusing to give up even a drop.

I looked up at him, knowing my eyes unsettled him. Set in the face of one of the old lands, our eyes were normally brown. When Sekhmet had created us to punish the wicked, she had made our eyes different. She wanted the punished to know their fate was coming for them. "She's a pretty thing. She did not look fragile to me. Daughters of Hecate rarely are."

"You will not mention that name again," the man shouted, coming one step closer. My breathing changed, and I lowered my eyes, not wanting him to see the predator in them any longer. Willing him a hairsbreadth closer.

"Why should I not speak to her?"

"She is fragile, like I said." The man was shrill. I tried to work through what could be happening, why the Church was using a witch, one who felt so inherently powerful, in the first place. In my time, they had hunted them with as much fervor as they did us.

"Does she know who she is?"

The man shifted his robes and stepped closer. A sigh,

almost of contentment, leaked out of me. I did not have much strength and would only get one chance at this. I dug my toes into the stone but made no other discernible motion.

"She is a girl. An orphan." He snorted with disgust. "Nothing more. I wanted to bring her here to sit beside you, but I was overruled. I will use her as I was directed, and you will not make her stray from her path. I was tasked with this mission, and it will bring me to the cardinal's seat."

Before I launched, I inwardly shook my head at myself. Why did men of little power always think others would shake at their might? This little man with his little ambition. He had no idea what real power was.

"Did you hear me? Have you fallen asleep, demon?"

I felt as much as heard the bars shake. And I launched. His screams were almost as sweet as the blood flooding from his forearm into my mouth. I ignored the stabs of the electric wands breaking down my body and concentrated only on the nectar of life I could suck before I completely lost consciousness. Part of me was sad that I wouldn't be able to send this man to his judgment, but his mistake at least would give me some strength. *Thank you, Sekhmet.*

The blackness came for me, as I knew it would, a bloody smile on my face. I faded out to the tall man's screams—my lullaby.

Three

Eliza

The bass beat through the room, over the floor, up my feet, exploding from my chest. My hips swayed to the music, the whiskey making my limbs loose. I stood in the middle of the crowded dance floor. The rectangular bar to my left lit up with soft bulb lights, and colored lights over the dancefloor blinked intermittently, creating an intimate but exciting feel. Someone came up behind me and slipped their hands around my waist. We gyrated together, and his excitement pressed against me, causing my own to pool. My hand reached up behind me, finding his neck, bringing his head closer until our lips touched.

I squeezed my thighs together and flipped around in his arms. My eyes met his, and I looked him up and down. He was handsome despite a little acne on his face, sandy brown hair matched with dark eyes. I motioned to the bathroom behind him, and his dopey eyes lit up.

Without any more encouragement, he grabbed my hand and headed for the door. This bar had unisex bathrooms, so they were singles. I closed the door behind us and dropped the bolt. The room was small, white walls covered in graffiti with vulgar sayings and catchy jokes, a toilet at the back, and a small ceramic sink to the left with a mirror behind it. He was on me fast, thankfully. I hated when they waited in the corner like timid puppies. What did they think I'd asked them in here for?

He lifted me up to the sink, his hand sliding up my skirt, and I felt myself clench, ready for his fingers. Mercifully, he didn't make me wait. Slow pants and clumsy hands followed. He dragged my panties down to my ankles, and I fumbled with his belt until I could slide his pants past his hips. Our lips and tongues and teeth were everywhere. I gripped him, happy with what I found, before I pulled a condom from my bra, ready for exactly this moment.

"You don't waste any time, do you, sweetheart?"

I opened the condom and slid it on smoothly, my hand going to the base of his throat. My hazel eyes met his brown ones. "Don't talk."

He laughed like it was a joke, but he caught my drift from my serious expression, and he moved forward again. I tried to recapture the intensity, the fantasy, as he pushed inside.

"Faster," I panted, frustrated when the orgasm that had been so close fled. Reminders of his judgment, of others, of the fact that I shouldn't be here, crashed in from his statement. I gripped his shoulders and buried my face, letting him finish. The spell had been broken, and I wouldn't recapture it tonight.

After he pulled out, his face the relaxed look of a satisfied man, I hopped off the sink. I went to the toilet to clean myself up and felt a hand on my back. Energy built up in my chest, and I opened my mouth to say something when he suddenly jerked his hand back. I turned around to see him shaking it. He looked at me with a lopsided smile, "Static. Listen, I'd love to call—"

I cut him off, smiling gently but keeping my voice firm. "We both know that's not what this was."

He moved toward me, cupping my shoulder, trying to pull me close. "But it could be. I've never seen you around here. I'd love to—"

I removed his hand from my shoulder, then reached up to kiss him on his cheek. "Goodbye."

When I reached the door, his feet shuffled as he swung around to face me. "Don't you even want to know my name?"

I paused, gripping the handle. "No."

Wading through the crowd back to the parking lot exit, I pulled my leather jacket around me. Normally, it was exactly right for a spring day, but winter was having a hard time letting go this year. The chill seeped into my bones. Or maybe it was the old lady in the graveyard earlier. I was sure her cruelty would stay with me for a long time.

My car beeped as I unlocked it, and I climbed in. I looked around, ensuring I was alone, and began shedding my sparkling skirt and slinky top for jeans and a modest crew neck shirt. I rolled up the club outfit and put it under the passenger seat into a hole I had made in the bottom for better hiding. Opening the glove box, I remade myself for the Catholic Church. Makeup wipes to wipe away the mascara, eyeliner, and the deep red stain on my lips. Baby wipes to wash away the sweat and shame of what I had been taught was wrong my entire life. Mouthwash to wash away the whiskey and the stranger's taste.

Disappointed and angry tears threatened. I hadn't even gotten any satisfaction for the guilt I would carry with me. Sometimes the energy built up so much that I needed some kind of release. My short stint in the real world had exposed me to how much dancing could do that for me.

Eventually, the overwhelming need to feel close to someone, to feel more, led to encounters like in the bathroom. But after what happened during my gap year, after what I'd done when I let people get close, I didn't trust myself to let anyone in again. Besides, the habit kind of prevented me from being able to date and see where it went. Still, I ached to be close to someone, to matter to someone. I might have accepted my place in the Church as my lot in life, but I never stopped wishing I could have a different kind of family. A real family.

When I finally finished and stuffed everything in a small throwaway bag, which I'd toss at a gas station before hitting the highway, I sighed and closed my eyes for a minute. Swallowing, I tried to push down the shame and guilt of what I had just done. I had been conditioned to hate myself, to feel dirty for it. But the truth was, I needed it. I needed an escape from the closeted halls and the downcast eyes. I needed a night of debauchery and pleasure to help me gird against the weeks of service coming up. Sometimes who I felt like and who I was told I should be didn't reconcile. Sometimes I needed something to quiet the noise.

Living in bucolic Vermont, and so far from city lights, it had been tricky keeping up the double life. But as striking as I've been told my cheekbones are, when I transformed myself into a normal twenty-five-year-old woman with my chestnut hair down and makeup bringing out my hazel eyes, frequenting the kind of places the people I know usually tried to "save you from," I was never in danger of being recognized. Opening my eyes and taking a cleansing breath, I turned over the ignition and dropped the car into gear.

Against everything I had expected, Father Paul had selected me as one of the postulants to be a part of the new patient's exorcism. This next week was going to be intense, and my one weekend a month of personal time away from the convent was over. My headlights shone on the white line, guiding me home.

I readjusted my habit for the second time, twitching from nervousness. This wasn't the first time I'd gone out to Burlington to release some of my pent-up energy, but guilt always weighed me down when I came back. The nameless pleasure, the pure wantonness of every part of my night, went against everything I was taught since childhood. What I never understood was why was fear of judgment the only part that felt bad?

"For the love of God," I whispered under my breath, mentally slapping myself for the curse, as I saw Olivia practically skipping her way up the hall. The woman was a freakin' saint, and I was tarnishing her lovely halls.

As expected, she slowed and faced me as we came alongside each other. "How was your weekend, Eliza? You look tired."

I swallowed my snort. From anyone else, the statement would have been a passive-aggressive dig, but from Olivia's guileless blond haloed head, I took it for the concern it was. "It was just a long drive taking in the sights."

"Aww, taking in God's bounty. You are such a good Christian, Eliza. 'Pledged to God' your name means, and you always prove it."

The guilt and shame wrapped around my bones like shrink wrap. I gave a little cough. "You're too kind, Olivia." I looked forward in the hall, desperate to get away from this conversation, the kind of expectations and accolades that had driven me to that club in the first place. My gap year had taught me what a release some whiskey and dancing could be. "I really should shower and get to bed; I have a big day tomorrow. I hope your weekend was good as well?" I tacked on the question at the end, reminding myself to take an interest.

She smiled, her teeth showing all around, her eyes crinkling at the corners. "It was lovely. Thank you for asking! I had a trip to the lake and just sat on the coast with a bit of ice cream."

I shivered. It had been a low of forty degrees this weekend. I returned her smile and said, my voice a little wispy, "Lovely."

She was nodding enthusiastically as Mary approached. I gritted my teeth and dipped my head as she came alongside us. "Sister Olivia, we should be going." She looked at me, her nose in the air. "We don't want to miss our nightly devotionals."

My eyes narrowed slightly before I reminded myself to drop them. Mary was practically Mother Superior's right hand. She had never liked the interest Abigail showed in me. I could never figure out if she was jealous of it or just disdainful in general. She had been one of the loudest detractors when I was added to this convent and to the class of postulants. She had shouted at my lack of Christian purity: an orphan of unknown origin, someone who so obviously struggled with the path of righteousness. I wanted to pull her hair and grind her into the dirt.

"Oh, right!" Olivia looked at me apologetically. "Well, I'll let you get on, Eliza. See you later!" I nodded with my lips pressed together tightly.

I didn't bother to look Mary's way. "See you later." I continued down the hallway, relieved I would finally get to shower, wash away Mary's judgment and my stupid guilt, and begin my time in the infirmary on one of the most anticipated cases our branch had ever seen. *Not as a patient*, I reminded myself. As an exorcist.

Four

Eliza

I teetered between that weightless feeling you get on rickety rides and the nauseous one of eating too much funnel cake. Swallowing the bile rising in my throat, I stood in the semi-circle of postulants before the infirmary door. Olivia stood to my left, Sam to my right, and Michael across from me. I thanked whatever kismet had allowed both Sam and Olivia to be in this group. Maybe I would make it through this.

A door slammed, and our heads snapped up. Father Paul walked toward us in his cassock, immaculate as ever. He began talking as soon as he was in earshot. "You are all here because you have displayed, through your research and approach, that you will have the best opportunity for success. I don't need to remind you of the evil possessing the man downstairs. Your success means everything. Remember, once you start an exorcism, it is important you complete it, or you welcome the demon to try invading your soul as well."

My hand shook a little, so I clasped it with my other in front of me. I forced myself to breathe normally, ignoring the gooseflesh on my arms and the sweat down my back. This wasn't my first time participating in an exorcism, but the expectations lauded for this case weighed on me.

Father Paul's heavy looks and my fellow postulants'

shifting insinuated this wasn't a normal exorcism. This wasn't the teen from down the street who couldn't stop his sticky fingers or the grandmother who had suddenly started speaking in tongues. Half the time, I thought they needed a short stint in county and a neurologist, not a prayer book.

Father Paul looked my way, but instead of his usual probing stare, his eyes seemed to land somewhere between Sam and me. "The Church has high expectations for you and your class. I would hate to see you disappoint them." It was clear by his tone that he didn't expect that to be a problem. Looking away from us, rubbing his hands together as if he were wiping off dirt, he turned back to Olivia and Michael.

"Today, we will not be administering any rites. The demon's body seems to be broken down to a weakened state already, but we have no idea what his natural state is. This demon has possessed this man for an unknown amount of time, keeping the mortal flesh alive while the spirit most certainly must have fled. This is possibly the most powerful demon we have ever encountered. We will make his physical conditions intolerable to help weaken the demon further before we start."

My gut turned. I knew Father Paul's cruelty intimately. Memories of some of the simpler nuns enacting their "discipline" under the direction of Father Paul's surety of my suppressed possession made me shiver. How much more intolerable could he make this man's conditions? Thankfully, he was looking away and didn't notice my discomfort. He loved weakness in others. A squeeze on my forearm had me looking over at Sam. One corner of his mouth lifted, and he nodded at me reassuringly. I put my hand over his and squeezed back.

My attention drifted between Olivia and Michael. Olivia was studious, a little wrinkle between her brows. Michael looked gleeful, rocking back on his heels and then onto the balls of his feet. He would be excited at the idea of exerting power over some poor soul. I had grown up with Michael in the orphanage. He had never been able to tolerate the idea that he was unwanted or a reject of society in any way. He had overcompensated the way men do, in the gym and with an overinflated ego he hadn't earned.

Father Paul walked away to speak to someone at the infirmary door. One of the nuns who were part of the patients' nursing staff. A dirty blond curl lay sweaty against her forehead, her face unnaturally white, even for hours spent underground. They were too far away, their voices too low, to make out what they were saying, but Father Paul shook his head sharply and turned away from her while her mouth was open mid-sentence. She met my eyes for a moment, hers imploring, before she gathered herself. She shook herself and turned swiftly, swiped her badge, and went back in.

"That was Emily. She's been assigned to the demon's care. Apparently, he is feeling more spirited than he has since he woke up. We have measures of protection, however. Today's tasks will proceed. When we are done, we will gather in the classroom and plan the rites we will use for the exorcism."

With that, Father Paul led us to the infirmary doors, swiping his key card, and we walked through to the more palatable frosted doors. As we continued down the hall to where I knew we'd encounter the dank conditions and rusted iron bars, I wondered again what more he planned to do to Luk and where the line should be drawn. As I fretted, it dawned on me that Father Paul hadn't once used his name. One of our edicts was humanizing the victims of demonic possession. They weren't misbehaving children or dangerous criminals. They were victims of an evil entity. Father Paul wasn't separating the demon from the man, giving me a bad feeling of how today would go and where he thought that line lay.

We stopped before the bars of Luk's prison. The bars were classic, like a jail cell at Alcatraz. The floor beneath us was tightly packed dirt, the sound of water dripping on the stone walls like an ominous background track to today's activities. Father Paul stood at the front of our foursome, his arms spread wide as if presenting at a carnival. "The devil incarnate. We must soften him so that his exorcism proceeds successfully." We all looked forward. Luk was huddled in on himself, head between his legs and arms over his knees. A tattered blanket sat around his shoulders, hiding most of the rest of him. Looking at him, I felt cold from the inside out.

Emily squeaked when Father Paul addressed her. "Gather the guards. They'll know what to do. We'll subdue him, and then we'll begin."

She nodded jerkily and rushed off. I frowned. Everyone else shifted. Nobody spoke, and anger rose in my gut as I grew more certain that Father Paul didn't even see a line. "Guards? What are we doing today exactly?"

Father Paul's callous gaze made my heart race. "Our Christian duty."

I snorted. I couldn't help myself, even if it earned me extra prayers tonight. "And what exactly is that?"

Olivia raised her brows. Michael gave a good imitation of the father's disdain, and Sam wouldn't meet my eyes at all.

Father Paul stepped closer until we were almost toe to toe. "Our Christian duty is to uphold the Lord's name and honor under any circumstances. To worship Him and to show Him our humility. To follow His laws and edicts. And to do that, we must exorcise this demon. Do you have a problem with that?"

I opened my mouth to answer, but another snort

interrupted me. We all jumped, even the father. That hadn't come from me.

Luk's long form unfolded, and he walked closer to the bars. As he took his first step, Father Paul stumbled away as if in fear. *Curious.*

Luk wrapped his hand around the rusted bars, and as he came into the light, I saw that his hollow cheeks seemed a little less sunken. The strong line of his jaw and aquiline nose was less pronounced. His brilliant blue eyes seemed brighter. "Your god is a vain, selfish god, priest. He's a number in the pantheon and not anybody's favorite."

I was surprised Father Paul didn't rush toward him immediately. He spoke his sharp words from a distance. "Our God is a benevolent God and the only God there is! He gave his son for us, for our eternal life!"

Luk let out a raspy chuckle. "He gave his son's life, priest. But not for you. He gave him up for power."

Father Paul faced us instead of addressing Luk again. "You see! You see, he thinks he knows things nobody could know! Look at him. Hear his vitriol! Know this man is possessed."

I swallowed. We all had the list. The list of the signs of possession. And Father Paul wasn't wrong. Luk was landing on quite a few of them.

Luk didn't look concerned or affronted. He didn't look insane. He curled his full lips into a lazy smile. "Things I couldn't know? I may not have been alive at his rising, but I was there during the slaughter of the old people. The Crusades the Catholics made in his name. My kind feasted on yours. It's where most of us earned our rebirth."

Rebirth?

Before Father Paul could respond, muted footsteps brought our attention around. Emily entered in front of four guards, all carrying sticks with a two-pronged end. As they neared us, the guards snapped the sticks in front of them, and the ends sizzled with electricity. I gasped. Cattle prods.

Father Paul seemed to change gears, the red in his face fading, the vein that had started popping on his forehead smoothing out. "We'll see what you know, where you came from, soon."

The guards stepped toward Luk, who didn't try to hide from them. He didn't try to move to the back of his cell or flinch away from their prods. He looked straight at me right before the first prod hit him. Then he convulsed, his face contorting in pain. He cried out, but he fell against the bars, not away from them, allowing the prods to stay on him. Soon his screams turned into laughter, but he lay with his hand curled like he couldn't move.

It took me a moment to pinpoint the feeling that rushed through me at his audacity, at his defiance. It was envy. It was the kind of stand I wanted to make against Father Paul every day. It was…admiration. I shook myself out of the revelation, putting it away for later. Everyone exchanged glances again. "Open the doors." Father Paul sounded so sure, but Emily whimpered. The guards moved to obey the father's command. As they stepped into the cell, Luk continued lying there limply. His laughter had died off.

One guard passed him with a tool kit I hadn't noticed before in his hand. He went to the back of the cell and opened it. My gut clenched, and my eyes widened in horror when I saw his purpose. He began drilling chains into the wall. *Chains.*

"Father Paul!" I objected.

"You can't be serious!" Olivia cried.

"Silent!" He didn't even look at us. He didn't step near the entrance either, I noticed. Emily tried to back away, turning to leave when Father Paul's next word stopped her. "Emily."

She turned back slowly. A tear tracked down her face. "I want you to go in and minister to the demon."

The demon? Why wouldn't he call him by his name?

"Sir… Father." Her voice was soggy with distress.

"I'll do it." I stepped forward. This wasn't how exorcisms normally went. This was awful. This was abusive. This was *insane.*

Father Paul slashed the air with his hand. "You'll do what I tell you to. And that is to stand there and learn." Looking back at the young nurse in her habit, her tears flowing freely, he said, "Emily, go."

She nodded, obedient as we were taught, and walked toward the cell. She gripped the bars as if they were holding her up as she walked slowly to Luk. Her hands gently felt his face and turned him from his side to his back. He breathed easily, but his eyes were closed. He seemed to have passed out.

She looked back at the father. "He's unconscious, Father. It is safe to restrain him."

"Then restrain him."

Emily shook visibly, but she nodded.

"I'll help," Sam said, making for the entrance of the cell.

Father Paul fisted his cassock as he walked by, pulling him back. "You will also watch and learn. This is the nurse's job."

We all shifted. Even Michael began to look uncertain. None of this was what we'd learned in class. None of this was how an exorcism had gone before. The guards finished in the back of the cell, tugging on the spike that held the chains to ensure they were secure.

"I can't lift him alone." Emily's voice rose, on the edge of hysteria.

Father Paul's face remained stony, unmoved by Emily's fear. "Guards, assist her."

I tried to get a good look at the guards. Typical army types with short buzz cuts, black uniforms, and boxy shoulders. Two just grunted their assent and headed to help Emily. They crouched down, each grabbing Luk under an arm, dragging his legs behind him as they moved him to the shackles. *Shackles. Jesus Christ, how can this be what you want?*

Emily began enclosing one of Luk's wrists in a cuff. Through her tears, I could make out that she was saying something, but not what it was. As the cuff's click rang through the hall and she moved to the other one, everything seemed to happen all at once. Emily was pushed out of the way, falling on her back. The crack of the back of her head on the stone echoed. I rushed forward without thinking, without caring what Father Paul said.

As I rushed into the cell to Emily's side, screaming drew my attention. Luk had one of the guards against the wall, his screams slowly turning to gurgles, blood flowing freely down the stone wall behind him. The other guard had the electric prod on Luk, steadily zapping him. I didn't know how he was still standing.

My breath sawed in and out. I sat frozen by Emily's side. She began coming to, right as Luk looked at the other guard. A bloody smile engulfed his face. He seemed more vibrant somehow. Before my eyes, his skeletal frame gained muscle and sinew, his shoulders filling out with the strength you would expect from a man of his height. He turned to me so I could see his full face, and I was stricken by how handsome he was. His piercing eyes were set against strong cheekbones, the rest of his features now suiting him instead of standing out. He looked like an Egyptian warrior, clothed in nothing but thin, tattered linen pants. Without much effort, he ripped the cattle prod out of the guard's hand.

"No, please, no! I was just trying to help him!" The guard

threw his hands up in front of him and backed out of the cell. The prod zapped a couple of times before it went out, and Luk threw it to the cell entrance. Then he trained his eyes on us.

Emily was conscious enough that I helped her up. I pushed her behind me with one arm and began backing us out of the cell. I didn't know if the shackle would hold him, and if it didn't, how fast Luk could reach us. He had been lying there one second and sucking the life out of the guard the next. Luk watched me with hawk eyes, the eyes of a predator trained to catch the slightest movement. I followed the length of his body, his stomach, where before I had seen hollowed ribs now had a slab of muscle, the sharp indents of his hip bones exposed, his ill-fitting pants hanging low, striking me with awareness despite this situation. As we stepped over the cell's threshold, the bars slammed. Sam stood there sweating. He had been waiting to shut them when we came out.

"You see this devil! The demon in him thirsts for blood. Look how it changes his appearance!" shouted Father Paul, sounding half-mad. I was shaking. The guard Luk had attacked lay forgotten, dead, at his feet.

"Your exorcism begins tomorrow, devil," Father Paul spat at him.

He led us out of the cells, and all I heard as I left, too sick to look back, was an amused voice. "Looking forward to it."

Five

Eliza

We sat across from each other in the annex next door to the church we used as our library. Everybody stared at the table or the floor or into space. Stained-glass windows lined the long hall, with oak tables and chairs spaced evenly along it. Rows of bookshelves held the Church's knowledge and the history of exorcisms. Nobody talked, though Father Paul had sent us here to strategize.

"Come up with two separate prayer lists for the exorcism. Do not disappoint me." Then he left abruptly, rubbing his bandaged forearm like he'd been doing since we had left the cell.

I inhaled sharply, ready to break the quiet, when Olivia, sitting across from me, beat me to it. "That was insane."

She echoed my thoughts from earlier perfectly.

Michael spoke from beside her, his hair still too long, a soft brown to match his eyes. "I wasn't expecting that. I mean, the trust Father Paul has placed in us. I've never heard of a demon this strong. And to let us novices take it on!"

I stared at him hard for a moment. *Of course,* that would be Michael's takeaway after that situation. He practically worshipped Father Paul. So much for not having idols.

Olivia spoke next, her voice almost timid. "I've never seen an exorcism go like that."

Michael shrugged. "Father Paul knew it was necessary to be that extreme. That dude is *evil.* Did you see the way his appearance changed when he drank blood? He went from looking like a victim of starvation to a gladiator."

Sam didn't look up, still staring at his hands. "Is nobody going to talk about that guard we left on the floor like a flour sack?" I shifted. "We didn't even try to help him."

I had seen his spirit after Sam slammed the bars shut. I knew it wasn't worth going in and risking more lives or injuries. But Sam was right. At the moment, none of us had even mentioned it.

Michael scoffed. "There's no way that man was alive. His throat was torn out. Jesus, how was the demon even able to do that?"

Olivia coughed primly. Michael looked over. "Oh. I mean. Oh, whatever, you know what I meant." She just sniffed, almost making me smile. Almost.

Sam grabbed a book from the middle of the table. *Of Exorcisms and Certain Supplications.* "Should we get started then?"

Everyone nodded. As we began poring through the different liturgical texts and ceremony rites, something nagged at me that I couldn't push completely away. Luk was obviously evil. What he'd done to that man? There hadn't even been the smallest shred of remorse. But Luk didn't feel evil to me. Not that my radar for that sort of thing was a hundred percent accurate with the living. I could tell inherently when a spirit passed through me what their true nature was, but I was also generally good at reading people. Luk didn't read like an evil man who would carelessly end another's life. But he had.

Books spread in front of us, Michael and Sam argued. Sam said, "I say we go with the Rituale Romanum, and then ad lib from the nine Psalms and five Gospels. This doesn't feel like something we're going to be able to do with a few Hail Marys."

"We should have a more structured plan. This isn't the time to wing it."

Olivia shifted in her seat. Her eyes swung from Michael to Sam, arguing their cases. As they swung to me, her forehead puckered, and I realized she was concerned. I started to ask her what was wrong when Sam interrupted me.

"Come on, Eliza, back me up here."

Sam had slung his arm across the back of my chair, and I felt his body heat as he drew close to me. He made moves like that often, trying to press in, to make me more comfortable with his touch.

As usual, I shifted away, just slightly, just enough to discourage, but gave him my full attention. Looking at Michael, I raised a brow. "Let's be honest. We all know Sam has a gift for picking out the ritual text. He's had more positive outcomes than almost any other novice."

Sam relaxed into his chair, his lips curled in satisfaction.

Michael glowered at me. "You just have a crush on him, Eliza. First, you commune in graveyards, probably bringing the demons to our congregation in the first place, and then you try to tempt away our seminarians!"

He slammed a fist on the table as he said the last, but it felt more like a slap across my face. Sam's smirk fell, and the blood drained from my face.

I knew people thought horrible things about me, but rarely was it said to my face. The Church had more of a "bless your heart" kind of bully system going on, less of a mean girl's vibe.

Sam's voice lowered. "You are out of line. Take a walk." When his arm dropped onto my shoulder, leaning me into his chest, I welcomed the comfort instead of pushing him away. Michael's words were raw against all my insecurities, like a knife cut while I had been slicing a lemon.

I couldn't bring myself to look at Olivia, to either see her pity or her censure. Michael huffed but stormed out without another word. I swallowed thickly, pushing down the sob climbing up my throat, and finally looked up to see Olivia's expression. She wasn't looking at me, but at Michael's retreating back, eyes narrowed.

When she turned back to me, she softened. "Don't take anything he says seriously, Eliza. Michael's always been a bully."

I shrugged, trying to clear my throat without being obvious I was close to tears. I didn't want to be so affected. I was an adult. Being bullied wasn't supposed to matter anymore. But I'd been seen as the dirt on somebody's shoes my entire life, so it was hard not to feel the slice to my self-esteem as acutely as I had as a youth. The truth was being ridiculed hurt at any age.

"I'm fine." I coughed again, covering the crack in my voice on the word *fine*. This was, after all, the life I'd chosen, I reminded myself. I'd tried to get away and couldn't hack it. "Anyway, he was right in one respect. We need to have a plan."

Sam gave me a gentle shake, keeping me clamped to his side. The proximity finally started to make me squirm. I enjoyed my time in town, and I wasn't exactly down with the prim life I had agreed to, but I knew the way Sam felt for me. His puppy dog eyes and devoted champion embraces weren't innocent. He wanted more, but I knew better than to go there with him. It would only lead to drama and disaster and possibly expulsion from the only home I knew.

Sam frowned as I shook him off but tried to hide his

disappointment. "What do we do once we exorcise the demon? The man killed someone today."

I froze. Sam was right. But still, he had killed someone under the influence of possession.

There was something about the man, something about his eyes, the way he watched me, the way he hadn't touched Emily or made a move to intimidate her, the way he'd let the other guard go—it seemed so deliberate. Something about him drew me, even though he shouldn't.

"Has this ever happened?" I asked.

Olivia answered. "It has, but mostly in small uneducated villages where the possessed victim wasn't properly restrained to begin with. This hasn't happened at any of the infirmaries sanctioned by the Church.

I swallowed. "What did they do in the villages?" *What were they going to do to Luk?*

She looked at me with her brows knit together. "They stopped the exorcism altogether, and they executed the victim to release the demon back to hell and the victim to God's afterlife.

"You mean heaven?" Sam asked.

She started. "Yes, of course."

"But we didn't kill him. Father Paul wanted us to come here and strategize. He's a victim himself," I reminded everyone. I knew I should hate Luk. Today had cemented the vileness, at the very least, of the demon possessing him. But I couldn't. And it still worried me that nobody called him by his name. Nobody was treating him like he was afflicted. They were treating him like *he* was the demon.

Olivia nodded, a small smile on her face. Sam scoffed, making my gut sink. "He's a monster. Don't forget how dangerous he is. Maybe Father Paul is just keeping him around for practice."

Olivia and I both looked at him with horrified faces. That was something I'd expect Michael to say, but not Sam. Could he be right?

"What kind of practice? Breaking down his mortal body to weaken the demon spirit?" I asked, remembering what Father Paul had said when the guards had brought out the chains.

Even Sam shifted at the question, uncomfortable. We had heard that radical exorcisms had been performed, like in the movies. They might not get all the details right, but they originated from stories passed down of true attempts to send demons back to hell. But as novices, none of us had encountered a reality this gruesome.

Olivia's voice was quiet when she said, "Do you think Father Paul plans to punish him for what happened today?"

Sam looked back grimly. "How could he not? That guard had a family. I'm sure they'll be notified."

"Weren't the cattle prods and chains punishment enough?"

Sam looked at me incredulously, and for once, I didn't see an ounce of adoration on his face. "For murder?"

I shifted under his damning gaze. Olivia saved me on a sigh. "I think it's time to disband for the day. Sam, you really do have a gift for the rites. I say we go with your plan."

Sam dragged his eyes off me to look at her. "Yeah, yeah, okay."

The sound of our chairs scraping as we pushed them back echoed in the large room. I thought of Luk, the blood, fresh and drying, covering his cheeks and chin, dripping to his chest. Of the way his body had seemed to inflate with each swallow of blood, like from a story or a movie. He'd stood proudly, and for the first time, I'd noticed the line of his broad shoulders. His face was striking, his nose bold, his eyebrows thick, and his eyes piercing.

Something drew me in—the same something that craved sweaty dance floors and shameful bathroom sex. That scared me. That part of me had always scared me, even more than the part of me that saw ghosts.

Deep in thought, I barely remembered leaving Sam or saying goodbye to Olivia once we reached our halls. I opened my plain brown dorm door and walked into my nondescript room: Twin bed against the wall. A blue paisley comforter I'd bought at a fair covered it, but that's where the color ended. A cross nailed to the wall, a Bible on the nightstand by my bed. A small area rug so my feet weren't chilled from the floor. The same bedroom as almost everyone else.

But on my bed sat something that wasn't in everyone else's room. Or if it was, they didn't know it. A ghost. The guard from earlier, to be precise. He looked like he'd looked in life. Same buzz cut, same stocky shoulders on a thick body.

I suddenly felt very tired, knowing what was coming. "I'm sorry," I said softly, holding my hand out for him. He came toward me, his jaw tight, anger emanating from him. I braced myself for his emotion. A death like his would make anybody angry. As his hand touched mine and he began to pass through me, I gasped, and my eyes opened wide.

I stood in the room, arms thrown out as I absorbed the life he'd lived, the afterlife he was being sent to. This man was horrible. He had abused his wife, expected everything in life, and become embittered when it didn't hand him what he thought he deserved. He hurt those smaller than him because it helped ease some of the sting and forced whatever he thought he could get away with on those weaker. Innately, from the door on the other side, I knew he wasn't going to a good place.

As the rest of his essence departed mine, it left an oily sensation behind. I fell to my knees, blackness dancing on the edges of my vision. I didn't always lose consciousness after a passing. This had just been a particularly bad week. First the woman, and now him. I took deep breaths and willed the blackout to stay at bay. After a while, the spots began to get smaller, and light filtered in. With one hand on my chest, I sat back on my heels and looked up at the ceiling, trying to look past the old building, the chipped white ceiling, to something more.

My door opened abruptly, forcing me to swing my head around. Mary stood rudely in the entrance, one hand braced on the door, the other on her hip. "What are you doing?"

"Praying," I said, thinking up a fast lie. "Why didn't you knock?"

Her expression soured. "Mother Superior called for you. She wants you now."

I sighed. "Okay. Mind giving me some privacy to collect myself?"

Mary just sniffed and slammed the door behind her as she left. I looked forward to where the guard had sat, waiting for me, so he could cross over. Reflecting on the lie, I thought, *the Hail Marys are adding up for me this week.* I stood, brushing off my clean skirts that suddenly felt dirty, and headed out the door to face whatever new problem awaited in Mother Superior's office.

Six

Luk

The power threaded through me. After drinking that vile guard, their lightning sticks had felt like a tickle. I tested the weight of my wrist against the shackle. The iron ground against the stone. I could pull it easily when the time was right. I tried to sit down, but of course, the father had made the chain too short.

Instead, I kicked my leg up behind me, leaned against the wall, laid my head against the stone, and closed my eyes. Letting my breathing become as shallow as possible, I listened. Throughout the day, nuns passed between the rooms through doors that whooshed when they opened. They'd minister to patients, most of whom sounded mad. One was truly possessed by a demon from the house of Asmodeus. I had laughed at hearing his story. The man, who was already predisposed to taking lovers outside his marriage, had been caught cheating. His wife had sent him to this place, sure he would not cheat under his own volition, and miraculously, she was right. Well, partially right.

Listening to them taught me the language and colloquialisms of this new world I found myself in. It helped pass the time while I waited. I knew the father had been angry when he left and expected retribution. I knew I'd have to wait. He kept me waiting less time than I thought.

"Hello, devil."

"Is it devil now?" Hearing my voice, the strength in it for the first time in centuries, sparked hope. Maybe I would get out of here and still have a chance to earn my rebirth.

"You sound amused."

"I wonder if you've looked in a mirror."

"You are the one with a body at your feet, with blood on your face, and with my own flesh in your teeth."

I smiled at that last part. I looked down at the body next to me and laughed darkly. "This man, if you can call him that, wasn't worth the rebirth he was given."

The father followed my line of sight. His face gave a good impression of a mourning friend, his eyes heavy, looking down. Maybe he really was. "He was a Christian soul."

"For what that's worth."

"What is that supposed to mean?" The father stepped closer, his face a mask of rage before he remembered himself. His eyebrows drew together in consternation, but he still took two steps back. I smiled at him, dropping my fangs so he could see them. He gasped.

"What do you think it means, Father? I remember when your religion gained its following. Nobody thought much of it. Different gods and goddesses had been more popular at different times, often called different names. Nobody expected the effectiveness of your god's son's love for him. Or the following he would inspire when he became a martyr."

The priest tilted his head in confusion. "Jesus gave his life for our sins. He was reborn and brought to heaven."

I laughed at the idiocy of mortals. How easily they accepted the information spoon-fed to them. How quickly millennia-old propaganda slipped into their psyche.

"He gave his life. But not for your sins. He gave it for the greed and wickedness of other gods' games. And the soul his father gave him allowed his rebirth. Not his reanimation."

Father Paul's brow wrinkled, trying to work out what I had said. Finally, it smoothed. "This is the demon in you speaking. Trying to tell me history that isn't real to sway me away from my creator. But I will not falter. I am a Christian. Coming to walk the path of righteousness is what gave me purpose. It saved my life, and I will uphold the Church's teachings!" The father slipped into the Lord's Prayer, and I snorted. I lay my head back against the wall, waiting for him to finish. He wasn't the first lost soul I'd met who clung to any kind of meaning he could give his existence. People could do terrible things in the name of their gods.

There was silence for a while. I could hear dripping condensation and murmurs from the other rooms. I waited for the father, and after a time, I was rewarded. "Why did you kill that man?"

I took a deep breath. "Because he was bad, and I was hungry."

"How do you know he was bad? And hungry? I've seen your teeth. I've seen what you eat. Do you mean to tell me you're a vampire?"

I opened my eyes and looked at him. He was a tall, skinny man with a wan face and dark hair. His soul was blacker than any I'd encountered before. I wondered what events led him to believe that his Christian faith would help him escape his Karma. Either way, the earnestness with which he tried to understand prompted a true answer. "I am a child of Sekhmet. We were made to punish the breakers of Ma'at. The wicked. The irredeemable. For that, we were given gifts. I know the man was bad because I felt the stain on his soul here." I tapped my chest.

The father paled slightly, and I smiled, my fangs peeking

out. I typically would have retracted them, but watching him squirm each time he saw them was too enjoyable.

"Are you a vampire?"

"We've been called many things. Vampire is one of them."

The father glanced down the hall, watching for anyone who could overhear. I already knew the coast was clear, but I enjoyed his discomfort. His paranoia. "What are your weaknesses, demon? How can I free the mortal flesh from your influence?"

I tilted my head at him and sighed. I was disappointed. I had given him too much credit. "Why would I tell you my weaknesses, Father? The answer to your question is I have none. And I will take pleasure in ending your life and sending your own black soul to recycle. Maybe in your next life you will find more kindness in yourself."

The father cursed, not very priest-like, and turned away, rubbing his jaw. Curious about something myself, I asked, "What are you doing with a daughter of Hecate, a death witch, in a nun's habit?"

The father swung around at that question. He walked toward the bars, his face reddened, that vein on his forehead protruding, his anger overwhelming his fear. He probably thought he was safe since I had at least one arm chained. I wouldn't waste my opportunity to get free completely to prove him wrong.

"You will never say that again!"

I frowned, and my head tilted again in question. "Why is that, Father?"

His breath sawed in and out, his fists clenched at his sides. I let out a full belly laugh. "She doesn't know what she is, does she?" Straightening, I squinted at him. "What did you do?"

"Never mind that. Never say that again, or I will stop this foolish game, and I will end you immediately."

I bared my teeth and hissed. He had no idea how to end me, and at this point, I had enough strength to prevent it if he figured it out. Either way, soon, I would be out of here. I only needed an opening, for my cell to open one more time.

Suddenly, the priest straightened, and his eyes narrowed. He looked more certain of himself than he had before. "I know how to torture you now. You've told me without even realizing."

No longer amused, I watched him wearily.

"Nobody will enter this cell again. I will make a line around it, ensuring no matter how far you stretch, if you were to get out of that shackle, you wouldn't reach a soul on this side. You eat the wicked? You feed on blood? Then none other than the most innocent will come near you. And if possible, not even then. I will starve you to death until the demon leaves this mortal body."

Anger rose in my chest. I schooled my face as best I could, but my jaw ticked, leaving the father more satisfied than he should be. I was a fool. I was centuries old, but I had only really lived fifty years of it. I'd been a baby when I was desiccated, much too young to earn my rebirth, and much too young to learn many of the lessons my predecessors had.

The father began to walk away, amusement in his voice. "I know how to defeat you now, devil. Exorcism begins tomorrow. I suggest you just give in."

I gnashed my teeth, wishing I had taken the chance after all. I would have been able to hold him close against any onslaught. No matter what came, I could have at least ended his life.

To my sensitive hearing, his steps echoed around me as he left, victory in every step. Not bothering with the pretense anymore, I snapped the shackle out of the wall. I kicked the guard's body toward the cell door and went back to the wall, sitting down heavily. Resting my arms over my knees, I glared into the hall, out toward freedom.

"Never."

Seven

Eliza

By the time I had made it to Mother Superior's office, the door was closed, but faint yelling penetrated the thick walls and mahogany door. Her secretary's eyes had widened. Abigail, our Mother Superior, seemed to follow me throughout my life. First, she had presided over the orphanage where I grew up, and then this convent, where I had finally taken my vows.

Abigail rarely raised her voice, and in all the years I'd known her, she had certainly never had a screaming match. The girl, Sarah, I think, had wrung her hands as she watched me.

"She really did want to speak to you, Eliza. I believe it was urgent, but I think it might be best to come back tomorrow morning before your duties."

I had nodded, dumbstruck, wondering who could be in there. Nobody yelled at Mother Superior. She was one of those people whose presence commanded obedience and respect. I had given Sarah a weak smile and agreed to come back in the morning, then went back to my dorm to start my nighttime routine.

The extra free time had allowed me to finally do some research. After locking my door to ensure there would be no more abrupt interruptions from Mary, I pulled my phone out and began searching for it. Thinking back to the first thing

Luk had told me, "Our mothers are friends," I tried to remember what he called me. Hecate's daughter. I googled the name Hecate.

I swallowed, a sick feeling in my gut as results began to populate. The first thing that came up was her origins as a Greek goddess. That's why her name had sounded so familiar. I enjoyed reading about mythology. As I kept going, more and more results mentioned witchcraft. Associations with the moon, with doorways and hell hounds. It reminded me of what I called it when ghosts went through me—crossings.

I clicked my phone off, unable to go through anymore tonight, and lay down to sleep. That night, I dreamed I was being chased by dogs with acid dripping from their mouths, chased through endless doorways as a woman desperately called my name.

Now, here I stood. Bright and early, wishing we kept coffee in the commons in our building. I usually snuck into town to "take the morning air" and get a cup of coffee.

I sat in the hardback chair that lined the wall to the left of the secretary's desk, waiting for Mother Superior to invite me in, trying to hide my impatience. I'm sure I was failing. Sarah sat, shooting me sympathetic glances intermittently, the large oak door behind her like a doorway to judgment. Doorways. I shook myself, my research from last night still haunting my subconscious. Finally, Sarah called, "She'll see you now."

Despite how eager I'd been to get this over with, nervousness churned my gut at the idea of sitting in front of this woman. She had been the architect of my entire life. It hadn't been a soft life. She had joked once that our promotions seemed to come in pairs.

As I walked in, she sat behind her desk, shuffling papers, ignoring me. Despite the proximity we seemed to always find ourselves in, we'd never been close. She wasn't as cruel as Father Paul, but I would never call her warm. I'd never called her anything other than Mother to her face, though I knew her real name was Abigail. A bit ironic and creepy. I didn't dwell on that too long.

Without looking up, she spoke, remnants of an English accent giving her words a lilt. "You can sit." She intently read one of the papers from a stack while I settled myself. Finally, her gray-blue eyes rose to meet my hazel ones. Her hair curled in a halo around her head, remnants of the blond still visible but fading to white. Though slightly wrinkled, her face held dignity and beauty. Her thin lips pursed to a single line. I sighed. I sensed a lecture coming on.

"Good morning, Mother."

She nodded at the greeting. "I heard that Father Paul selected you for the exorcism of our newest patient."

I shifted, surprised. Mother Superior didn't usually involve herself in priests' work. She was assigned to the school but oversaw the care and behavior of the nuns, not their work within the infirmary. "I, uh, yes." I coughed.

Her piercing stare pinned me in place, and I stilled. Finally, she looked toward the bookshelves lining the walls on either side of the room. I sighed, relieved from the intensity of her examination, which had always tied me up in knots. "This case seems a bit extreme, doesn't it? Do you have any concerns about this assignment?"

I thought back to yesterday. To the chains that Father Paul had ordered the guards to drill into the wall. To the man the possessed Luk had killed by ripping out his throat. *Concerns? I was questioning my entire life.* "No, Mother."

She looked back at me, jaw tight. "Hmmm." She stood and walked around the large oak desk, resting against it and facing me. Her habit was impeccably ironed. She always looked pristine. "I may not be part of the school, but I am given reports when it affects my charges. I know what happened down there."

I twisted my hands together in my lap. A shroud of shame always seemed to follow me. I wasn't doing enough, I wasn't honest enough, I wasn't chaste enough. Living up to the standards of those who came before me, trying to earn my way into the good graces of those in charge, trying to do it for the "right reasons" so that I was worthy of the rewards. I was so tired of trying to be good, whatever their definition of it was, I wanted to scream.

"I'm sorry, Mother, I wasn't sure if those events were supposed to be public knowledge. Of course, they were upsetting."

She scoffed, and my eyes swung from my lap to her derisive face. I had never heard such an unsightly sound from her. She put a hand on her hip and paced the length of the shelves as if looking for something. Finally, she paused and lifted her other hand to lean on a shelf, head bowed. "I think upsetting may be an understatement."

I cleared my throat. "Well, yes. But I'm devoted to my duty. We will save the victim."

She looked at me then. "The possessed man?"

I nodded. "His name is Luk. We don't know much about him because the demon in him is strong. But we've come up with rites to free him. We'll save his soul."

She considered that, then walked back to her desk and settled herself in her seat. "That's good. That's good, girl. Has this possessed man...said anything? I heard he was found in unusual, almost unbelievable circumstances."

At first, I thought of what he'd said to me. "Daughter of Hecate." And all I'd learned that could mean. Then finally, it dawned on me what she meant. The way he'd been buried under a tablet that dated back over three centuries and had seemed to come to life from the drippings of a murder victim's blood.

"I'm not sure. This is the most," I looked at the ceiling, trying to figure out how to phrase it, "complicated exorcism I've ever heard of. I'm not sure if Luk is the name of the demon or the man. The victim might have been placed there more recently than we think, or maybe there really is some way for a demon to trap a soul and preserve the mortal flesh. I think we may be in uncharted waters, Mother."

She watched me closely. Her head motioned in a barely perceptible nod. "Astute."

A small zing of pride shot through me. I hated myself for being so susceptible to her praise. But no matter how much I'd tried to reprogram myself to be independent, to not be like the Marys of this convent, completely dependent on the approval of the church leaders, it didn't change the fact that this woman had practically raised me. I glowed in the warmth of her approval like a child.

I sensed the meeting was at an end and, agitated with myself, was happy about it. I started to rise, ready to say my goodbyes. Speaking of unprecedented exorcisms, it was time to get to mine.

I nodded my head in deference and made to exit with a parting, "Mother." Her words stopped me at the door.

"Daughter."

I looked back. She rarely called me that. Normally it was girl, or postulant, or when I was young, child. "I want you to be careful. If this being is that old, he may say unusual things. The older the demon, the more adept he will be at shaking your faith, at shaking you. Nobody must see you falter. Your place here is precarious, given your history. We granted you this chance to be part of the school, but some remember

Father Paul's suspicions. Some of the nuns at the orphanage were not happy he could only bring you to the infirmary as a postulant, not as a patient."

My teeth clenched, and my stomach got that weightless, organ-floating feeling, making me sick. She had hit on one of my worst fears. I couldn't tell if it was on purpose to rattle me or if true concern was behind her imperious expression. I swallowed down the bile and said, "Yes, Mother."

We stood outside the infirmary doors, waiting for Michael. Of all of us, of course Father Paul would entrust him with a key card. He had been a hotheaded, conceited boy, and those qualities had only amplified as he'd grown into a man. Sam leaned a shoulder against the wall, and Olivia kept casting glances between the infirmary door and the floor.

"You, okay?" I asked her.

She looked up and smiled, but her normally fair complexion looked a little green. "Of course, just antsy waiting for this to begin, you know? I mean, yesterday was so crazy."

I nodded. I knew what she meant. A man had died yesterday, and we were all acting like it was a matter of course. We didn't even know who Luk was or where he came from. That was the name he had given and part of the name on the gravestone where he was found. But that grave was from 1292. Who was he, really?

I looked over to find Sam watching us. "We will succeed today, Olivia. We'll send the demon back to hell and find out who the man is beneath."

Michael's arrival interrupted anything further he wanted to say. Sweat dripped down his forehead, and his cassock was askew. He must have run here. "What are you all waiting for?

Let's get started," he said on a labored breath. Sam laughed, kicking off the wall. Olivia nodded, still looking worried. I rolled my eyes.

I trailed behind everybody, walking through the hallway with the frosted glass doors leading to patient rooms. I jumped when a hand slammed against the glass to my right. I could make out the person's outline behind it, staring at us as we passed. "Do you think he needs help or—"

Michael glared back at me, impatiently motioning us to hurry up. "That's what the nurses are for. He can wait. Let's get started. This demon is returning to hell today!"

His energy and optimism were off-putting. The way he and Sam acted in sync, I assumed they'd talked after we had all left the library. Still, after yesterday's events, I would have expected us all to be more solemn. More cautious, like Olivia. But Michael's infectious energy ramped up Sam, and even Olivia's brow had smoothed.

We stopped alongside the gate, and my hand went over my mouth. The guard's body lay against the bars of the door. A hole gaped in the wall where yesterday Luk had been shackled, and he sat leisurely on the floor, head leaning against the stone, watching us. Or rather, watching me. I couldn't tell if it was my imagination, but his eyes always seemed to draw and settle on me.

Michael drew out his Bible, and the rest of us followed suit. He began with the Lord's Prayer, eliciting a laugh from Luk. I watched his eyes sway to Michael, even though all our voices carried the memorized words.

"What are you trying to exorcise, boy? There is no hitchhiker in me."

Michael interrupted his prayer to say, "I'm not a boy."

We all looked at him sharply, continuing our prayer. Stupid sexist rules made him take lead on this. Olivia was further in her classes, not to mention more even-tempered. She didn't even seem to notice Michael breaking ranks. Sweat dripped from her temple, and I frowned in concern as I watched her utter the prayer's words. After we finished, we began the ritual, to be followed by the first of three psalms we'd picked out. Michael held a large cross out in front of him, and Sam and I lit frankincense, moving our hands so that the smoke drifted lazily away from us, clockwise. Olivia used the aspergillum to splash holy water toward Luk's cell.

Luk got to his feet and came toward the bars. We were well out of his reach behind the chalk line drawn on the floor. Father Paul had briefed us this morning; nobody besides the possessed man's nurse was to cross the line.

As we switched gears, uttering the first psalm, Luk's advance faltered. A hand flew to his chest, rubbing as if to relieve an ache. His expression didn't change. Half amused, with the barest hint of his eyebrows tightening, showing what looked like...pain? My stomach tightened. He *was* possessed. The prayers were affecting him.

Michael's voice rose as if he could taste victory. Olivia looked at him uncertainly, her eyes drawn tight and sweat rolling down her temple, slowly following suit. I found her hesitation curious, but I focused on my own part in this ritual. Luk caught himself as he stumbled into the cage bars. He was breathing hard like he'd run a mile as fast as he could. Instead of opening his mouth to taunt us, however, he began his own prayer.

It sounded like Arabic, but I couldn't be sure. The only word, or name, I understood was Sekhmet. Pressure began building in the room like I was inside a balloon about to pop. Olivia screamed and fell to her knees as we began the second psalm. My Bible dropped in my surprise, and I moved toward her, but someone caught my arm.

Sam shook his head, but his voice sounded like it was coming down a tunnel. "We have to finish. Even if it doesn't work, we have to finish the ritual."

"Let me check on her!" I cried. She was curled in a ball on the floor.

At a shove from my other side, I turned toward Michael's stormy face. He didn't say anything, merely pointed at the Bible I'd left forgotten on the floor. Jerkily, I picked it up, angry tears falling from my eyes. I continued chanting, feeling helpless and wondering why. Why did I stay with the Church? Did I even believe in this? Why did I abide by an institution that would let one of their own lay crumpled on the floor? That would allow a contractor who did their bidding to be murdered and not even give the pretense of mourning?

Then I remembered I'd tried to leave. And what a disaster it had been. After only a year, the small life I'd built for myself crumbled, and with it, the lives of several others had come crashing down. I shuddered, remembering my attempt at autonomy hadn't just hurt me. It had hurt others too. I hurt others just by being around them. When I'd sat in the front pew of the closest church, crying my heart out, staying at a shelter because I'd been kicked out of the home I'd rented with friends who refused to look at me, a kind nun had sat next to me. She had remembered me from my childhood. She had encouraged me to take my vows. She had promised me the Church would give me discipline and direction, and I had seen it as a saving grace. Enough grace to save me from myself.

As the second psalm ended and we began the final one, the pressure in the room continued building. My ears rang like there was a distant bell, and a phantom wind flowed through the halls. Luk held himself up by one arm, muscles corded, his belly clenched. Sweat trickled down his neck, down his bare chest. He continued his own chant, and I followed his gaze, focused on Olivia, his face a mask of determination. As we said the last words of the final psalm, Michael held forth the cross and shouted, "Be gone, demon, be gone!"

Luk's face contorted, and he bared his teeth, long fangs on either side of his mouth, as he hissed at Michael's words. We all gasped, and then Luk collapsed to the floor. I spared him a glance but rushed to Olivia's side. She groaned as I helped her up.

"Are you okay?"

Michael frowned down at her. "What happened to you?"

She opened her eyes slowly, her forehead clammy and skin pale. "I don't know. I just felt this pressure and panicked. I fell and hit my head."

Gently, I checked her head for any bumps or bleeding but found no injury. I opened my mouth to reassure her, but her pleading eyes stopped me. I quirked an eyebrow at her but switched gears. "That's a fine lump you have. I bet a concussion too. We all felt the pressure. Let's get you back to the dorm."

Her face relaxed. "That sounds good."

I rose, helping her up. Sam took her under an arm, and she leaned on him thankfully. Michael stood in front of us, stopping anyone from leaving. He stared at Luk, who lay, eyes closed but breathing steadily.

"We should wait for Emily. She's the only one allowed in, and we need to know if it worked."

I huffed. "Michael, whether it worked or it didn't, Olivia needs to rest, and he's unconscious. He's breathing. Let's get her somewhere safe and come back."

He looked around, frustrated, his hand fisted at his side. "Where is that damn girl?"

My nose curled in disgust, and I shook my head. "Yesterday, he threw her and knocked her unconscious, and then she watched him kill a man. She probably ran far away."

He frowned, realizing I was right. "You go in."

I blanched. "What?"

"Olivia is hurt. You are the only other girl here. You go in. He didn't try to hurt the girls yesterday."

I gave an incredulous laugh. "He was chained to the wall; he couldn't hurt anyone else yesterday."

Michael suddenly advanced on me, his fist looking ready to swing, and I stumbled back. "Do your Christian duty for once, Eliza, and go in there. I command you."

I gritted my teeth and squared my shoulders. "You aren't my commander."

He smiled back meanly. "I am right now."

I ground my teeth together, narrowing my eyes. I looked back at Luk. Part of me was concerned for him. The ritual had obviously hurt him. If we had successfully exorcised the demon, the man left behind might need help. I looked toward Olivia. "Fine, but let Sam take Olivia back to the dorms first."

Michael knit his brow and suddenly walked over to take up Olivia's other side. I think it just dawned on him that I would have to open the door. He shoved keys at me as Sam and he walked by and said, "Sam and I both will take her. Meet me in the library with a report."

My jaw went slack. He was serious. He insisted on knowing if the exorcism had worked but wouldn't put himself in danger. He'd leave me here to die and send in guards if the demon ripped out my throat. I opened my mouth to argue when Olivia moaned. I swallowed my words, looking back to Luk, indecision warring inside of me.

Finally, I nodded and looked at Michael. "I'll report back." He smiled triumphantly and made a show of adjusting her under her other arm. Sam shot me a worried glance, but I waved him forward. As they ascended the stairs to the main part of the infirmary, I whispered to myself, "If I can."

Eight

Eliza

I walked cautiously to the cell door. It already felt normal. His cell. I swallowed thickly, and sweat dripped along the back of my neck. I rested a hand on the gate, my fingers on the keys, ready to unlock the door and swing it back. Trying to summon the courage. We had sent the guards away for this exorcism. I would have no backup.

Luk moaned, rolled over, and then stilled. The motion and sound pushed me into autopilot, and I flung the door back. The dead guard at the entrance gave me pause, but I gingerly made my way around him and dropped to my knees at Luk's side. My fingers went to his throat, checking for a pulse. Despite how he looked, it was strong and steady. I didn't know what I had expected—all this talk of vampires and him being around since the Crusades, would he even have a pulse? It was the first time I'd been this close to him.

He didn't move his arms or legs, but he cracked one eye and looked at me. I fell back, startled.

"I won't hurt you, little witch."

My brow wrinkled. I kept a little distance between us, ready to bolt if he moved too fast. "Why do you call me that?"

"Because you are a daughter of Hecate. That's what you are. A little witch."

My indignation rose. I may not have always been the best

Christian, and the Church and its rules may have often chafed, but still. “I’m a child of God.”

He chuckled. “That’s true. All you humans are. But Hecate has a greater claim to you, little witch.”

I huffed. “I’m not little. And I’m not a witch.” This conversation was ridiculous, but I couldn’t help a thread of fear after what I’d read about Hecate online. Shaking myself, I moved cautiously closer. He continued to lie still, giving me some semblance of ease. “Are you okay? Do you need medical assistance?”

He made a point to keep his limbs in place, but his chest, bare and carved like a statue of David, shook with his humor. “Yesterday, you were standing by while they chained me to a wall, and now you want to know if I need a bandage?”

I frowned. “Yesterday, I didn’t have a choice.”

His smile faded. “We all have choices.”

I sat back on my heels. That statement stung, and shame, somehow deeper than what I usually felt when I went into town for a quick lay or a night of dancing, settled in my chest. “I was afraid.”

He nodded seriously. “Of what? Of me?”

I thought about it. Taking the chance he would murder me without my eyes on him, I peeked out of the cell to check if anyone was around, studiously ignoring the body thrown like trash at the door. The stench of rot was beginning to demand attention. After suffering his soul passing through me the other day, I couldn’t feel as disgusted by his murder.

“Nobody can hear us.”

My head swung back. “How do you know?”

His face kicked up in a small grin. “Because Father Paul wasn’t wrong about everything.”

My eyebrows raised. “You are the devil?”

He cocked his head, his right arm moving unconsciously

before it stilled. He was staying still so I'd talk to him, I realized. "And if I was?"

I stared into his brilliant blue eyes, their color entrancing against that olive skin. Something stirred, something I didn't want to admit or pay much attention to. Want. "Even the devil needs prayers."

He smiled, and this time it wasn't in irony. It crinkled the skin around his eyes. He took a deep breath, and I thought he was testing me. He very slowly sat up, scooting farther away, but so that we were eye to eye. My heart beat rapidly, fear and adrenaline surging. His body had transformed into a fantasy the other day. Stubble covered his chin, shading his jawline and tracing around his full lips. Muscles bulged in his shoulders. I wondered absently if my small hands could even fully cover them. His waist tapered, carved with sinewy abs. My mouth went dry. I watched him but didn't move. He nodded his head as if he understood. No closer.

"That's true enough. But no, I am not the devil. I am a vampire. A child of Sekhmet."

Nothing I had read last night mentioned Sekhmet. I thought back to some of the mythology I'd read as a child in school. The Church wasn't big on it, centering more on Christian history, but there'd been some, and I'd read more for fun. "Sekhmet's from Egypt."

He folded his hands in front of him and rested them on his outstretched thighs. A position he couldn't move from quickly. My heart rate slowed just slightly.

"Sekhmet is ancient. She is the mother of order and war. And healing."

My brow wrinkled. "There's a lot of contradictions there."

"Not as many as you think."

My ankles were beginning to hurt in this position, so I

took a chance and sat back on my butt. "Maybe. Why do you say I'm a daughter of Hecate?"

He stared at me a while before looking at the wall of his cage, and the breath I held slowly hissed out. I should have been scared, but instead, curiosity thrummed through me. "Do you know where you're from?"

I rolled my eyes. "New England. America."

Amusement danced in his eyes. "I don't know what either of those places are. But that wasn't my question anyway. Do you know where you're really from?"

I looked at the floor. "No."

He nodded, no judgment on his face. "That's because the Church is hiding it from you, little witch. You should find out."

I huffed. "How would you suggest I do that?"

"Find a coven, to start."

I shook my head at the ridiculousness of this conversation. "I came in here to see if you needed immediate medical care." I rose. I didn't know what had made me sit down and talk to him like this in the first place. "But from the look of it, you are fine. I need to go." Pausing, I turned back. "Have you eaten? Been given water? Anything to wash?"

He rose too but didn't come closer. "No."

Horror rose in me. "When's the last time?"

He looked curious at my concern. "I haven't been offered food or water since I woke."

My eyes widened, realizing he had meant since he had gotten here.

"Don't come closer, please. I need to close this door, but I'm going to get you some things to refresh yourself with."

"Okay, daughter of Hec—"

"And stop calling me that. My name is Eliza," I said sharply.

His mouth quirked up. "Okay, Eliza."

I dragged the guard's body out of the cell with me when I went. Locking Luk in felt wrong, but I did it. It was what I was supposed to do. I found the kitchen in the main part of the infirmary. It wasn't possible he'd received nothing since he'd been here, was it? It must have been more than a week. The burden of guilt from my inaction weighed on me, but then I shook myself. "He killed somebody yesterday, Eliza. Get it together."

Gathering a couple water bottles, a warm soup, and some bread, a basin, and soap, I headed back to his cell with the tray. After setting it down, I opened the door to his cell and went back in. He was in the same position I'd left him in, but his olive skin tone was a little yellow.

"I thought you said you were okay," I said accusingly as I sat the tray down halfway between us and backed toward the door.

He scooted across the floor, taking the water from the tray and drinking thirstily. As he spoke, he began to wash, using some of the water and soap in the basin I'd brought him. "You used magic to try to force me from this plane litt—Eliza. While it was a fool's mission, I spent the last hour combating you so you wouldn't accidentally send another. I'll be okay, but for now, I'm a little spent. Thank Sekhmet for her assistance." He kissed two fingers and raised them to the ceiling before taking a piece of bread, dipping it into the soup, and taking a bite.

I watched the water drip from his chin and hands, mesmerized by the droplets. I'd forgotten to bring him a towel. "What do you mean magic? We used the Lord's words to exorcise your demon. We're just trying to help you, Luk. And protecting who?"

He swallowed his bite and considered me, ignoring most

of what I had said. "I am not possessed, Eliza. I am an enforcer. Some call me vampire. Sekhmet created us to punish the wicked. If I complete my purpose to her satisfaction, I will be granted rebirth." He pointed to me with his bread before dipping it in the soup and taking another bite. "Like you."

I processed what he had said. None of it made any sense. "What do you mean you're a vampire? Vampires aren't real. And why do you keep mentioning rebirth?"

He swallowed his bite. "If demons are real, why not vampires? Rebirth is how we are given a second chance. To find our loved ones. To live a better life. To stay a part of existence. God granted you an automatic rebirth; that's true enough. But some of us must earn it. Some of us aren't even given the chance."

Confusion swirled within me. None of what he was saying matched the doctrine I'd grown up with. Luk's eyes suddenly shot to the hallway that led to the main infirmary. "We need to end this, little witch." He motioned to his cell door. "Get out of the cell. Hurry."

I did what he said, panicking at the urgency in his voice. I couldn't believe how comfortable I'd become in his presence in the first place. I closed the door with a resounding click. When I looked back, the food tray, basin, and water I'd brought were gone. My brows lowered in confusion until I found the smallest part of the tray peeking out from Luk's blankets. Before I could ask, Father Paul called sharply from the stairs.

"What are you doing here?" He walked side by side with Mother Superior. Abigail pursed her lips.

I smoothed my habit, now dirty and wrinkled from kneeling, giving away what I was doing here. I mentally slapped myself. Michael had *ordered* me to be here. I wasn't doing anything wrong. And we were supposed to *try* to get the demon to talk. It helped with the exorcism. Though somehow, that thought didn't feel right.

"I was told to nurse the patient. Emily was unavailable."

Father Paul advanced toward me until he was in my face, trying to make me back down with his size. At five foot seven, I wasn't short, but I was slight. Still, I stood my ground, my hands fisted beside me. I tried to make myself relax. I didn't want him to know how nervous he made me.

"You weren't supposed to be left alone with the devil."

"The—" I huffed. I was so tired of this. "*Luk*, the *patient*, was unconscious after the attempt. I was left behind to ensure that he was okay."

The father looked over at Luk, who now stood close to the bars, watching the priest intently. Mother Superior made a noise of argument when Father Paul grabbed me by the arm, forcing me a few steps toward the infirmary door, his grip bruising. A growl, rising in intensity, brought all of us around.

Luk stood there, his long teeth—his fangs, I realized—extended, his face crumpled in anger, glaring right at Father Paul's hand on my arm. As surprised as everyone else, I gave the barest shake of my head. Luk's expression didn't change. Instead, he turned away abruptly. Father Paul turned back at me. "It looks like the exorcism didn't work. Get out of here. We'll talk about this later."

He shoved me away, causing me to take a couple stumbling steps. A crack echoed through the room, like a fist smashing into the stone wall. I didn't dare look back this time though.

"You go too." I heard behind me.

"You don't order me." Mother Superior scoffed.

I listened intently, walking as slowly as I could as I headed toward the stairs.

"Hello, devil. I think it's time you and I talked." My

brow wrinkled in confusion as I finally reached the steps and started up to the main infirmary. That wasn't Father Paul's voice I'd heard at the end.

Nine

Luk

Anger rose from my chest into my throat. I bit my cheek and tasted copper. The beat of my heart pounded slow and steady in my ears. I wanted to rip his throat out. I wanted his warm blood flowing over my chin and his terror feeding my adrenaline. I wanted his lifeblood over my hands for touching her. The strength of my reaction surprised even me.

It took me a moment before I could turn around and answer the woman. When I did, I took in her appearance. Her coif gave her away. I cocked my head, refusing to show her respect. "Yes?" The question was evident in my voice. *What do you want?*

She curled her nose at the slight. *Good. I'm glad you recognized it for what it was.*

"Devil, I hear you are called."

I spit against the stone steps, blood splattering, to show what I thought of that. My hands balled in fists at my side, and I gestured with my chin toward the dead priest walking. "That's what the coward calls me. I let him because I find it amusing. But that is not what I am called."

The mother tsked, her lips downturned. "Then what are you called?"

"Lukman." I gave her nothing more. After what the priest had told me, knowing that the little witch had been stolen from her family, I had been curious. But after meeting her, speaking to her, I was quickly forming an attachment. Her chestnut hair framing her ever-changing almond eyes and sharp cheekbones had initially drawn me in. But it was the way her delicate frame contrasted with her iron inner strength that made me want more of her. She didn't seem to know what had been done to her, seemed to swallow the Catholic Church's promises whole. But after her eyes were opened, after she understood what she was, that would change. From what I remembered, the daughters of Hecate had a close bond with their patron goddess.

This wasn't the time to be getting distracted from my purpose, but right now, I didn't care about that. Maybe it was that death beat in her like it did in me, finding kindred in this dank, dark place. Maybe I craved the companionship every being needed on some level. Or maybe it was just *her*. Something about her pulled me. She was kind to those she feared. She was thoughtful of those around her and insightful but open to things she might not understand. I lived to earn my rebirth, but Eliza made me remember that I was working hard to earn it for the things life offered.

Olivia, the other woman present at the exorcism, had looked afraid but resigned before falling ill. Eliza hadn't understood her fear or her sickness, but she'd understood Olivia needed a cover. She'd provided it without hesitation. That had endeared her to me immediately. But when she'd told me even the devil needed prayers, when she'd offered kindness despite the possibility that I was the worst entity she'd been taught to fear, I had succumbed to the precipice of feeling all men eventually fall victim to. She would be mine.

"How did you come to be here, Lukman?"

"I was part of an army. To combat the likes of you."

The mother cocked her head, the fine wrinkles of her face doing nothing to diminish the loveliness of it. If anything, it enhanced it. She was mortal, able to experience the excitement of life in a way that no immortal ever would. Her hair, white in ringlets underneath her coif, was a halo of wisdom around her. Or it should have been. I hadn't found wisdom in the way she'd merely squealed at Father Paul's rough treatment of Eliza rather than intercede.

After considering me, she said, "And what are the likes of me?"

That was an easy question. My stasis had left me with the burning anger of the Crusades, like the sand had been between my clothes and the blood had been on my hands only yesterday. "The likes of someone who would decimate a nation, a people. And do it in the name of religious righteousness. Who would take a lesson from the ancient Egyptians and erase the doctrine of every other god before you in favor of yours, using the uneducated masses to win your war. For the sake of salvation, you'd say. But we knew the truth."

Her breathing and heart rate had slowed. "What truth?"

I leaned closer to the bars. As the rust abraded my skin, I swore I'd get out of here soon. "That you didn't do it for salvation. You did it for power."

"This is ridiculous, Abigail. You need to leave and let me deal with him."

"You will not address me so informally, Father Paul. And you will stand down, or I will speak to the pope himself about that cardinal seat you covet."

I didn't have to be a child of a God to feel the animosity rolling off the priest at the reprimand. He raged at being so easily controlled by a woman. But whatever her connection to the highest seat of the Catholic hierarchy was, it was real enough to temper his hate for now.

Looking back at me, the mother arched a brow. "The Church in those times did it to save souls. But it's true we only endeavored to save God's souls. Do you claim to be from those times?"

I smiled, my fangs still descended. "Do you claim not to believe me?"

She smiled back mildly. This woman's feathers weren't easily ruffled. "No, I don't claim that."

I waited for her to make her point.

"I'm going to tell you something. And I'm going to reveal this information only because you've just demonstrated you have some kind of feeling for Eliza."

"Mother Superior, you are not authorized to do that! You are not authorized to deal with demons in order to achieve your own ends!"

The mother whipped her head over, rounding on the priest. "And what of your dealings, Father Paul? When you discovered an entity had awoken that might have the power to disprove my hypothesis, you jumped at the chance. You couldn't pass up the opportunity to have Eliza in a cell and any of the rewards such a capture might bring you."

"Her kind killed my family! And you prop her up, give her everything she wants, and tout her as the next coming to the upper clergy! She is nothing but an infection I intend to cure. And when I achieve that cardinal seat, I will ensure you and your blasphemous endeavors are ended for good."

The mother made to smile at him, but it came out more like a grimace, her eyes narrowed, and her posh accent dripped with malice. "Good luck, Father. I have the pope's ear. I've kept her alive this long, and I'll see her become the

Church's weapon. Your bigotry blinds you, and it's a weakness in our war."

"What war?" I broke in. The mother had been about to tell me something important about Eliza. I wanted that information.

She looked back at me, her pale face reddened from her confrontation with the priest. His shoulders heaved with the breaths he took, trying to get himself under control. She curled her hand around the bars of my cage, unafraid despite the fact that she must have heard what I do when people get close. She knew she wasn't in danger. Her soul was not black, and I would not risk missing whatever information she had on the little witch. My blood ran cold, realizing Mother Superior couldn't know about my discernment on whose blood I took and that she knew she had me with Eliza's safety.

"Eliza was taken as a child..." As she went on, I felt my fangs prick on my bottom lip, anger turning in my gut, my jaw clenched so tight my molars felt like they'd shatter. Mother Superior was smug as she finished telling me, as she beckoned the cowed priest behind her as she left.

Over her shoulder, she gave a last farewell, a slap in the face. "God Bless, Lukman."

I listened to their steps fade on the stone stairs and whispered to the empty air, "Sekhmet, help me save her."

Ten

Eliza

I stood in front of the closed door picking at my fingernail, an old anxious habit. Luk's words flipped over in my mind. *Hecate's daughter. Find a coven.* I thought of what I'd read about Hecate, the goddess of doorways and witchcraft. Of the crossings. I shook myself. *Utterly ridiculous.* Obviously, his demon's word trying to tempt me to sin. Tempt me away from the father. *I am a child of Sekhmet. She is ancient. Mother of order, war, and healing.*

The abrupt opening of the door shook me out of my thoughts. I gasped, still shell-shocked from my conversation with Luk. My shock didn't end when Olivia stood in front of me. My mouth hung open. Her normal appearance, doll face and porcelain skin shrouded by her coif and halo of light blond hair, had completely changed. Her greasy, sweaty hair stuck to her face, her complexion had grayed, and her green eyes stared back at me, sunken in their sockets like she was coming back from a prolonged illness.

I pushed into the room, taking her arm and guiding her back to her bed. A wooden twin bed, like mine, her sheets rumpled and sour from sweat and sickness. "Olivia, I just left you. How did you fall so ill? Michael and Sam didn't stick around to make sure you were okay?"

She put her clammy hand on my arm to stop my tirade.

I tried not to wince. The sour smell of sweat wasn't only in her sheets.

I took a shaky breath and sat down beside her, taking her hand to hide my reaction. Michael was a testosterone-filled Father Paul wannabe, but I expected more of Sam. To leave her like this and not even call for another sister to take care of her was outrageous. We were supposed to model our lives after the Bible's edicts. Where was love thy neighbor? Where were compassion and kindness?

"I sent them away. I just need time, and I'll be alright."

I was confused by her dismissal; she was obviously not okay. "Olivia, what happened during the exorcism? Is that when you first felt ill? You told Michael you hit your head. Why did you lie?"

Olivia and I weren't close, but she had always been kind. I wanted to help her, but I wasn't sure how. I wasn't even sure what the problem was. She laid back against the pillows propped behind her and took a deep breath. The walk back from the door and our conversation had winded her. My concern deepened, but also my suspicion. *How could she have gotten this sick so fast?*

"I don't want to tell you, Eliza. I like you. You're one of the few I like, and I don't want to have to leave, and I don't want you to hate me."

My eyebrows tried to climb to my hairline. "What are you talking about? Nothing you say is going to make me hate you. I won't let you leave. Why would you leave? You have one of the best reputations of all the postulants."

She laughed, the sound turning to a cough. "I'm certainly not a model postulant, Eliza."

"Why?"

"Because I'm not a human. Because I'm not here to exorcise demons, I'm here to bring them in." As she said the words, her eyes widened, and her hand left mine to clap over her mouth like she couldn't quite believe what she'd said.

I was backing toward the door before I realized I'd stood from the bed. I stopped my retreat, forcibly stopping myself from running. This couldn't be happening. Olivia? The most innocent of the sisters. The one we all measured ourselves against, the one even Sister Mary was kind to.

She lowered her hand, and her eyes drooped forlornly, but she didn't try to stop me. Her mouth drew down on one side, and her eyes became watery. "It's okay." Her voice cracked. "I get it."

I took a deep breath and felt for the doorknob behind me, ready to bolt. This was insane. This wasn't real. This wasn't— I stopped, a thought forming.

I licked my lips and, instead of turning the knob, leaned against the door. Maybe Luk had been possessed, but the exorcism didn't fully work. Could he have passed on his demon to Olivia? But he was still talking crazy, so that didn't fit either. I timidly walked back into the room and took a seat at the end of the bed again. Olivia lay still, reminding me of when Luk had played opossum so I would come talk to him.

"What made you sick during the exorcism, Olivia?"

She lay so still, one tear falling from her eye, tracking down her pallid cheek. She didn't move to wipe it away. "You were saying prayers to send a being from the other side back. And you have a unique ability to do it. Even though you weren't concentrating your ability, even though you didn't know you were using it, you're a conduit, a gatekeeper, and just being there during the words gave it more power."

I tried to digest what she had said, reconcile it with the dogma I had been taught was the only acceptable view of this world and the next during years of Catholic school. "Why would I have a unique ability?"

She furrowed her brow but otherwise remained still. "Because you're a death witch, Eliza. Don't you know that?"

I swallowed, glancing toward the door. *Little Witch. Who are your people?*

"I've never heard the term death witch."

"If I move, will you run away?" she asked.

My eyes were locked on her every movement, wondering how fast a demon could move, thinking of Luk and the guard. Despite my fear, I wanted to know. My entire life had been laid out for me. My one attempt to leave had lasted less than a year and was disastrous, with the Church my only place to turn to. They had told me how to be, how to think, and who I was my entire life, and I had been so sure I was bad or wrong that my only hope was to listen. But I had seen ghosts since I was a child. I felt things during exorcisms that no other postulants talked about. I had never felt *right* in the Church. And with everything thrown at me lately, I was beginning to wonder, was it because there was something more? Could it be that I wasn't bad, that what the Church had taught me was a lie?

I nodded to her and held my breath.

She scooted herself until her back was more firmly against the headboard and pulled her legs to her chest. "You're a daughter of Hecate. I heard the patient, Lukman, say it to you, and you didn't seem shocked. I've seen you go into town to feel the energy. I figured you were here on some kind of mission like me."

My face was a mask of confusion, my heart a riot of uncertainty. I let the breath out. Luk was crazy. Olivia must have been possessed by the same demon. But how did demons get down to the infirmary? I thought we had prayers and wards.

"The first time I went down to the infirmary, he told me our mothers were friends and called me a daughter of Hecate.

I researched who she was after that. Do you know what Luk is?"

She tilted her head. "I know of his kind. Sekhmet is a feared goddess where I'm from, and we all know of her children. They've had varying degrees of success in their mission throughout the centuries."

I picked at my finger again. It started to bleed, but the sharp pain helped center me. Bleeding still hurt. Everything wasn't different yet.

"What is their mission? What are her children? Gods?"

Olivia laughed, and the impression of bells made me think of the Olivia a moment ago. Who I had thought she was. Enchanting and beautiful and kind. I shook myself. Was she not still those things?

She didn't notice my internal battle. "Children is a euphemism. They are her creation. Her pet projects. When God began to smite those he didn't agree with by using his own children, she took it personally. She felt a need for balance. She created what you know as vampires. They were to punish the wicked. They subsist on blood, but they can also be tempted by earthly means. However, if they stray too far from their path, if they don't fulfill their intended purpose, they won't earn their rebirth. While they have longevity granted by their maker, they aren't infallible. They can be killed. Many have fallen to gluttony and greed and been killed by their blindness to their wants."

It was too much. I felt like my skin was shrinking too tight around my bones. If Oliva was telling the truth, nothing was what I had been taught, what I had been raised to be. Nothing was within the lines where I knew how to survive. I thought I had been ready to be shown that, but I hadn't looked far enough ahead. To what lay on the other side of the unknown. To what the freefall of stepping off that cliff would feel like. I stood and began pacing, absentmindedly picking into the wound of my thumb.

"Olivia, this sounds crazy. Have you become possessed? I don't want to turn you into the infirmary—"

The stark fear on her face stopped me. I had intended to explain how I had been threatened with that as a child. I began to go to her, already forgetting she might be some monstrous thing, but she scooted away from me like I was the monster. She huddled in the corner of the wall and the bed, looking for all the world like a frightened child.

"Oliv—"

"Please don't. *Please.*"

"I—"

"You don't understand. I have a purpose too, Eliza. I was sent here by my maker. And if I fail, if I'm found out and sent forcibly back, I won't get my rebirth either. I'm a lower-level demon, Eliza. I won't even get a second chance."

I had been vaguely thinking maybe Olivia had been possessed by a demon, but she had just told me she *was* one. "You're, y-you..." I stuttered, not sure how to say it. Not wanting to really confirm it.

She nodded. "A succubus. It's my job to infect as many of the congregation here as I can, to cast as much doubt on this infirmary as I can. The underworld isn't happy with the Church establishing more of them. Their efforts are usually scattered and below the Lord's attention, but this infirmary is organized and effective. It's my job to help the hitchhikers get their hooks in and keep them in."

"Hitchhikers," I muttered.

She looked at me curiously. "You really didn't know what you are?"

What I am. "What am I? I'm a postulant. An orphan. A woman. But then they throw me into this exorcism, and I meet this man. Is he possessed? Is he a *vampire?* Then I find out one of the purest postulants, the one Mother Superior tells us to live up to, the one Sister Mary is even polite to, is a *succubus demon.*" I laughed at the ludicrousness of it all. My hands flew to massage my temples, and my eyes closed tight against the words I was beginning to accept were true. One last attempt to keep the insanity at bay. *Don't be a coward,* I whispered to myself. Dropping my hands and looking up at Olivia, I asked, "Olivia, did you seriously think I *knew* what I was? I still don't."

She didn't let her legs go, but she relaxed more. "I really did. You act like one of the touched. The way you dance, the way you sneak around and throw off suspicion. I've seen you in the graveyards too. Sure, people think you're odd, but the fact that you aren't a prisoner in those cells yourself, I really thought you were more skilled than me at infiltration."

I shook my head. "What do I do with this? I can't believe you saw me. Did you follow me?"

Olivia shrugged. "Well, yeah. I mean, you're a gatekeeper, and I was trying to stay on this side of the gate. I kept close tabs on you and always tried to stay on your good side."

I plopped onto the bed, leaning back on my hands, giving in to the exhausting revelations and the fact that I was accepting this new reality. Another thought wiggled in. I wasn't afraid. Not only was I beginning to believe all of this, it felt more like home than anything in the Church ever had.

"Olivia, how do I find out who I am?"

She scooted a little closer to me. The fact neither of us were screaming at the top of our lungs was a good sign. We were starting to trust each other a little more. "Finding a coven would be a good place to start." The repeat of Luk's words earlier chilled me, but at this point, I figured they were probably true.

Eleven
Eliza

We weaved through a bustling crowd of contradictions. There were couples dressed up, coats held tight against the chill, homeless with their hands outstretched to passersby. Music called out to me from the different bars and restaurants we passed. Soon, the clubs would be opening. I felt a prick of disappointment. The idea of losing my troubles to the beat of a good song and a stranger's hands sounded wonderful right now.

Unbidden, the image changed, the hands no longer a stranger's, but Luk's long olive-tone fingers crawling over my belly. I thought of him, blood dripping down his chin after he ripped out that guard's throat. I thought of him when I had left the infirmary last, livid at Father Paul for touching me, and I shivered.

"It's not too far off the beaten path, just close enough to get the occasional tourist, but far enough away to attract the intended clientele."

I nodded to Olivia and followed her away from the familiarity of Church Street and farther into the darker streets of the wharf. Olivia had been surprising me since our conversation. How could the most innocent-seeming sister at the Church be a succubus demon?

As we walked down the steep hill, I asked, "Break this

down for me. What exactly is a succubus?"

Olivia side-eyed me. We had dressed in regular clothes, our habits left behind when we had snuck off the church grounds. Her jeans and crop top accentuated her curves, and her long blond hair, normally hidden in her coif, flowed in wavy curls down her back. She'd opted for light eye makeup and lip gloss. The overall effect changed her from an innocent angel to a blond temptress.

"I was created to tempt men. Lilith was angry at how easily God replaced her when she didn't conform to what he had envisioned for his precious humans. She was a woman of power and vision, and she wanted to be Adam's partner, not his servant. When she wouldn't get in line, God replaced her with Eve. In retaliation, Lilith made the succubae. It really wasn't fair to Eve, she was sweet, but it didn't take Adam long to stray."

I gawked at how airily she told her story. "Adam and *Eve.*" I raised my voice higher than intended on the last word. Olivia cocked a smile.

"How old are you?" I asked, wondering if she had been the succubus who had tempted Adam.

She seemed to read my mind. "I'm only one hundred years old. Really not that old. Delilah has long since earned her rebirth. She was born again as a human sometime around the eighteenth century, I believe."

I turned my head away from Olivia and mouthed the words, "Only one hundred years old." My mind boggled at the world I was falling into. I had gone back to the Church because my attempt to live on my own had ended in pain and fear. It was a prison, but a safe prison. Olivia was showing me my world had never been as safe as I had thought, and there was more around me I hadn't even known existed. It's like I had spent my entire life with my head in the sand, just trying to exist. But my eyes were opening. Somehow, it felt like I was starting to…live.

"You seem to be taking this well. Are you just in shock? Think I slipped you some shrooms?"

I faced her and ran a hand through my brown hair, then looked at the sky, tripping a little on an uneven paving stone on the sidewalk. "I was enrolled in a school for exorcism. I believe in demons, and I believe in God. I've heard of witches and vampires, though I just figured they were misunderstood demons that hadn't been exorcised. It's not that this is easy to take in. It's just that, I don't know. I feel like I'm peeling back the layers of something I guess I already kind of knew existed. And somehow, it feels right."

She nodded. Pointing to our right, she said, "We're going that way. Look for the tarot sign."

We walked in silence to a Victorian-style house, complete with a gable roof, stained-glass windows in the tower, and a winding porch with a banner that said "Tarot." "A tarot card reader?"

Olivia turned to me, her eyes serious. "A powerful divination witch. I'm not sure how much we can trust her, to be honest. Sarah Lee has her own motivations. But she should at least know what happened to your family. To you."

I picked at my thumb, the wound a scab now. "Do we just tell her I think I'm a death witch? What did you call it, a gatekeeper?"

Olivia's already large eyes went comically wide. "Are you insane? Didn't you hear me say we can't trust her? We just say we want our cards read. I'll ask some casual questions about thinking I felt a gatekeeper around here and see what she says. Maybe she'll be able to read something in your cards that will point us in the right direction to search next."

I nodded, biting my lip. My head was a mess right now,

vacillating between curiosity—part of the reason I never felt like I fit into my life was because I didn't, but there was somewhere I did fit—and wondering if I'd gone crazy. I fought demons; I didn't befriend them. Witches were curse-happy devil worshippers, trying to steal God's power, not my parents, who I was somehow taken from as a baby. Vampires were monsters akin to the devil, not hot men who I ached to feel over me. Except now that I was faced with it, none of that seemed to be true. And right now, Olivia felt like my closest friend.

"Let's go then. You take the lead."

Olivia threaded her arm through mine. "That's the spirit."

As we neared the porch, the door opened. A dark-skinned bohemian woman with white dreads leaned against the doorframe. Her long skirt swayed against her solid frame, black liner painted her eyes, and a small frown formed on her mouth. "I heard there was one of you around these parts. Didn't expect you to darken my door."

Olivia, open and innocent, trotted up the walk and two steps to the woman's porch. "We were out for a night on the town and thought we'd see what the cards had in store for us."

"Bit of an odd pastime for a succubus, don't you think?" She crossed her arms and eyed me up and down, probably wondering where I fit in. So far, everyone could tell what I was by being around me. I stared boldly back at the woman, trying to feel for something. Anything. But I just felt the chill of a Vermont spring night and unease in my gut.

Olivia shrugged one shoulder. "Is my money not as good as any of your other patrons? I want to see if my rebirth is coming."

The woman's eyes finally shifted back to the succubus demon. She sniffed. "We both know you're too young for that. Keep your secrets, then. Come in if you have cash. Business has been slow."

Olivia had a forced smile on her face, but tension creased the corners of her eyes and tightened her jaw. Eyeing the empty doorway, I forced a foot forward. I wanted answers. I wanted to know who I was and why these entities were telling me I was one of them, not one of the Church's.

Olivia tugged on my arm, her feet dragging in hesitation, but only for a moment. She followed me over the threshold into the house. I looked around, unsure what I would find. It seemed like the typical antique furnishings found in an older Vermont home. Luxurious Persian rugs added warmth and cushion to the old marked-up hardwood floors. Curtains cordoned off most of the house, other than the foyer and the living room, bringing in a bit of the fortune-telling vibe I expected.

The woman rifled through a drawer in an old sewing table. After taking out a deck of cards, she headed to the sitting area, a small circular table surrounded by a garish flower-patterned rolled arm sofa and mismatched armchairs. She sat in one of the armchairs, and Olivia and I took a seat on the sofa.

"Whose cards am I reading first?" she asked.

Olivia and I sat arm to arm. I could feel her intake of breath, ready to name herself, but I had grown too impatient. "Me!" I blurted before she could speak.

She elbowed me, but I ignored it. The woman eyed me again. "And who are you, girl?"

I felt a prick of annoyance. "I'm Eliza, and I'm a twenty-five-year-old woman."

The woman, Sarah Lee, Olivia had called her, scoffed. "For a mortal, I suppose that would feel like a great deal of time."

I frowned at her. "And you aren't mortal?"

The woman turned to Olivia with a droll look. It seemed to say, what kind of noob did you bring me? I shifted, annoyed, uncomfortable, and feeling like I had stuck my foot in it.

"I am a daughter of the Carmantae. I am human, but my mothers have touched me, and I live no mere mortal life."

Olivia rolled her eyes and moved as if to whisper to me but said loudly for Sarah Lee to hear, "Witches get a *little* boost in longevity. It's nothing compared to most, a few hundred years max, but they do live longer than most mortals."

I breathed as the edges of my vision darkened. A heavy weight settled on my chest. I swallowed and bit my cheek, tasting the tang of blood. I needed to keep it together. I needed to get answers. But everything being thrown at me, the rate at which my world was changing, was starting to give me whiplash.

My voice was hoarse when I said, "Right, longevity. My bad. So." I coughed, clearing my throat. "Me first, then?" I ended it like a question.

Sarah Lee sniffed again, her eyes resting on me this time. It seemed to be her favorite way to show disdain. "Fine. Let's begin."

She shuffled the large deck of cards in front of her, their backs covered in an intricate tree, notes of music hung like fruit, and in the middle was cradled what looked like an infant. I watched carefully, never having been to anything like this. I had seen tarot readers and psychics at fairs, but as a sister, it wasn't something I encouraged or patronized myself. Sarah Lee hummed, her body folded over her hands, where the cards shuffled almost too fast for me to follow. The harmonized melody and soft shuffle of the cards mesmerized me, making me sway, and my eyes began to grow heavy. I imagined I was in a field, with spring all around me, and everything around me felt alive and awake. The grass with opinions on the flow of the wind, the wildflowers singing a sweet song, the insects harmonizing with the flutter of their wings. Sarah Lee's humming grew sharp, rising in intensity, bringing me back to the moment. Suddenly, she snapped up, staring at me with nothing but the whites of her eyes. I gaped. They matched her white hair and contrasted dramatically against her dark skin.

"What is your question?" The voice she used wasn't the same one it had been before. Her speech amplified like she was speaking through a microphone. My gaze slipped to Olivia, but she just shook her head and motioned toward Sarah Lee. I swallowed. What was my question?

"Where…" I thought about it, wondering how I could ask my question without giving myself away. "Is my family alive?"

I couldn't tell where Sarah Lee looked anymore. The whites of her eyes seemed to gaze into space and time itself. She held the deck out on one outstretched palm. "Cut the deck."

Wiping suddenly sweaty palms on my jeans, I scooted to the edge of my seat and leaned forward to cut the deck. I placed a third of the deck onto Sarah Lee's other empty palm. She combined the two decks together and drew three cards off the top, placing them face up in a row. Then she placed the rest of the cards to the side. I jumped when she snapped her eyes closed. When she opened them again, they were her normal dark brown.

She looked down at the table and back up to me almost immediately. "Your first card, your past. The queen of swords in reverse. You've grown up denying your true needs. You felt that to nourish your soul would be selfish, would be wrong. It has withered due to this neglect." She frowned. The tip of her fingernail, sharpened to a point and milky white, touched the middle card. "Your present. The devil."

An involuntary sharp intake of breath brought her attention back to me. Olivia's hand dug into my thigh. I kept my face blank, but my attention was rapt. The card showed a man on a throne with fangs just like Luk's and two people below him. "You are facing a crossroads where you won't be able to ignore those needs much longer. There is something coming, something that will open your soul to all it's been missing. Something that will feed it in a way it's never been fed. You need this if you are to bring yourself back to life, back to what should have been."

I swallowed. *What did that mean, what should have been?*

Sarah Lee looked down at the last card and sharply back up to me. "Who are you?" she demanded suddenly. Olivia rose next to me, grabbing my arm.

"You know, I don't think I need to be read after all. I think we're actually good here. Right, Eliza? Let's go."

We began to walk hurriedly to the door, more questions than answers swirling in my head. "Stop!" Sarah Lee demanded behind us.

"Let's go," Olivia muttered urgently, keeping us moving toward the front door.

"Who are you to draw the moon as your future?" Sarah Lee sounded mad but didn't follow us over the threshold of the front door. "Who are you to claim Hecate's blessing?" she called as we hurried up the road, our breath puffing in front of us in the cold.

Twelve

Luk

"Baby, we can't get caught."

"Please, you know I need it. You know I need *you.*"

"Oh, baby, I need you too."

I heard a scuffle and then a fall. I looped my long arms over my bent knees. I was weakening again, nowhere near desiccation, but I was filtering all the energy I had left to my hearing and sight. Saving the succubus might have been misguided, sapping much of what I'd regained from the guard. I sighed. Strength wasn't going to be what helped me get out of here anyway. It would be my wits. I needed as much information as possible to use against those around me, those in charge of the keys to my cell. After our talk, Mother Superior had sent down some refreshments, water to wash with, and a new pair of pants, this time with a shirt. If she thought it would soften me toward her cause, she wasn't as smart as I'd given her credit for.

Shortly after the commotion on the level above me, I heard the swoosh of a patient door sliding open, then closing. The door to the actual prison they called the infirmary made a louder, more echoing noise when it opened. Before the woman left the underground completely, I called out, hoping she'd hear my shout from down in my dungeon, assuming only she would, and she was clever enough to ensure nobody else was around to hear her feeding.

I sighed in relief when she approached the stairs. I knew her footfalls by now. She'd been coming to see the man who had an Asmodeus hitchhiker since I'd woken. It's how I'd known she was a succubus demon. I had learned her name since she'd tried to exorcise me, almost sending herself back instead.

The footfalls stopped outside my cell. She smoothed her hair back under her coif, eyes settling on me. I needed an ally. I wanted to know how I could see Eliza again. "Olivia."

Her face was expressionless, her lipstick half rubbed off, her coif askew; she looked ridiculous. I swallowed my laugh, turning it into a cough.

"What do you want, vampire?"

Her words were slightly exasperated, turning my amusement to annoyance. I frowned. Jealousy spiked, and I quickly pushed it down. Jealousy that she was free to complete her purpose, that she seemed to be having some measure of success, and that she was able to interact directly with Eliza.

I forced my features to smooth and cocked my head instead. "I want intel. How are you doing, succubus?"

She pursed her plump lips. Olivia was beautiful, a buxom blond somehow perfectly packaged as an innocent angel in her plain white and black habit. Considering the dichotomy of her projected image, she probably tempted the men of this congregation with ease. Meaning, she was smart too, I reminded myself. No stupid demon would have had the guts or the skills to pull off masquerading as a sister in an exclusive school. She must be hurtling toward earning her rebirth.

"Don't play with me, vampire. If this is your attempt to charm me, it needs work."

I dropped the pretense and leaned against the bars. I was

tired anyway. The blood I had taken from the priest had fueled me enough to be able to function. The blood from the guard had made it easier to think straight, past the hunger, and returned me to my normal state. But the exorcism had taken its toll, their god's magic warring with mine, and I was back to feeling like a starving man. Since the succubus didn't seem to want to play, I wouldn't expend the energy trying.

"How is Eliza?" I asked plainly, hunger of a different kind making me wonder if she was alright.

Olivia's eyes slanted, and her shoulders hitched. "Why are you so curious about Eliza?"

I swallowed. What might she want in exchange for the information I needed? I rubbed a hand over my mouth, letting out an involuntary chuckle at my bloodstained cell, the lingering smell of the corpse they had removed, and the useless shackles lying in a pile at the back. I had nothing to trade. I decided to show my hand and ask for what I wanted, determined to give whatever I could in return.

"She was kind to me. And she's in danger. I'd like to repay the kindness."

Olivia stood straighter. "How is she in danger?"

The interest in her voice was unmistakable, quieting my own hopeless thoughts.

I turned back to her. Maybe I did have something to bargain with after all. "I'll tell you that if you tell me how she is."

Olivia tsked in annoyance, shifting her weight, looking toward the stairs, the path away from my dank cell. Turning back to me, she said, "Eliza is fine. She's how she always is."

My mouth twisted in annoyance. I gave her the same meaningless answer she'd given me. "Eliza's in danger like every mortal is in danger. She's dying from her own humanity."

Olivia threw her hands up. "Well, I don't know what you mean by 'how is she?' What are you asking? She's a sister who is doing sister things. I can't read your mind, vampire."

I frowned. What did I mean? "I— is she…." I stopped, realizing I didn't even know what I meant. "Does she seem more troubled than usual?"

Olivia hooked a hand on her hip, keeping her body turned toward the stairs and hall, striking a pose that was probably more natural to her than the demure subservience of her Catholic nun persona. "Yes, but not because of anything you need to know about. Now, how is she in danger?"

I recognized the urgency in her voice. "You like her?"

She rolled her eyes like I was ridiculous, but the crease in her brow gave her away. Something troubled her. Finally, she spoke in a clipped voice. "Well, like you said. She's kind. Now hurry up and tell me. I can't stay here much longer without getting caught."

I leaned closer to the bars. If the succubus had a soft spot for the little witch, maybe she'd help me protect her. "The Church took Eliza from her parents when she was a baby. They killed her entire line. She's the last gatekeeper, the last of the Hecate touched."

Olivia's jaw dropped. Her gaze became distant when she said, "That's why they haven't been around the last couple of decades. That's why there's been a shift in the underworld."

"What do you mean?"

"The two, no, the last *three* decades..." Her voice trailed off. "There was a shift, and the Catholic Church seemed to be getting stronger. It's why I was sent here. It's why I was tasked with taking such a risk. The underworld determined that the Church is becoming too powerful, and the power is shifting. So many of us haven't been able to earn our rebirths, so many perished for eternity because we haven't been able to access this plane. I was sent to try to undermine this infirmary, so it can't become as effective as the others for sending us away."

"What if they mean to use Eliza to send hitchhikers away? To send demons away?"

Olivia's eyes widened as she realized I was right. "Oh, Lilith." Her mouth set in a thin line, and she said, "We can't let them find out. Despite growing up in their orphanage, she's different. She isn't like them, Luk. She's kind, she's open-minded. We went to a Carmantae witch just last night; Eliza knows she's something else and wants to learn about her real family—"

"You did what?" My voice was low and dangerous. Olivia had exposed her to a Carmantae witch? To someone who would be jealous of Eliza's inherent power? Of her birthright? "Did you let her read her?"

Olivia bit her lip, and her hand dropped from her hip. "Yes," she squeaked.

I closed my eyes, a growl starting in my chest. My hands clenched into fists, the nails digging into my palms. "You put her on their radar? You lit her up like a supernatural beacon?"

Olivia was so nervous she danced from foot to foot. "I—yes, we didn't know what she was. I knew she was a death witch, but I never thought the Church would have been able to eradicate her line. We were trying to figure out how she could find her family—"

"Bring her to me." I cut her off, anger barely kept at bay. No matter how much I wanted to crush the little succubus for putting Eliza in danger, I needed her while I was trapped in this cell.

Olivia stilled, some of her sassy strength coming back. "Why?"

I narrowed my eyes. "Because I can teach her about her family. I need to make her understand without exposing her to any more entities that could try to harm her, capture her for their own use, or steal what she has."

"How can you teach her?"

I scoffed in disgust, my anger renewing my energy. I paced the length of the short space. "Stupid succubus, do you know the time I'm from? I was there when the death witches were at their most powerful. I knew them. I worked with them. I can tell her about her history without exposing her to more danger."

Olivia looked at me skeptically. "Why do you care?"

I stopped pacing, standing before her. I looked at the stairs, searching for an answer. Realizing the little witch already meant more to me than she should, my breath hitched. I thought back to the tranquility I'd felt, lying still, curious about what Eliza would do. Her soft words when she said even the devil needed prayers. Her outrage when she learned I hadn't been given food or water. I looked back at Olivia, and whatever she saw in my eyes, her shoulders relaxed. "Because she's kind."

Thirteen
Eliza

My hand fisted the sheet, my chest hitching as the sharp sweetness caused a pool of wetness to form around my finger. I groaned and turned my head to the side, pushing it into the pillow. I moved my finger faster, letting a second join it, gritting my teeth and rolling my ankle against the building sensation. Unable to take it anymore, I flipped over, breathing fast and moving my hand faster.

I mentally scrolled through a few of my go-to fantasies, settling on my hands held firmly over my head as my hips worked. I swallowed as I slowed my movements, not wanting to work myself to a finish too fast. I wanted to draw this out a little bit. Needed the cascade of warmth to last more than a few seconds.

As I thought of strong hands lifting me under my ass, slamming me against the wall to drive inside me, my thoughts changed. The strong arms' owner wasn't faceless anymore. I imagined staring into Luk's eyes. Not his eyes as I'd seen them the first time, vivid blue against a gaunt face. I imagined him the way he was now, his strong cheekbones and defined jaw blooming with health. And exertion. I imagined his broad shoulders, muscles contracting as he held my ass firmly, working me with his dick to finish with him. In my fantasy, the muscles in his neck corded, and he grunted from the buildup, almost too sweet.

I bit into the pillow, the fantasy so visceral I practically felt him instead of my own fingers pumping inside me. I pitched over the edge, that moment when the feeling became so sharp it was almost painful, so good I couldn't stand it anymore, right before it released into a rush of relaxation. Electricity rushed up my spine, and even my tensed shoulders relaxed, contributing to the feeling of overall ecstasy. I closed my eyes and loosened my jaw around the pillow filling my mouth. I breathed around the sheet as I rode the wave as long as I could.

I was jarred out of it sooner than I wanted by a thump outside my door. My head snapped around, and I quickly pulled my hand from my yoga pants. I jumped out of bed like it was on fire, yanking the small quilt over the pillow. I whipped my head left and right like the entire room would showcase what I had just been doing.

My pulse skyrocketed at the tentative knock. I rushed to the door, not wanting whoever stood on the other side to think there was a reason for the delay. Opening the door, slightly out of breath, I tried to look nonchalant. The effect was ruined by Olivia, apple cheeks red, sweat on her temple, pushing forcefully past me. I glanced both ways down the hallway, then quickly closed the door and turned to face her.

She leaned against my nightstand, fanning her face. "Girl, if I knew I could just walk by your door and have a feast, I wouldn't waste my time on that greasy slimeball down in the infirmary."

I laughed nervously. *She couldn't know. She couldn't know.* "What do you mean?"

Finally catching her breath, she gave me a level gaze. "What do you think 'What do I mean?' The sexual energy reached me through your door. I was afraid I'd be caught lurking outside, but it was worth it. I didn't want to risk interrupting," she waved her hand at me, "whatever was going on."

I flicked my thumb, wincing from the scabbed wound's pain. "I didn't...I wasn't...I..."

She looked at me quizzically before understanding dawned. "Eliza, I don't care. That was hot. Like, actually, do more of that. Like, do that all the time."

I fidgeted, walking over to the bed. "I know I shouldn't. I know it's wrong. But sometimes, the energy gets so built up. I just need a way to let it out. I've prayed and prayed about it. But the older I get, the more exhausting it is."

I sat down on the bed. It dipped when she sat beside me.

We sat in silence for a while, me flicking my thumb and her drumming her fingers on her thighs. She blew out her breath and finally spoke into the silence. "You remember what I am, right?"

The familiar shame that accompanied my nights on the town weighed me down. I thought about what she had said, but before I could respond, I started to laugh. The ridiculousness of it. The irony. I couldn't take it. Olivia laughed too. I wiped tears away from my eyes, finally getting myself together.

"I guess my impression of Olivia the postulant hasn't completely been overridden yet."

She chuckled again, then wrapped her arm through mine and rested her head on my shoulder. "Good. Because I'm both. Sort of. Well, I just mean I'm still the me you met before I told you where I'm from."

I laughed. That phrase usually meant someone's state or country, not their existence. I sighed, the awkwardness creeping back in. "Anyway, I'm glad I...filled you up?"

Olivia wiped an arm across her brow. "Phew, did you! I guess it makes sense, though, considering last night."

I frowned. "What do you mean?"

Olivia shrugged. "I mean, it must have been a lot of energy to channel, what happened with Sarah Lee. Not to mention, I imagine you had to contend with that dead guard last week, and we haven't had a break. I'm sure you did need to blow off some steam."

Turning slightly to see Olivia better, I asked, "How did you know about the guard? And why would you assume that all made me have to blow off steam?" I felt like every time I was around Olivia, or Luk for that matter, I learned something else. Something that made my nature, my habits, the things that tied me up in knots at night, make sense. I was beginning to feel like there was a space and time in which I belonged.

Olivia cocked her head. Shaking herself, she muttered, "I keep forgetting. Eliza, you're a gatekeeper, a death witch. The only one around these parts. If he passed, he passed through you. And I mean, even I could feel the energy that Carmantae witch was putting off last night. She was pulling from you. You must have felt a spike of energy, even if you don't know how to properly channel it."

I ran my fingers through my hair, pulling it to the side. "What does that have to do with what I, with your," I huffed, telling myself to stop being a child, "with your *feast*."

Her mouth tilted in a half grin. "You need some way to expend that energy. Where do you think the legends came from of witches dancing naked under a full moon? Energy doesn't get destroyed; it transfers. Before I realized you didn't know who you were, I just figured it was how you released energy. You're more naturally powerful than any other witch I've met. The power fills you sometimes to bursting. It's too much to hold, and you need to let it go."

"Do other witches need to let it go? Is this how we all let it go? Sex and dancing?"

She shook her head. "Some do spells to store it for later. For some witches, the way they get their powers is through offerings and blessings. They do ritual sacrifice or hours of praying in order to earn their energy, and they do it for a specific spell. That spell expels the energy. Or some try to store it in sacred objects, like an athame. What is it like for you? When you're full like that?"

I laughed and turned back away from her. Looking at my hands in my lap, I once again got that feeling. What was it? Vindication? That I wasn't just an outcast, bad, a constant fuck up? That I wasn't just the dirty square peg that was dropped into this pure group of round holes? That the way I felt, and my coping mechanisms, were understandable?

"I guess, after a crossing, or some of the more difficult exorcisms, I feel this, like, heartbeat. It's next to my own, and it's thumping like a bass drum steadily faster and faster. I feel like I need to move with it—to it. If I haven't been able to get out for a while, and it builds up even more, it's like there's static on my skin, like I was near a lightning strike in a thunderstorm. Like if I don't move, if I don't relax, I'll explode next."

Olivia shook her head, eyes wide. "That sounds intense."

I coughed, feeling a little uncomfortable. I decided to change the subject. "What brought you by in the first place?"

Suddenly, Olivia seemed serious, a little withdrawn. Her shoulders hunched in, and she looked at the ceiling. "Oh, yeah." She kicked her legs against the bed and started to whistle. I waited her out. Finally, she started. "So, I was down in the infirmary with the slimeball, feeding."

"Feeding in the infirmary?"

She shrugged her shoulder casually and brought her hair

over her shoulder, playing with the ends. "Oh. Yeah, one of the guys down there has one of my hitchhikers. Honestly, it was easy. He already had the inclination and had done it once. He had repented due to his nature, of course, but not really. I just encouraged it until the hitchhiker took hold, and he did it…a lot."

"Did it?"

Olivia smiled big and winked. "Did it."

We both laughed. "It got him put in the infirmary, and since he's so handy and it's relatively low risk, he's the easiest for me to feed on right now."

"How do you feed?"

She shook her head. "Later. What I have to tell you is actually kind of important."

I nodded my head, though I felt like learning how a demon fed was pretty important.

"So, while I was down there, I talked to Luk."

Never mind, this is more important, I thought, remembering my fantasy.

"Okay?" I prompted when she stopped.

Olivia started kicking her legs against the bed again, lowering her head like she was unsure about something. I held my breath, wanting to know what had happened between her and Luk to make her feel like that.

"Luk is worried about our visit to Sarah Lee."

I jerked back. "You told him? You talked about me?"

She looked at me through a curtain of her hair as if she was hiding. "Uhm, yeah. He, uh, anyway, he made some good points. Nothing major. But he, well, he's offered to tutor you or whatever. I mean, he's offered to tell you about your dead family."

I sat dumbfounded by a few things. Hearing the words "dead family" that bluntly for the first time was a bit jarring.

I shook that off, pushing it to a corner of my mind so I could deal with it later. I concentrated on the tutor part.

"What do you mean tutor me?"

Olivia blew out an exasperated breath and turned to me. Taking my hands, she said, "Listen. There's a lot going on, and I don't want to spook you. But I think you need to go down and talk to Luk. I think he has a lot of information that can help you. And I think there's more going on with the Church, with how you came to be with the Church, than you know. I think you should go see him soon."

I stood, needing to move to process what she was saying. "How am I supposed to even get down there? I've been forbidden from interacting with him. And why would he, of all people, have information I could use? I mean, he's a supernatural entity who was conscious during the Crusades. Things have changed a little since he was around. And by a little, I mean this isn't the same world he left. He wouldn't even have known my great, great, great, great-grandma.

Olivia brought a finger to her mouth as if deep in thought and then smacked her lips. "Actually, he could have known your great, great, great, great-grandma. Death witches were beloved by their mistress and often granted longevity."

I rolled my eyes at her flip response. Swallowing, I tried to think about why I was really putting up any resistance. Didn't I want to know where I came from? I was worried because I was attracted to him. He excited me in a lot of ways, not the least most likely because he was forbidden. But those were all things I could suppress, urges I could channel into something else. The idea of trusting him with finding my family, or what happened to them, felt insane. How could he know anything useful, anything about my family in particular?

"What?" She shrugged her shoulders defensively.

I shook my head, walking away.

"Listen, Eliza. He wouldn't tell me everything. I'm not exactly sure what he's going to help you with myself. But for some reason, he wants to, and he says he can. And I'm worried. Things have been off lately. Father Paul has been taking secret meetings with the seminarians, and Mary has been getting shifty with me. It isn't like her. If something is happening, I think you should find out all you can."

I crossed my arms, cradling my elbows. Olivia was fast becoming my closest friend, but she was asking for a leap of faith I wasn't prepared to make. Sneaking into the infirmary to see a forbidden subject could land me next to him.

"How am I supposed to sneak in to see Luk in the first place? We don't have access to key cards unless given them for exorcisms. Saying I want to have teatime with the guy isn't going to go over well."

She looked troubled but nodded. "That, at least, I have covered. I needed to be able to get in myself. After seeing how Emily reacted when Luk killed that guard, I cozied up to her. I offered to do her duties for her at night when the guards are absent. I told her if she doesn't tell, I won't. Win, win."

I looked at her skeptically, my eyebrows drawn down. "The guards aren't on duty at night?"

Olivia shook her head at me. "The patients are given a call-bell-like thing that triggers a pager, and a nurse is put on duty. After Emily was put on Luk's duty, she became the permanent night nurse. There's one other rotating nurse on call in case it gets busy, but she isn't stationed in the infirmary. She just has to keep her phone on and be on the grounds."

I took a deep breath. It wasn't without risk, but it sounded like I could get down there. We'd have a short window of privacy. It was hard to keep coming up with reasons to avoid finding out the truth. Or whatever truth Luk might know. Even if it wasn't everything, maybe it would at least start to point me in the right direction.

"Okay. I'll go see Luk."

Fourteen
Eliza

Goosebumps rose on the back of my neck. The short hallway past the patient rooms to the iron jail they kept Luk in felt like a long winding tunnel. My steps echoed around me as I walked, a cacophony where normally sound was muted. I tried to quiet my heartbeat, to slow my breathing, to not be so neurotic. I carried a wash basin, soap, and some water for washing and drinking, and some bread and meat. This time, I remembered towels. An offering. Before I was ready, I was at his cell, and he stood, his hands behind his back, his head bowed, waiting.

As I came to a stop, my arms clutched the various items to my chest. He raised his head to look me in the eyes. For a second, an image flashed of him standing there, looking the way he had before, with sunken cheeks and an emaciated frame. But then his broad shoulders, bold nose, and strong jaw came into focus. His stubble was growing into a thick black beard that gave him a distinguished look, all of this after drinking the guard's blood. Someone else must have had the same idea because he was cleaned up. Dark gray sweatpants hung where the threadbare linen ones had, and a white shirt clung tightly to the muscles of his torso. My mouth felt dry as the desert he must have come from, and I tried to work moisture into it before talking. "Olivia said you can help me learn more about my family."

The corner of his mouth twitched. "I can help with a lot more than that."

I stared flatly at him but shivered at the implication in those words. He laughed as if he knew I wasn't as unimpressed as I was trying to act.

"Come in. Sit with me."

The request sounded ludicrous. I had watched him rip a guard's throat out. He called himself a vampire, and the way his starving body had transformed after drinking blood, I was beginning to believe it. But I remembered how still he lay, trying to ensure I felt safe. And I remembered the softness in his eyes when I had brought him food and water the first time. I let out an exasperated breath and headed to the cell door, pulling the keys Olivia had given me from my pocket. My new best friend was a succubus. How ludicrous was sitting and having a chat with a vampire after all?

He watched me carefully, backing up to the far wall, the one area of the cell that wasn't marked with blood. The smell threatened to overwhelm me, and I breathed as shallowly as I could. The dead body was gone, but death and rot clung to the place.

"I'm glad you came." Luk sat down, crossing his legs, looking up at the ceiling. I sat next to him, keeping space between us. I set down everything I'd brought between us, drawing his eye.

"Olivia said that you could help me. How do you know what you told her? About my family. About what the Church wants from me."

"Because your Mother Superior told me."

My eyes widened, my heartbeat going erratic. "Why would she tell you that?"

Luk's eyes lowered to my chest, which I thought was weird. I was slender, and it wasn't that big to begin with, and my habit covered me completely. Then I realized he was looking at my neck. Self-consciously, I swiped my hand over my pulse. The movement caught his eyes, and they narrowed. Like lightning, he reached across the space separating us and grabbed my hand, knocking the bowl I'd brought to the side. The quick movement made me gasp, and without thinking, I tried to move away, but he held fast.

"You're hurt," he said with a growl, and I couldn't decide if I was more frightened or turned on.

Licking my lips, I said, "It's nothing. I…it's a nervous habit."

He followed the motion with his eyes but was quickly absorbed again by the sore I'd picked near my thumb. Smoothing a finger over it gently, he said, "I don't like to see you hurt."

I nodded dumbly. "Why do you care?"

He looked back up, his expression so serious. "I'm not sure."

He kept my hand in his but didn't try to move closer. "Your family, the Hecate touched, they're gatekeepers, but we called them death witches."

"Because they let death pass through to the other side?"

He shook his head. "Because when they wanted, they forced souls, or demons, to the other side."

I frowned. "Really? I can't do that."

He tilted his lips up in a half grin. "There are many things you can do that you don't realize. And some that you may be able to do one day if Hecate blesses you."

I sighed. This was all so much. "Luk, why am I here? Is that what you wanted to tell me? Couldn't you have passed that along to Olivia when you told her the rest?"

He squeezed my hand. "I don't know how witches do magic exactly. I've only seen them do rituals and ceremonies that they spend their entire lives learning. They didn't teach vampires the methods, but they worked their magic around us. And I do know, the death witches I met, most of their powers were inherent. The powers lived inside of them. You need to find a temple dedicated to Hecate. You need to reach out to her. And in the meantime, when you meet people like me or Olivia, you need to be careful. Especially other witches. They will be jealous of what you have and try to steal it."

"Steal it, how?"

He didn't say anything for a while. He rested his head back against the wall like he was tired. Concern for him bloomed in me. Finally, "They could try to steal you, try to force your power out of you, and take it. Or they could try to make you join their coven for power. Last time I walked this Earth, it was all everyone cared about. Leaders traded in it, fought for it, murdered for it. You need to be careful."

I swallowed. Our hands, still clasped, rested on the ground. His thumb began moving over my hand, and my eyes zeroed in on the motion. "It's not like I run into a lot of witches in the Church."

He shook his head, opening his eyes. "You need to leave. The Church is more dangerous to you than jealous witches. I haven't told you yet what your Mother Superior told me. They plan to use you to complete exorcisms. It's why they stole you. And if you aren't able to exorcise me, they plan to put you in a cell next to me. They plan to kill you."

"But that's what I do. I am an exorcist. Why couldn't I just complete an exorcism? And what do you mean stole me?"

"Because they want to prove it with me. And it doesn't work that way. I'm not a hitchhiker. I'm a vampire. I am a corporeal being. You can kill me, and I will cease to exist, but you can't send my being to the other side. I exist on the plane my body exists on until I gain a soul. And to send a body across planes requires more than just prayers."

I pulled my hand out of his grip, and this time he let it go. I started to pace the cell, stopping short when I encountered the edge of dried blood. Turning back, I absentmindedly began flicking my thumb, feeling the familiar bite of pain.

"Stop that!" Luk said sharply. I gave him a look but stopped picking at my nail.

"What exactly did Mother Superior say to you? Why do you keep saying I was stolen?"

Luk watched me pace my small circle. "She said that you were taken as a baby, the rest of your line killed. The death witches had become a thorn in the Church's side they couldn't ignore. They didn't banish all demons that were brought to this plane; magic is about balance. They facilitated crossings of the dead, and it kept other less-powerful witches from being able to call on the ancestors easily, making them jealous. They thought the witches of Hecate just wanted the power for themselves. The Church saw an opening. The Church banded together with whatever covens they could, and they came for the Hecate touched. They killed them all. But Mother Superior, part of the effort at the time, couldn't bring herself to kill everyone when she found a swaddled baby girl crying in a hole hidden in the floor. She convinced the clergy that if they raised you, if they brought you to their side, you'd help turn the tide in the supernatural war. She wasn't wrong. You have a unique ability to send spirits and ephemeral beings across the line.

My breaths came short, and I had to close my eyes to stave off a panic attack. I brought my hands to my temples and massaged, trying to absorb everything I had just heard. Finally, I put it away in the back of my mind to deal with later. Opening my eyes, the pressure of tears building behind them, I tried to make sense of what my world was becoming. "I don't understand why this was urgent, Luk. If everything you're saying is true, this has been a lifelong effort. A lifelong, Jesus, indoctrination." I didn't chastise myself for the slip, taking the Lord's name in vain.

He watched me, shifting slightly but staying where he was. "Mother Superior said that, thanks to Father Paul and some other detractors, they have been making some noise. They don't believe their efforts and the risks they took have paid off. You've barely been a part of exorcisms of unconfirmed possessions, nothing more spectacular than any other postulant. They plan to make you prove yourself soon with an upper-level demon. With me. Or they plan to eliminate you while they believe they still easily can."

Fear and betrayal ripped through me. The Church had raised me. I might not see Abigail as my actual mother, but she was the only mother figure I'd ever had. The Church might not have been the supportive, loving family I'd always wanted, but they were the only one I'd ever known. And it was all a lie. I paced the length of the floor a couple more times, trying to collect my thoughts. Finally, I asked. "Why didn't you just tell them what you told me? That you need to be killed, not crossed over."

He gave me a bland look. "Because I'd like to stay alive."

I laughed, feeling stupid, wiping a hand down my face. Of course he wanted to stay alive, Jesus. What did I think? That this stranger who had managed to survive centuries in a shallow grave was trying to throw himself on the proverbial stake for me? Distantly, I realized I was getting real comfortable with those small blasphemies. I couldn't quite reconcile everything I'd been told. I wasn't even sure if I was ready to accept it all wholesale. I needed to research. I needed to do what Olivia and Luk had suggested and find a coven.

I was walking from one family spoon-feeding me what I'd always wanted, a place to belong, to another. At least this one seemed to do it with softer hands. It was like the difference between the kind souls and the bitter ones when they passed over. Coming to a decision, I said, "What a strange world I've walked into. I can't just run. I've been with the Church my entire life. They've taken care of everything for me. I wouldn't know where to go. I wouldn't know how to pay for it. I tried once and failed."

"What do you mean you failed?"

Familiar pain seeped in. I was ashamed—of what happened, of failing. "I left the Church at eighteen. Growing up in a Catholic orphanage isn't easy. I went to New Hampshire, thinking it would be a new start. I started bartending, living in a crummy little apartment. It wasn't much, but it was mine. But I blew it all up. I made a mess of myself and everyone around me. So, when one of the sisters found me near where I was working and offered to help me take my vows, I did it."

"How did you blow it up?" He hesitated on the phrase, and my lips quirked. He was either a good actor or the common expression sounded odd to him.

"There was this coworker of mine. I knew he liked me. I didn't feel the same, but I also felt so alone. I encouraged him just enough, so he wouldn't lose interest. So I could feel the balm of his company but not have to commit to anything. Eventually, he grew impatient. He took my smiles and my cuddling as a green light and thought I just needed encouragement. But his encouragement was forceful, and..." I huffed. I was trying to explain this without making it as ugly as it had been. "He tried to rape me. And when he did, something came over me. I'm not sure what, but what I do know is he ended up in the hospital, and the police gave the place I worked at, where it happened, a bad name. The hit to the little mom-and-pop bar's reputation cut deeply into its sales, and they almost shut down. The place had been around for generations. If I had just been clear, if I hadn't hurt him, maybe the police never even would have gotten involved."

I trailed off and looked up. Luk had moved close to me lightning fast, with fire in his eyes. Even if he had come from the time of the Crusades, rape was part of a universal language. "Who was this man?"

My brow wrinkled, wondering why he'd ask that. It's not like he'd know him. "Some guy I worked with. He—"

"No, I want to know who he is," Luk growled.

My eyes widened, realizing what he meant. "Luk, you can't go after him. You can't even leave here."

Luk was intent on me, his chest heaving. "I could leave here easily, little witch. Even weakened as I am, with that door open, I could walk right out. Nobody could stop me."

My breath began coming in pants. Luk's anger and indignation on my behalf were a huge turn-on. He hadn't censured me for leading on the coworker who'd gone too far. He didn't tell me that I had destroyed lives the way Sister Ruth had when she'd softly urged me to join the Church to earn forgiveness. He was ready to murder anyone who had ever hurt me. And I was ready to jump him, how it looked or what people thought be damned.

"Then why don't you?"

His eyes narrowed. "Because when I go, I'll be taking you with me. And because if I were to go right now, I wouldn't know how to keep you safe."

My breath hitched, and my eyes dipped to his lips, then darted back up to his eyes.

"What if I don't want to go?"

Luk didn't miss my glance. His lips curled into a lazy smile, and he stepped closer until he was fully in my space. "You'll want to go."

He leaned his head down until our breath mingled. I breathed him in, expecting him to smell of death and rot. Instead, he smelled like sweet licorice and spice. I inhaled sharply, tilting my head so our lips lined up. Without further encouragement, his lips met mine, his tongue sweeping into my mouth.

My hands went into his hair, pulling, tugging him tighter to me. His arms came around me, gripping my hips to that part of him that apparently worked *just* like a man. I felt devoured as he kissed every part of my mouth, his lips brushing mine in an erotic dance. Just as I began to hope he'd pull my habit over my head and rub his skin against mine, he pulled away, holding my shoulders an arm's length away from him.

Luk looked at me with softness in his eyes, breathing hard. "Wait. Not like this."

Insecurity began to set in. What was I doing? Telling this man, this vampire, this patient, my darkest secrets. Jumping him like a horny teenager… and then he rejected me.

Luk seemed to see the war in my eyes because he tugged me closer. Instead of kissing me, he held me, drawing me back toward the wall, pulling me down to sit next to him. He swallowed. "We need to talk more first."

I bit my lip, my mind a riot. Questioning myself for why I'd let what just happened happen, wanting it to again. "I know you're from a different century, buddy, but these days, you don't need to talk that much first if you don't want to."

His eyes danced at my words. "I'm a supernatural being, Eliza. We were never wrapped in the same constraints of mortal ethics. I want you. And I will have you. I knew it before and only stronger now. But I want you to understand me. I want you to understand this world. Because understanding will make you safe. And I need you safe."

Most of the sting of rejection faded at his words. I was becoming insane. I was already insane. But his words excited me. Despite knowing I was rushing into this too quickly. He was saying everything I had always wanted to hear. He cared about my safety, about me. And he had a body that made me want to sin. Giving myself to him, his lips and tongue, would be how I would repent. I whispered, "What do I need to understand?"

Luk looked at me with soft eyes. "My purpose is my entire reason for existence. Sekhmet doesn't play us like puppets. We can indulge in all the vices of humans. But then, we won't earn our rebirth. Any of our loved ones, when we die, will be lost to us forever. Different vampires react to that in different ways."

I cocked my head, wanting to know more about him. "What kinds of ways?"

He shrugged, looking away from me. "Some ignore their purpose and kill for the fun of it, enjoying the gifts Sekhmet gave us. Some indulge in everything they can take with their power: women, beautiful things, good food. Some turn away from anything they fear could tempt them: comfort, relationships." Looking back at me, he said in almost a whisper, "Love."

My mouth hung slightly open. The smells of the cell faded, the wet and fearsome surroundings distant, and I stared into Luk's mesmerizing eyes. He snapped me out of it when he said, "I barely had the chance to choose my path. I was captured and desiccated at fifty years old. I had barely begun to exist and thought my chance at deciding was taken forever."

"What is your purpose, Luk?"

"Vampires are here to punish the wicked. To strike fear in their hearts and to send them to their judgment. Sekhmet is a lover of Ma'at. She is war and peace, pain, and healing. She requires balance, and we are here to help her keep the balance. It's something my kind and the witches used to bond over."

Luk's lips quirked, and his head fell back against the wall as if exhaustion suddenly hit him. Like this conversation was taking everything out of him. "You look horrible. How can I help you, Luk?"

He rolled his head along the wall until he was looking at me. "You need to go soon. You've been here too long already."

I shook my head. "How can I help?"

He considered me for a while. He seemed to be at war with himself, his lips pursed at my question until they were in such a thin line, they disappeared into his beard. Finally, he said, "I need blood."

I gulped. *Blood? Of course.* "I'm not going to help you kill somebody."

He smiled faintly and shook his head. "I'm not asking you to. I'm not asking anything, really."

"Can I get you blood without hurting someone else?"

He looked into space. "Hurting? No. Killing or permanently maiming, yes. I just need the nutrition to subsist, just like you with food. Sekhmet's way of encouraging us to do as we're told."

I sighed deeply and jerked my head in a nod. My thoughts raced, but I knew what the answer was. I stretched my arm out between us, offering Luk my wrist.

"Take my blood."

His gaze sharpened, and his head lifted from the wall.

Like a snake striking, he grabbed my outstretched hand. "Don't play with me."

"I'm not." Fear zinged up my spine, and my adrenaline spiked. Goosebumps left a trail from where his hand touched my skin all the way up my arm.

His gaze turned shrewd, and he narrowed his eyes. "Tell me, Eliza. Are you kind because you're supposed to be? Does your compassion come because you want to be a good girl?"

I gave him a frosty glare. I knew I had been a puppet. It must look like I was a naive girl to him. But I had my own mind, and I would prove that to him. I'd prove it to myself. "The Church didn't teach me to be kind. It taught me to be ruthless. It taught me to lie, to hide myself, and to be scared. I'm kind because you're a human being."

His gaze softened but was no less intense. "I'm not a human."

I went to throw my hands in the air, exasperated, but he held fast, reminding me of when we first sat down. Annoyed, I said, "A being then. You live and breathe and feel, and I don't want you to feel bad."

"Why not?"

I felt like he was holding his breath. Something about how still he sat, watching me, waiting for my answer. I stared him square in the eyes and revealed more of my heart than I meant to. "Because I know what it feels like. And it hurts. And I don't want anyone or anything to hurt like that. Especially you."

He muttered something in Arabic and, without ever losing my gaze, lowered his mouth to my forearm. I felt him lick across my skin, and where his tongue traveled, my skin tingled, numbing. I watched as fangs descended past his normal teeth, and he sank them slowly into my flesh. The sting wasn't as sharp as I had expected, but either way, that wasn't what made me gasp. The feel of his tongue, his mouth as he replaced the sharp sting with firm suction, made me think of other things. It brought me back to my room, to that moment of sweet relief. It made me think of a possible future where Luk was in my bed, protecting me like he had said he wanted to. It made me think of new fantasies.

Fifteen
Eliza

I closed the door behind me, and Olivia popped up from the bed. In the short time I'd known her true identity, she'd transformed from a seemingly naive and innocent young woman to a vibrant, entrancing one.

"Tell me everything. What did he say?"

"Let's sit." I headed farther into the room, taking a seat on the simple high-backed chair at her desk while she sat bouncing on the edge of the twin bed.

"So?" she prompted.

I looked down at my nails for a second, specifically at the sore spot, buying a little time. I thought about Luk's thumb stroking my hand. I thought about his tongue and lips, the bite of his fangs on my forearm, hidden now by the sleeve of my habit. I wasn't sure I was ready to share all I'd learned, to rehash it. Besides, what would it change? My ugly family history, the truth of where I came from. Olivia already knew I was a death witch; that wasn't in question for her. My toes curled, and I lifted my head. "He didn't tell me much more than you, honestly. Just to be careful of other witches, and that I needed to run."

Olivia's face fell. "Run? Run where?"

I shrugged my shoulders, my stomach rising to my throat like I was in free fall. Then anger rushed back in. Anger at the

Church, at the lies and manipulation my entire life. It gave me the strength to keep going. "I have no idea. I wouldn't even know where to start. I've been with the Church almost my entire life. I've wanted to start over so many times. I just thought…I don't know what I thought. That I was bad. That I hurt people around me just by being there. But either way, I was wrong. I don't know where I'll go, but wherever it is, I'm taking Luk with me."

The familiar fear of going out into the world was like a tsunami coming straight for the banks. I'd volunteered with the Church to clean up the aftermath of a tsunami once before, and the damage was incalculable. That's what leaving the Church had been like to my life the first time. It's why, even though I'd never felt like I fit in, never found true contentment, I had never tried to leave again. Sister Ruth had told me all that the owners of The Raven, the bar I had worked at, had almost lost, the sentence Mike was being given because I wasn't clear. After all, if I had just been clear, I wouldn't have driven him to it. Sister Ruth had practically confirmed he was a good guy to everyone else; everyone liked him. It had to have been me. I figured, at least I was alive and had some kind of purpose. At least it was something I knew. But not anymore.

Olivia pursed her lips and began kicking her feet against the bed. It was her tell; she was thinking hard about something.

"I haven't made nearly enough headway here. I have another hitchhiker ready to go. I'm about to release him at the next Sunday sermon, but Lilith already spoke to me. She wanted me to be further along by now."

I gaped at her, and when she finally caught my expression, she paused, tilting her head. "What?"

"Lilith? Like *the* Lilith? You talk to her?"

Olivia lifted a delicate shoulder, soft where I was bony. "Yeah? She's my creator, and she's pretty hands-on with her subjects."

I swallowed. Lilith was different things in different Christian mythologies, but it was pretty universally agreed that she wasn't good. I looked at my friend, studied her soft feminine features, the delicate slope of her nose, the apples of her cheeks, and the warmth of her eyes. Cursing myself for my stupidity, I reminded myself I was dealing with divination witches and succubae. I had the hots for a vampire, and I was pretty sure he felt the same way. My mind drifted for a second to how steadily he had looked at me when he told me some vampires were tempted by relationships, by love. Coming back to the present, I shook my head. Weakly, I lifted my hand as if to wave away my silliness. "Right, go on."

Olivia nodded, oblivious, like I was really just clarifying who Lilith was. I held back a snort.

"Anyway, my point is, I can't leave just yet. But let me get a couple more hitchhikers in, and maybe I can help. Maybe I can go with you."

Warmth spread through my chest until that anxiety of a lonely future faded to a distant ache. What if I could escape? What if I wasn't alone? What if the Church wasn't the only home I had?

"You'd really want to come?"

Olivia rolled her eyes, hopping off the bed and settling her curvy form on my lap, startling me. Hugging me around the neck, she said, "Of course! With the way you blow off steam, I'm sure there will be plenty of places to feed and chaos to sow."

I laughed, and for once, it wasn't guilt that filled me but mischievousness. For once, I didn't feel dirty or shameful. I felt hopeful and excited. Before that wonderful new feeling had time to take hold, there was an abrupt rap at the door. The person knocking began opening the door before either of us had a chance to answer.

Olivia jumped off me like I was on fire; it wasn't exactly proper for us to be sitting on each other's laps. Unsurprisingly, Mary's head appeared around the door. Apparently, I wasn't the only one she inappropriately burst in on. Few others would dare be that intrusive. She looked between Olivia and me with narrowed eyes. "What are you doing here?" she asked me.

Olivia bowed her head slightly, face somber at Mary's accusatory tone. Betrayal was written on her face. Mary didn't like to share her friends.

"Sister Eliza requested council. Our last exorcism didn't go as planned. She wondered if I could tell her what she did wrong." Olivia folded her hands in front of her, looking neither guilty nor worried. I marveled at her ability to lie and to feed right into Mary's vanity and prejudice.

Mary sniffed, nose in the air like a cartoon character. "Of course it didn't. I've wondered how you've lasted this long. They've barely put you on easy, unconfirmed cases. Maybe that's what Mother Superior and Father Paul want to see you about. They looked very serious when I left them."

Normally, I would laugh at the gleam in her eye, but considering recent events and what Luk had told me, my gut twisted with fear. I was careful not to look at Olivia for comfort as I left, not wanting to break her facade of magnanimity regarding my incompetence. But I wished I could. That feeling of friendship, of a sort of family, even if fleeting, was something I had been searching for my entire life. Instead, I girded myself against whatever was going to happen and said to Mary, "Lead on." She practically skipped to deliver me to whatever horrible fate I knew she hoped waited.

Mary wasn't wrong. When I stepped into Abigail's office, she was seated across from Father Paul, and both wore grim masks. The room was silent enough that our steps echoed like a resounding clap as we entered the room.

"Mother," Mary said, with a freaking curtsy. She waited, head bowed, hoping to witness whatever reprimand, or worse, I was about to experience.

I didn't know why Mary and I had instant enmity. As soon as I had stepped foot across the school's threshold from my old convent, she had pinpointed me as a menace. Maybe it was because of the whispers about my oddity that had preceded me. My tendency to hang out in graveyards and pass out. Or maybe it was because I was a successful orphan when so many of us, after our tenure with the nuns, spent our lives rocking in a corner.

All I knew was nothing noteworthy had happened between us. Mary had known before she spoke a word to me that she hated me, and she hung on to that conviction ever since.

Abigail looked at her impatiently, one eyebrow raised in question, and finally said, "Thank you, Mary. That is all."

Disappointment pinched Mary's face. Her thin nose curled, and her lips puckered. But she nodded her head again and left the room without complaint. Father Paul sat silently through the entire exchange, staring at me steadily. I shifted. I had been in similar situations before. The last time, Father Paul had made a play to send me to the infirmary as a patient, not as an exorcist. His most earnest attempt. He'd had what he claimed was a folder full of evidence—accounts of my stories of ghosts as a child, backed up by a couple times I had been found talking to the air or passed out over gravestones.

He had shouted of his proof of my demonic possession and demanded I be cleansed, if for no other reason than to avoid infecting the innocent souls around me. I remember feeling like some grotesque thing that could taint others by breathing their very air. Like my existence was poison, and I had to keep myself apart to save anyone around me. My encounter with Sam only confirmed it. I made a fist, digging my nails into my palm at the memories I had buried down deep. You couldn't carry the trauma of your childhood with you forever.

"Eliza, take a seat."

I cringed. The only seat available was next to Father Paul. But I dutifully said, "Yes, Mother," and moved to the small cushioned chair. I tucked my arms close, hoping the arms of my chair would shield me from whatever horrible thing, whatever horrible evidence, Father Paul had against me this time. From today alone, there was plenty for him to pack away in his folder now.

Mother Superior, Abigail, sat down and shifted until she was comfortable, her white hair visible just around her habit. She picked up a pen and began twirling it through her fingers, a habit that betrayed when she was ready to make a momentous decision. Bile rose, but I swallowed it down.

Instead of speaking, she looked pointedly at Father Paul, who cleared his throat. I turned to him, telling myself to accept whatever fate this was. I thought briefly of Luk. The way he had kissed me with abandon. The way he had said he needed me safe. Of his arms, strengthening around me as he drank. My entire life, the Church had made me feel like a problem, like something bad, and in one afternoon, Luk had made me feel like something precious to be cherished. I had wanted time to explore that, but I comforted myself, knowing he would only get stronger. He would escape. Even if I wouldn't.

"Eliza, Mother Superior and I have come to a decision."

I squared my shoulders. I wouldn't feel any reproach for my actions this last week either. Everything I had done, everything I had learned, felt right. It wasn't what the Catholic Church preached; it went against everything I had been taught as a child. But Olivia went against what they taught. She was evil for her very nature, according to them. I thought of her kindness, the first hand of friendship extended without any kind of ulterior motive. And I found I no longer believed anything that said I must regard her as indiscriminately evil.

Father Paul seemed to want something more than my stoic silence, so I gave it to him. "Okay. I'm ready." I was ready to be jailed. I was ready to be put in a cell next to Luk. I was ready for whatever was required for me to find myself and to stop being led by a set of arbitrary principles put down in a book and fed to me since I was a child. I was ready to find my own way.

He seemed satisfied with that answer, pursing his lips but turning to face Mother Superior. "While we let the devil we plan to exorcise soften so that the exorcism is a success, we are going to train you further. There is another exorcism planned to help a man of the congregation who has found he cannot resist the desecration of his marriage bed. You will help him."

I was confused. I had heard the words; thanks to Olivia, I even knew what he was talking about. But my mind reeled as it came back from the precipice of what I had thought was my doom to the realization that I had more time. I thought of Luk, and instead of dread clenching my stomach, I felt a flurry of butterflies. I had more time.

"When do we start?"

Sixteen

Luk

I knew from the sound of the footsteps on the stairs it was her. At this point, I was attuned to every part of her. The way her breath puffed, the lightness of her steps, the tension in her muscles when she was nervous—or excited. Eliza came into view, and I couldn't contain the desire to burst through my cage bars to get to her. To touch her.

She looked a little harried, her normally smooth hair messy, like she'd run her fingers through it over and over, putting me on edge. "Hi." Her voice was almost shy, and possessiveness thrilled through me. I didn't imagine she was innocent, or at least I hoped not. As a Hecate witch, despite whatever thrall the Church had on her, whatever part of her she felt needed to be hidden, there was a larger part that would crave wild abandon. I wanted to tease that part out. I wanted her to dance naked under the moon like the witches I had watched when last awake. When the vampires and the witches worked together to put the evil of the world away.

"Little witch." I smirked, waiting for it.

Her brows drew down in annoyance. "I told you not to call me that."

I couldn't fully suppress my grin. "My mistake. Twice in one day. You couldn't stay away? Wanted to say goodbye before you left?" I hoped that was why she'd come.

Her brow smoothed, and she grabbed the bars as she approached me. "There's a lot I have to tell you."

Annoyance made me tsk. "Open the door. Talk to me in here."

She shook her head, looking back to the steps that led up to the infirmary above us. "I can't. Olivia gave the keys back to Emily and won't have them again until tomorrow. I told a guard I was coming to examine another patient to get past the main doors. I had to see you, had to tell you something."

I gripped the bar above her, letting my fingers slide over her fist, feeling the softness of her skin under me, even if not in the way I wanted. My voice softened, the playfulness fading along with the excitement of seeing her, which turned to worry. "Why haven't you left yet?"

"That's what I needed to talk to you about, so Olivia gave me her next shift and promised she wasn't hungry and could go the whole day away from here. I guess I filled her up enough."

"What do you mean you filled the succubus up?" I growled. Rage swept through me, halting any thoughts of her danger, her softness, or how badly I wanted her between my legs, not my fingers.

Her cheeks pinked, and she shifted as if to move away, but I tightened my hand on hers. Violence stole from my chest, and I made a concerted effort not to put too much pressure on her hand, trapped between me and the iron. I'd grown to like the succubus, but if she tried to steal what was mine, I would crush her.

"It's nothing. I was— She walked by my room when I was just, whatever, she's not hungry. I didn't fill her up like you're thinking. I didn't fill her up that way."

It took a moment for the haze of my anger to clear, to realize what she was saying. When I did, I felt myself react, hunger replacing rage, and wanted to crush the barrier between us to dust.

"Bad little witch."

Her cheeks went from pink to scarlet, proving me right. When I got out of here, I'd find her wherever she went. And I'd show her she was mine.

"That's not the point. There's been some new developments. I don't know what they have planned for you, but they've moved me off your case. They're having me take the lead on the exorcism of a man upstairs."

"The one the succubus placed her hitchhiker in?"

Eliza nodded. "I don't know why they changed their minds, but it isn't all or nothing now."

I looked down at her, and my chest tightened with pity. The Church was all she'd ever known. I struggled with what I would do when I got out of this cell. When last alive, I had moved with a nest of vampires, all intent on earning our rebirths. The times I had lived in made it easy; there was an army of men with depraved intentions to feast on. Thousands to send back to the afterlife to cycle again. Part of me understood her reluctance to step into the unknown. Being trapped in this dungeon, battling with corrupt priests of the Church, is what I'd known. When I left here, I'd need to start over. What did the world outside look like now?

"Eliza, you can't stay. Even if the execution has been stayed, they're still sharpening the guillotine. It's coming eventually. You need to get out while you can."

She bit her lip, pulling my gaze. I imagined my own teeth skimming that lip, drawing the barest drop of blood to sip while I ravished her mouth. I hardened, the evidence impossible to hide, even in the thicker cotton pants I'd been given.

She didn't catch it right away. I let her pull her hand

away this time when exasperation had her wanting to pace. I watched her carefully as her eyes came back to me, her huff right before she was about to answer me, her eyes drawn down the length of my body the way they had been since I'd replenished most of my strength with the guard.

Her throat moved as she swallowed. The color rose up her neck, and her heart beat faster, more erratic. I smelled her arousal. The bar I held cracked under my grip. Her wide eyes flew back to mine.

I struggled to get myself back under control. She walked toward me, putting her hand over mine this time, thinking she was helping. I trembled at the touch, from wanting her, from consuming her mind and body.

"Olivia said she'd go with me if I waited. I just need to wait a little longer. We need to figure out a way to get you out too."

Her words were like a cold bath. "Are you and the succubus together?" I didn't mean to cut my words so sharply. But after hearing of her filling the succubus up, and now that she'd be escaping with her, jealousy consumed me.

Her brows knit together, and she frowned at my words. "We're friends, Olivia and me. I don't know how to live outside the Church. They've taken care of everything my entire life. I have my weekends away, but I wouldn't even know where to start. Olivia is going to help me."

My next words came without thought. Every part of me meant them; I meant them more than I wanted my rebirth. It wasn't a question anymore of how I felt for her. Eliza had become vital to me. "I'll help you."

She pressed closer, and I cursed everything in creation that there was anything between us. "I appreciate that, Luk, but Olivia and I need to figure out how to help you."

I growled, trapping her hand between the two of mine.

"I will take care of you, little witch. You don't need to worry about me."

She smiled, and it looked suspiciously insincere. "Nice sentiment, wrong century, buddy." While I tried to work out what she meant and why she kept calling me that, there was a crash upstairs that drew both our eyes. Eliza cursed. "I need to go. The guards will respond to that, and I can't be caught down here."

She turned to go, but I grabbed her arm through the bars, surprising her by swinging her back. Desperation filled me. Desperation that this would be the last time I'd see her despite both our promises. Desperation that I'd never get to touch her the way we both wanted.

She caught herself and opened her mouth to argue, but I reached my other arm through the bars and brought her close, crushing my lips to hers. I couldn't kiss her the way I wanted, I couldn't do half of what I wanted to her, but I could take this little taste. And by the dazed look in her eyes when she drew back and said her final goodbyes, we'd both be fighting for another taste. And another.

Seventeen

Eliza

"Eliza. Eliza!"

My head snapped up, the library coming into focus, the lamps bouncing light off the stained-glass windows, splashing blue and gold light across the table. Sam had asked me a question. My mind had been replaying Luk's kiss over and over. "What's that?"

His forehead creased. "Are you listening to me at all?"

"I'm sorry, yes. I was just…I'm sorry. Could you repeat that?"

Sam smiled kindly at me, affection sparking in his eyes as usual. His crush was harmless; we'd all taken vows of celibacy. Nobody knew I interpreted that to mean I just had to be celibate in a habit. Nobody knew, either, that I was currently fantasizing about how I'd like to get it on with one of our most notorious subjects. My cheeks warmed at the thought, and Sam's smile grew wider.

"No problem. I was just saying that the approach for this one should be pretty basic. I say we start with the Lord's Prayer and move on with the Anthanasian Creed. From there, we can pick from the Psalms." Sam's gentle and kind words held no reproach for my lack of attention.

Michael, on the other hand—his scoff dripped with annoyance. "Pay attention, Eliza. I don't understand why you're taking lead on this in the first place. A disgrace of a nun, a woman, and a freak."

Sam's face grew red, and he bit out, "That's enough, Michael."

Michael frowned at him. "I don't know why you're always defending her. You're better than that."

Sam opened his mouth to say something, but I placed a hand on his arm, silencing him. I pinned Michael with a hard stare. He had somewhat of a point; I should be paying more attention. But calling me out for Sam planning the exorcism was bullshit, and he knew it. Sam always picked the prayers, it was his gift, and this fight was getting old.

"Michael, if you feel so horrified by it, why don't you take it up with Father Paul?"

I couldn't help the narrowed eyes and slight smile. We both knew I'd won. Father Paul and his approval were Michael's greatest weakness. I'd never understood why he worshipped the man. Thinking of how I deferred to Abigail, I put it down to an orphan's need for a parental figure.

It didn't matter that there wasn't any warmth in Abigail for me or Father Paul for Michael; everyone wanted a mom and dad. The difference was I knew where my messed-up devotion came from and curbed it at every turn. Michael leaned into it. And Father Paul would never be a real father. After the way he had treated Luk, I believed that to be true in every sense of the word. Besides, after learning of how I came to be with the Church, that the very people who had been raising me may have been the ones who killed my real mom and dad, it was getting more difficult to stay. Every polite word, every second in their company, felt like a betrayal of their legacy. A legacy I didn't really know or understand. I thought again about what I had learned about Hecate on the internet.

Surprisingly, I had found a Pagan temple that said it had a tribute to her in a small town in Bristol.

"Whatever," was all Michael replied. Sam shot him an admonishing glare but got us back on track. It was just the three of us. Olivia had successfully gotten out of this round of exorcism for her "flu." Apparently, most of the postulants at this branch who performed exorcisms weren't particularly skilled, and she didn't need to duck out of them. She usually avoided exorcisms with Sam because, even when she knew they were working on a mentally ill human without a hitchhiker, his words alone caused an uncomfortable pull in her gut. But even then, she could withstand it.

With me, she had said there hadn't been a gentle tug but a violent yank. She had felt lassoed around her middle and wrenched across. She had only withstood it because Luk, apparently knowing she was supernatural and appreciating her ingenuity, had stepped in. He hadn't been chanting against his own removal but to keep her in place.

She had said, without his counter prayers and Sekhmet's intervention, she would have been tugged across, or at least exposed, and probably never would have earned her rebirth. I shivered at the thought. Olivia was quickly becoming one of my closest friends, and I was beginning to realize she might be my only friend. After most of my life spent in the Church, my lack of any true connections made me sad. I didn't fully understand Olivia and Luk's world yet, but I knew not earning her rebirth would have meant I lost her for good.

Wanting to move this along, I said, "I agree with Sam's plan. I think we should leave the Psalms for what feels right at the moment. I'll have copies of each ready and earmarked with what I think will be appropriate. We'll do the standard rites of holy water, and this time we'll burn lavender."

Sam nodded in approval, and Michael just grunted

again. The scrapes of our chairs echoed around us as we all stood to leave. Michael, apparently disgusted to be in my presence, charged out of the library. Sam hung back, walking beside me to the door.

"Sorry about him. I don't know what's up with him. He has no right to talk to you like that. He normally isn't so…so…" He seemed to be at a loss for words.

I raised my eyebrows at him. Michael had always been a bully, though he was markedly less so with the guys. Sam ducked his head, blond hair brushing his eyes, and muttered, "Yeah, maybe I'm full of shit. I can talk to Father Paul if you want."

I shook my head sharply. "That's the last thing I want. I can handle Michael. Really, it doesn't even bother me." It wasn't completely true, but it wasn't a lie either. When I had been working hard for approval, it would have cut deeper. But now, with people who knew and liked the real me at my side, his barbed words hardly left a scratch.

Sam just nodded, retreating from his white knight post. I sighed, wanting to get to Olivia. She had needed to feed again and replaced Emily today. The Sunday sermon would be happening soon, and I hoped Olivia was successful with whatever hitchhiker she planned to implant. I still wasn't sure how I felt about the embodiment of evil being casually placed into humans to tilt their natures, but the most selfish part of me shied away from thinking of it like that. If Olivia was successful, we were one step closer to escaping together.

Sam and I walked out of the library. The sun was just beginning to warm up the horizon. We had met early so we could get a full strategy session in before church. I was just about to say goodbye when I felt Sam's hand on my arm. I looked over in surprise.

"I know that I don't do enough. I try."

I nodded, my brow wrinkling. "I know, Sam. I don't expect anything."

He tsked. "I just, I want you to be able to depend on me." His arm slid from my forearm and traced up my elbow. I shivered, but not in a good way. Uncomfortable, I turned to face him full-on, knocking his arm off in the process. His hand let go and made a fist.

"I know, Sam. It's no sweat, really. Don't you have duties today?"

He nodded, his eyes still searching mine. I pretended to be lost in a gale at sea. Sam had never been this forward, and this was so not the time to start. "Yeah. But I wanted to talk to you about that. Do you ever just want to get out? Get away from the Church? I feel like you aren't treated the way you deserve." His hand came up to cup my face, and I couldn't help a flinch. He frowned but withdrew. "You deserve so much, Eliza."

My gut churned, and heat spread up my neck. It was like déjà vu, only this time, I was sure. I was *sure* I hadn't encouraged him. I had tried to be so careful and ensure he knew we were only friends.

"Where would I get out to, Sam? This is my calling, my life." The words felt like acid on my tongue. I knew now they were a lie. That this had never been my calling, but something forced on me. Something I had been trained to think was the only way I'd be good enough to have any kind of life. I was breaking away, just not with him.

"I could take you away from here, Eliza." He reached toward me again, but I took a step back. He sighed, his face crestfallen. He tried one last time. "I would leave the Church for you."

I shook my head, and I was sure the sadness I felt in my heart shone through my eyes. I had appreciated Sam's friendship. Before Olivia, I would have called him the person I was closest to. I had appreciated everything he'd done for me and how he'd propped me up like a bulwark when I was down. But I had always known it came with conditions, with my seeming to be available to him. But I was also sure I'd always been so clear. I was married to God, to the Church—it was my protection from his affections. Obviously, that wasn't enough. I'd be letting go of more than the Church when I left. Maybe it was time to let go of everything that was a part of it as well.

"I don't want that, Sam." I didn't want to be mean, but I needed him to understand. I hoped that would be enough to get my point across.

He smiled sadly. "Maybe you will one day."

Sam turned to leave, but I didn't want him to misunderstand. I didn't want another situation like what had happened in New Hampshire. I couldn't bear history repeating itself. As he neared the bottom steps of the library, my turmoil burst out of me on a shout.

"No, Sam. I'll never want that."

He looked up at me, features pinched. I couldn't tell what flickered in his eyes. Anger? Disappointment? Whatever it was, his mouth tightened, and he didn't say anything else. He turned sharply on his heel and kept walking toward the church to prepare for his Sunday duties.

I watched his retreating back and muttered to myself, "What in the hell was that?"

"What in the hell was what?"

I yelped, jumping into the air at Olivia's voice. "Where did you come from?" I shouted at her.

She raised her eyebrows, pointing to the right, where the garden path led to the street and back to our basement quarters. "It's almost time for church. I figured I'd meet you so we could get some coffee."

I held a hand to my racing heart. "Yeah. Yeah, makes sense. Sorry, I'm a little on edge. My entire life turned upside down, you know. And my last human ally—" I stopped, staring into space for a moment. I was beginning to realize I shouldn't assume. "Who I *think* is still human, just asked me to run away with him. Even though we've both taken vows of celibacy, I'm pretty sure I'm the only skank in this school who breaks those regularly."

Olivia guffawed. "Well, that's a lot to unpack. First of all, you are not a skank. Or if you are, I want to be a skank. If you are, then *every* girl should strive to be a skank. Second of all, don't look at it like your life got turned upside down. Look at it like it's turned right-side up. You know where you came from! You are getting *hot and heavy* with one of the most powerful supernatural beings on Earth. And third of all," she pointed at herself comically, "*succubus*!"

I couldn't help but laugh. As usual, Olivia somehow put me instantly at ease. She wrapped her arm through mine like she always did, and we started down the few steps to the street. Hanging a left, we headed to the boutique coffee shop on the small town strip.

"One kiss isn't hot and heavy. And thanks for the pep talk. I think I lost Sam forever. He actually asked me to run away with him. I tried letting him down easy, and he acted like he'd carry a torch for me until I said yes, so I made it clear. I'm not sure he appreciated that." My gut turned with worry about how Sam would react. I hated when people were mad at me—a long-ago instinct to make everyone happy so I could survive. But under that worry was a thread of pride. I rubbed the ache in my chest from the stress and guilt of losing a friend but tried to hold on to that thread, to tug it to the forefront.

Olivia's eyes widened comically. "Well, he better watch out. I got a tongue lashing from Luk today, telling me to stay away from what's 'his' while I was feeding down there. And he kind of likes me, I think. I mean, he did keep me from crossing over. I can't imagine what he would do to a male human he thinks is trying to steal you away."

"I am not his *turf*." I let annoyance lace my words, but secretly, a thrill went through me. After spending so much of my life feeling unwanted, the idea of Luk calling me his, of someone wanting me so much they claimed me, was a balm to my soul. The idea that, even weakened in a cell, he'd threatened to keep me safe felt like a warm blanket in a blizzard.

Olivia just scoffed and said sarcastically, "Okay." We chatted about nonsense on our way to the coffee shop. We were walking the four blocks to the town square, past a hodgepodge of classic New England bungalows with the occasional Victorian on a corner. I loved the spires and porches of those grand homes. Thinking of that reminded me of Sarah Lee, of that Pagan church. Luk had once suggested I find a temple of Hecate. Maybe it was past time I listened.

When we turned up one last street before the main strip. I felt a tug and looked over to my right.

In front of a blackened house sat a mother. On each side of her, she held a small hand. The mother was young, her face prematurely lined.

I pulled my arm from Olivia's, stopping at the creaking gate, blackened and hanging on one hinge. Spirits usually disappeared after traumatic deaths; I wasn't sure where to. They didn't come immediately for passing. This had happened a week or so ago. I remembered hearing the news and feeling so sad for the family. Olivia looked at me, then toward the house.

"Oh. I'll just. I'm going to give you some privacy." She continued up the street a ways, not leaving me but giving me space. My heart swelled with love for her.

I looked back toward the mother and let empathy pour from my eyes. I swallowed and walked to them, opening my arms in an embrace. I wept as they passed through me, sinking to my knees, thinking the world needed more of their purity and goodness. She had been a single mom raising her two children, their father killed in service. The house had been old. She hadn't known that when the breaker kept flipping, she should call an electrician, or maybe she just had hoped that she could keep flipping it a few more paychecks so she could afford one.

Either way, the wires the mice had chewed through in the basement had sparked a fire. The smoke had reached them before the fire. They had never even woken. By the time the smoke smell had reached their neighbor, they were already dead. And by then, the blaze had kept everyone out but the fire department.

The mother grieved that her girls wouldn't grow up on Earth and have full lives here, but a part of her was eager to pass on to see their father again. The guileless children felt the same way, not understanding what they might have lost or fearing where they might be going. For the first time in a long time, I wished I knew for sure.

I sat on my knees long after they'd passed through me, gravel digging into my skin. This type of passing didn't suck my energy out like the old woman or the guard. When someone evil passed through, they purposefully pulled at what I imagined was my life energy, my vitality. Sometimes, they would push their pain at me, overwhelming my senses even while they sucked away my defenses. When someone like the mother and her girls passed, they treaded as lightly as they could, like they were giving me the gentlest shock, two people shaking hands but trying to be considerate on a particularly staticky day.

Olivia's steps preceded her soft voice. "Are you okay?"

I sat back on my heels, sniffing back the tears, wiping my cheeks. The dusky morning was turning bright. "How long was I out?" I always called it "out," even when I didn't lose consciousness. During a passing, I was absorbed by the person, good or evil, and I stopped paying attention to anything else around me. I stopped paying attention to time.

"Not long. A half hour. We should head straight to church though."

I nodded, starting to rise to my feet. Before I got far, Olivia was there in front of me, offering me her hand. A weight pressed on my heart, and I had to hold back another torrent of tears. I gave her a watery smile as I took her hand. It wasn't the passing or sad tears that pressed at me now. It was comfort. It was the first time I'd felt comfort or understanding from another person after a passing.

I knew I could trust Olivia, and I knew it was time. I didn't suppress the sudden urge. It would take me a couple hours to get there and back and be able to find someone to talk to. Church services should cover that before we were due at the infirmary. "Olivia, I need you to cover for me. There's something I need to check out."

Eighteen

Eliza

Olivia had made me explain where I was going before she'd agree. I had a feeling Luk had charged her with my safety while he was locked away. I wasn't sure how I felt about that. While the idea that someone cared enough about me to demand my safety felt good, the feeling that I was losing all control didn't. It turned out that any idea of independence had been an illusion my entire life, but I didn't want that to be true forever. I didn't want to leave the Church and stop being their puppet to become someone else's. No matter how well-intentioned.

I stopped when the Google directions told me I was there and looked around, confused. I had traveled through the main strip of town and kept going up toward the mountains. The directions had led me to a road off the main highway and through the trees to a mailbox. It was a well-treed lot, but I hesitated. I didn't see any structures or anything like a church. Taking a deep breath, I whispered to the silence, "Be brave, Eliza. You can't let them lead you through everything."

My blinker clicked on, and I rolled the car onto the dirt driveway. The click when the wheel came around, turning the blinker off, resounded like a gong. I took in everything as I passed the oak and elm trees, with an occasional weeping willow stretching its drooping branches like arms to hug the ground. Eventually, the foliage, just beginning to bloom with greenery, parted enough for me to see the pavilion. The stone didn't stretch high into the sky, which must have been why I couldn't see it from the road. Stone steps led up to the posts, four in a circle with no roof.

I looked around as I stepped out of the car. There didn't appear to be a set parking place, so I had pulled to where the road met the grass. A typical New England spring, a soft drizzle wet my hair almost immediately, and I pulled the edges of my raincoat around me. I had changed into jeans and a T-shirt, not wanting anyone to meet me with preconceived ideas of who I was or why I was there. Now I was afraid I wouldn't meet anyone at all.

I walked up the steps, my Converse shoes soundless against the soft stone, clean and worn lovingly, like people had been stepping on the stones for ages. I had thought this was a Pagan temple, but there were no walls. As I went to the middle of the circle and looked up, raindrops falling on my face, splashing down my lips and chin, I saw there was no roof. How could this be a place of worship?

I swallowed, looked at the stone posts, and realized the base of each one had a different group of pictures and objects. They were altars, I realized. I walked to the one closest to me and looked down at the picture of a delicate woman in a robe. One arm held a bouquet of flowers, and the other held a fruit broken open with seeds falling from it. Beneath the photo was a board covered with cloth. I looked left and right but saw nobody. Moving the cloth aside, I realized what must be in the woman's hand. Pomegranates. There were also sprigs of lavender and blue topaz and amethyst scattered on the board. I put the cloth back and stood.

Moving to the next post, I stooped down to see the portrait of another woman, this time with her arms above her, as if holding up the moon. Her eyes were closed, her face beautiful. A white robe fell from delicate shoulders, covering one breast, leaving the other bare, to wrap around a delicate waist. Around her picture were more crystals I couldn't identify and dried thyme.

My legs hurt from crouching, so I stood and walked to the next stone post, its sanded white beauty against the green and brown backdrop soothing. My sneakers gave off a muffled click as I walked across the pavilion. One step, two steps, three steps. Suddenly, I wasn't looking at a backdrop of green anymore but a world of swirling white smoke. My footsteps weren't soft and muffled but echoing, like they called into a canyon, and the canyon called back. I stopped as the sound beat in my ears, fear and curiosity rising in my chest until it felt gripped in a vice. The only thing keeping me from panicking was the feel of the line. I didn't spend a lot of time thinking about it, but it was a line of life and death. When a spirit crossed over, I stood on the line of life, but somehow, I moved. Not my physical body, but the line seemed to pass right behind me, and when the spirit passed through me, they were on the other side.

I could feel the line now, and even though I was in this strange place, the familiarity of it was a comfort. "Hello?" I called, hearing the word echoing back to me. "Is anyone there?"

I moved to walk forward, but a voice, one that didn't echo but fell as if carried by a weight, answered back. "Daughter."

I gasped. "Hecate?"

Before I could hear an answer, everything went black.

I woke to someone tapping my shoulder and water falling on my face. "Hello? Hello? Are you okay? Wake up!"

I groaned, rolling to my side to sit up. Large wrinkled

hands, callused with dirt under the nails, hands of a gardener, lifted me. I looked up into kind brown eyes, the woman's dark skin framed by curly hair between shades of black and gray.

She looked at me with concern. "You gave me a fright. I came to replace the offerings, and you were out cold against the stone."

A headache pounded. I reached up and felt a tender spot on my temple, but when my hand came away, there was no blood. Looking quickly at my watch, I realized I could have only been out for moments. Thank whatever gods I was praying to these days because if I missed the exorcism, I wouldn't be able to explain it. I didn't have much longer as it was.

"I'm sorry. My name is Eliza. I heard there was an altar to Hecate at a Pagan temple, and I came to check it out. But my Google Maps led me here.

"I'm Emmaline. Your maps brought you to the altar, but the temple is a few streets up. We have various temples that are connected by paths through the woods."

I nodded. "But there's all these different pictures. Which one is Hecate?"

Emmaline stood and held her hand out for me. I smiled up at her gratefully and took the help to stand, stretching out various aches and pains.

"Well, it's not just Hecate. Persephone, goddess of death and rebirth. We pray to her for protection and for a good bounty. Phoebe, Hecate's mother, goddess of light and prophesy, we pray to, to show us the way and grant us wisdom. Hecate, the three-mooned goddess, we pray to for safety through our travels, both day to day and throughout life."

As she talked, we walked to each post. The woman with

the flowers had been Persephone, the woman with the full moon, Phoebe, and as she described Hecate, I looked at a picture with a woman with three faces, and above her, a waning full and waxing moon. Under her left arm walked what looked like a sinewy monster of a dog, and under her right arm, from a chain wrapped around her wrist, dangled keys. In each arm, she held a torch. Cloth covered another plate—her offerings.

"What's on the fourth post?"

We walked toward it, and Emmaline seemed to consider before she answered. "This is the origin of all things. The duality of feminine and masculine. The origin of our souls. We pay tribute to it at all our altars.

I looked down, and before me was a beautiful tree with long branches, heavy with foliage. Its trunk twined into three interconnected circles. I leaned down to get a better look. Emmaline hovered around me as if I would drop again. Tracing the lines, I asked, "What's this?"

"The triquetra. It is so many things." Her voice sounded fond, like she was talking about a favorite parent. I looked up at her in awe, my mouth hanging slightly open. "It is life, death, and rebirth. The past, present, and future. The origin and future of all that we are. We owe everything to the Tree, to the unity of the triquetra."

"Is it a part of the Wiccan religious belief?"

Emmaline's eyes sharpened on me, and I stood. Maybe she was just realizing I wasn't necessarily one of her. I could be an intruder. She crossed her arms. Her voice was polite but more clipped than it had been. "It's part of many religious beliefs, including Christianity, known there as the trinity. It belongs to all religions and none. It just is."

I nodded, not wanting to offend her. I looked around, trying to figure out a way to ask my questions so she would let her guard down again, when she saved me. "What made you seek out Hecate's temple?"

I swallowed. "I've learned lately about death witches. I wanted to know more about them, specifically about a family that might have lived in New England around twenty-five years ago.

Her eyes drew down. If anything, I'd made her more suspicious. She must not have considered the information dangerous, though, because she answered me. "There was a family of Hecate touched. The last of them died after a five-hundred-year period where they were hunted. They were originally from Greece, I think, but the family had emigrated to the United States decades ago. They had made their home in Washington State but had come this way when they were on the run. They had settled in Massachusetts, I believe, when the last of them were found.

She watched me closely, my reactions. And I couldn't completely stifle them. I felt the blood drain from my face. Sweat beaded on my neck. My voice was faint when I asked, "Found?"

She continued watching me, her arms relaxing until she held her elbows. "Yes, two generations of a family, their grandmother, and two daughters and their children."

Tears built in my eyes. I'd had cousins? Did I have a sister or brother?

I coughed to clear my throat. "Did you know the family?"

The woman's brow wrinkled. "What did you say your name was?"

I smiled weakly. "Eliza."

The woman's expression cleared. "Ah, pledged to God."

"Excuse me?"

"It's what your name means. No, I didn't know the

family, but I knew of them. The grandmother and one of her two girls. The fathers were murdered outside on the front lawn. Three children were killed inside the house—a little boy and two little girls. One went missing, but she was never found. We can only assume she's long dead now."

"What was her name?" I asked. What was *my* name?

"Lilah. She couldn't have been older than a year, maybe younger. Such a shame. It was a lovely family by all accounts, but carrying Hecate's touch, it seems, is both a blessing and a curse."

"Why is that?"

She looked at me and began to walk. I walked with her, holding my breath to hear her answer. "The power they wield is coveted and feared. Anything that people want that badly or fear that much is bound to make enemies. No matter how good your heart is."

"Sounds like it," I agreed, fear worming through me at her words. I jumped when a large whistle pierced the air. The woman looked at me and raised her eyebrow. I laughed, but it came out shaky. Silencing the alarm on my phone, I said, "That's my cue. Late for work. Thank you for helping me."

She nodded her head, watching me with suspicion as I jogged down to my car. I looked up at her one last time before climbing in. Before backing up and heading back to Saint Peter's, I brought up my phone and googled the name Lilah.

"Woman of the night," I whispered, laughing at how much more fitting that seemed. My head came up, checking the rearview, and then forward for my way out. Emmaline was still watching me. As I backed out, turned around, and headed down the dirt road, I glanced back. She watched me the entire way.

Nineteen

Eliza

The sound of the man pacing and muttering, and occasionally moaning, came through the door. Sweat beaded down my neck, and I went to pick at my thumb but stopped before my nail dug in. I remembered Luk's words, the worried wrinkle of his brow, the vehemence in his words contrasted by the gentle way he held my hand. It was easy to forget he came from a different time by his easy adaptation to the way people spoke around him, his mannerisms, and the abs sloping dangerously into those gray sweatpants. Sometimes I missed the threadbare cotton ones just a little. It was times like those, when his thumb stroked the top of my hand, and his eyes stared at me so intently, that I felt like a damsel. Even though I knew I was strong, sometimes him wanting to stand like a knight between me and any danger, even my own anxiety, made me feel protected in a way I had never experienced.

I took a deep breath, putting Luk out of my mind for the time being, and looked at the infirmary door. I stood outside the man with the hitchhiker's cell. The sound of his hand slapping against the frosted glass door made me jump. He was particularly aggressive with women due to the demon's influence over him, so I was waiting for Michael and Sam to arrive. A guard had let me in when I told him I needed to prepare. I'd been earmarking whichever of the psalms I thought would be most effective. Both the boys were late.

I was just getting antsy, the man must have somehow sensed a woman was near, when the swish of the door sliding open announced the two men's presence.

"Sorry we're late," Sam announced, his voice flat as they strode toward me.

I just nodded, bouncing nervously on the balls of my feet. I had talked to Olivia about the exorcism the night before. She had suggested I see if I could feel my way through this like I did when a spirit crossed over, that the reason my exorcisms were theoretically more successful was because I pulled the hitchhiker to the other side. Since I had only done a few exorcisms, which Olivia doubted involved a real hitchhiker, I probably hadn't seen the similarities. But this would be a good chance to see if I could connect to the magic. I thought of the white smoke, the voice calling me daughter. My magic.

It was a good theory with a couple major problems. They were named Sam and Michael. What if they noticed me doing something during the ceremony? And what if I succeeded? I had accepted what Olivia and Luk were. I had met Sarah Lee and felt her magic when she read my cards, been to the altar of Hecate and thought she had called out to me, but this would be the final confirmation that I belonged in this new world. But also that I didn't belong in my current one.

"No problem. Here you go." I handed out copies of the psalms I had picked out for the ceremony. "If you want to read through, we can get started."

Michael didn't look up, just grunted. "Father Paul said he was going to observe this time. Since things didn't go as planned last time. He wants to see our process."

I swallowed, my uncertainty deepening. Father Paul

suspected that I performed these exorcisms supernaturally. That was his end goal. If he witnessed something that confirmed it, it would land me in a cell. It's what he and Mother Superior were hoping for.

"Ow." I jumped and looked down. The nail bed of my thumb was raw. I had started picking it without even realizing it. I looked up at the guys, clearing my throat. Sam wouldn't meet my eyes, but his face was a mask of annoyance. "Sounds good. Let's review the psalms while we wait for him." *They won't put me in the infirmary. They don't think I'm possessed. They won't put me in the infirmary.*

Threatened with it since I was a child, the infirmary was like my boogeyman. It was ironic how much comfort I found in a purpose that brought me down here regularly. But I was down here to help people. I wasn't trapped down here.

I knew that Luk's hearing, better since he drank from me, was supernaturally sharp. He could probably hear everything we were saying. I wondered what he thought of all this. That train of thought was interrupted by Father Paul's shoes clacking against the stones with his arrival.

He strode down the hall purposefully, a scowl on his face, a picture of impatience, as if it was he who had been made to wait this entire time. Looking up from a letter he was reading as he reached us, he said curtly, "What are we waiting for?"

Michael flurried around him, explaining all that we had done to prepare. Sam stood quietly, hands clasped, projecting readiness. He still wouldn't look at me. I clenched my teeth. At least my dislike of Father Paul and my situation with who I thought was a friend helped dispel some of my fear.

"We're ready. I'm going to approach the subject. Michael and Sam, at the door with the accompaniments."

They nodded, though Michael still looked put upon because he wasn't lead. He'd perform as expected, especially for his hero. I pushed the button that opened the sliding door. Inside was a messy bed, blanket pulled to the side, pillows strewn all over. There was a man, moderately handsome with a slightly pudgy waist, pacing around the back of the room, flipping through a magazine. A lollipop hung out of his mouth—a bucket of them sat on his bedside stand, a bottle of water sitting next to it. He turned to face our group and looked up at the sound of the door, his pants undone.

"Hello, Mathew. I'm Eliza. I'm here with Michael and Sam to help you."

Something in his face changed. He went from a pleasant face, slightly weak jawed with a sensitive mouth, to a man super intent. "Oh, baby, you poor thing. They made you wait so long for me. You look so frustrated. Let me help you."

I pedaled backward until my back hit the door, surprised at how quickly he moved toward me. I had heard his impatience on the other side of the door but thought Sam and Michael's presence would be enough of a deterrent. Before either of the guys could grab him, he gripped my biceps, pinning me and smelling my neck. I just began to feel his lips and tongue, the protest dying on my lips as he was dragged off, Michael and Sam each on an arm.

Breathing hard, I wiped a hand down my neck before walking forward. I began the Lord's Prayer without another thought, the boys holding the struggling man on the bed falling in unison with me. "Our Father in heaven."

As the words pulled from me, said so often in my life they came like second nature, I tried to feel what was happening. I thought of the line I had imagined earlier at the altar, the vibration of it, and of when I did a passing. It felt like someone rattling my very essence, reaching inside me and playing with my intestines. It was deeply uncomfortable but not violent. This felt more violent.

The man gnashed his teeth, cursing at us and struggling as soon as the first words of the Lord's Prayer fell from my lips. As I continued into the creed, instead of feeling as if someone was tugging at me, I felt like I was tugging something toward me. I tried to put the feeling into tangible action, but pressure filled the room. With a *pop*, the feeling of an oily presence turned into a writhing black wraith struggling to reattach to its host. The wraith hovered above and reached like a child for the man, who had stopped cursing and struggling and lay with his eyes bulging, body bowed toward the ceiling. He didn't reach for his parasite, but his body bent toward it involuntarily. I began the first psalm, The Cantina.

The first words spilled from my mouth, and Michael grunted, gripping the man's arm tighter after taking a knee to the stomach. Mathew, the afflicted, contorted and began to scream. This time, it wasn't obscenities that spewed from his throat but a sound of pure grief. I wondered what his grief was for. The hitchhiker that was being wrenched from his spirit? His very soul? The actions he had performed under its influence, or the loss of his excuse to act indiscriminately, without recrimination? Or maybe this was actually painful for him, like an amputation.

Whatever the reason, his screams would haunt me, the torment in them making me wonder how the victim would be anything but a husk of a man when this was over. But instead of faltering, my voice raised. Michael and Sam had fallen off, not memorizing every psalm like I had, but I could feel the power in my words. I didn't know where that power came from. Maybe God himself? But as I began David's Last Words, the hitchhiker that had stubbornly hovered in his wraith-like form above Mathew began its own otherworldly screech. The men's wide-eyed stares told me it was audible to everyone, but they couldn't see what I could see. I reached one arm to the demon. It looked like I raised my arm to the ceiling, a common reverence performed during prayer or times of need. But I wasn't paying homage. I was demanding the wraith come to me. And satisfaction seeped in when it obeyed.

The demon's oily evil enveloped me as what looked like an arm came toward me. A hand formed and clasped mine. It went into me, through me, just like a spirit. But unlike a spirit, the pain of a thousand heartbreaks and broken families, a thousand broken spirits, also rushed through me. I endured the entity's echo—not what this entity felt, but what those it had attached itself to had felt. All their regret for losing their blind satisfaction and for what their actions had done to others resounded in me like the wails of a thousand broken homes.

One hand raised, my body stretched up, my eyes blind to what was around me but turned inward to what was passing through me. I felt like I floated, my tiptoes all that kept me connected to this earth. And there it was, that beating heart of the line just behind me. I felt as the wraith, struggling the entire way, passed over it, leaving nothing but the film of a thousand regrets.

And then it was over. My gasp was all I heard before blackness enveloped me, and I came crashing down to fully connect with the earth.

Twenty

Luk

I paced my cell, violence raging through me worse than it had during my most bloodthirsty battle. The men talked above me, but I couldn't hear Eliza. Since she had given me blood, my senses had heightened, and I felt back to full strength. If I strained, I could just barely hear her heart flutter, even from this far away. It was a small band-aid to the overflowing fear still coursing through me from when I'd heard her body drop.

I was unsurprised when I heard two sets of footsteps leave the infirmary and one come toward me. The noise in my head increased. There should have been three sets of footsteps. Before I could find any semblance of composure, Father Paul stepped off the stone steps toward my cell, his thin lips stretched in an evil, satisfied smile.

He hadn't come within an arm's distance of my cell bars since that first day I had managed to steal a taste. I hummed with the want of tearing his throat open and spilling that satisfaction down my chin. I knew he had come down here to gloat, and I was glad he was a sadistic bastard because I would let him if it meant finding out what had happened. Finding out how Eliza was.

"Hello, devil." His dig didn't amuse me like it usually did. If anybody in this room was a devil, it was the man purportedly following a kind God. Who claimed to have dedicated his life to his forgiving faith when all he held in his heart was hate. I would always regret that this man hadn't been born when I came into existence. I sensed punishment was much less cruel these days than it had been back then.

"Father. What brings you down here?"

"Why do you look so tense, demon?"

"Oh, is it a demon now? I thought I was the devil." I struggled to hold still, to not give this man any more fodder than I already did with the obvious tension and fear I projected. Despite my strength returning, I still wasn't strong enough to break apart these bars. Not to mention me going missing would get Eliza killed. I needed to find a way out of here that didn't involve her, didn't hurt her.

"Oh, you're a devil, alright. But I don't give you enough credit to be *the* devil."

I scoffed. This man's simpleminded view of divinity was less developed than a child's in my day. Zeus had finally had the perfect son, and he had elevated him to the highest seat of religious fanaticism. His record washed clean, his vices buried deep behind a face of magnanimity. Through the centuries, he had adopted different names, but his newest name, the simple moniker of God, was the most ingenious. And it had given him one of the longest tenures as the most beloved of divinities. I was unsurprised that the truth behind that curtain of worship produced men like this.

"What do you know of the devil, Father?"

He clasped his hands in front of him, enjoying the conversation. I clenched my jaw hard enough to crack my teeth. I was done with this conversation and regretted the question. All I cared about was what had happened to Eliza.

"The devil, ruler of the underworld, most famous of the fallen angels."

I couldn't help the laugh. "You think an angel rules the underworld? You ignorant, simple man. Get to the point of what brought you here. Where is Eliza?"

The priest had paused when I started, but mentioning the carrot he dangled before me gave him back his confidence. "Eliza. Such a promising student of the art of exorcism."

I ground my teeth, my chest aching from the pressure that sat on it. She should have run. This stay of execution was a trick. My hand clenched into a fist and released, over and over. I vowed I would find a way to kill this man.

"Where is she?" I ground out through clenched teeth.

His eyes sparkled, a self-satisfied smirk tilting one corner of his mouth, and he began to walk the length of my cell; back and forth. "She's okay. Probably." I growled at his ridicule. He stopped, facing me, hands clasped in front of him. His black hair was slicked back. His thin lips stretched in a sadistic smile. "She actually performed wonderfully. That was probably one of the shortest exorcisms I've attended, and I am fully confident she succeeded."

I swallowed, knowing there was a catch. Knowing he hadn't come here to tell me Eliza was safe. I had given myself away before I even knew that I cared for her. At this point, how much was apparent. "Why did you come? Why didn't I hear her walk out of here?"

That made the priest pause. "You can hear that far?"

I bared my teeth and dropped my fangs. Satisfaction thrummed through me when the priest took an involuntary step back. "I can hear farther." The lie instilled the proper amount of fear. The priest's eyes widened, and his feet shifted.

He coughed. "Well, then you know the exorcism took a bit of a toll. I've never seen anything like it. It was almost like she was possessed herself. I definitely think her fellow postulants will have questions for her. Abigail's attempt to stay the execution of her star pupil may have backfired. She may have succeeded and shown her value to the Church today, but do you think the Church's general population is willing to embrace a witch in their ranks? They won't even allow gay marriage. Do you think they're progressive enough to let an entity they burned a century ago stand shoulder to shoulder with them?"

My nose curled at my distaste for this man, though his insight surprised me a little. I hadn't given him enough credit to be that diabolical. I wouldn't make that mistake again. "So, you think you've won something? Tell me, priest, what is it you've won?"

His next words, ringing with victory before he walked away, left me cold. I prayed to Sekhmet, to Hecate, to whoever would listen, that Olivia or Eliza would visit me soon. She needed to leave now. She needed to run.

"I've won Eliza in a cell next to you. I've won revenge for my parents, killed by her kind. I have almost everything I need to be given permission to exorcise her myself."

Twenty-One
Eliza

I woke slowly, my sore muscles aching with every stretch. I groaned as the fingers of my right hand, hard to move and totally asleep, started tingling and then burning in pain as circulation returned.

"Whoa, whoa, slowly." The blurriness cleared from my eyes, and I realized Olivia sat on the desk chair next to my bed, her face a mask of concern. When I looked up at her, she smiled. "Hey there, slugger."

I tried to smile, though it felt more like a grimace, as I moved my fingers to get feeling fully back. I started to sit up. Olivia jumped up to help me. I gripped my forearm with my left hand, rubbing the blood flow to where it should be. "How'd I get here?"

She tilted her head. "The guys carried you in. They were pretty spooked when they dropped you off though. Michael took off like a bat out of hell. Sam stuck around a little longer, but he wasn't super touchy-feely. Do you remember what happened?"

I tried to swallow, but my mouth was so dry my throat felt stuck. I coughed. Olivia uncapped a bottle of water and held it out to me.

"Thanks," I gasped, swallowing the fluid down. Coughing a little more, I sat back, trying to find my words.

"It worked. Olivia, it was like nothing I've done before. I've been a part of other exorcisms—I said the words, I saw people behaving insanely and seemingly be normal after. I mean, I've never taken lead before, but I saw it, Olivia. The demon or hitchhiker or whatever. It was like this black shadow that could form a head and arms and legs."

Olivia sat back, her face a solemn mask of a cherubic, buxom blond. She didn't move a muscle as she hung on my every word. It made me want to go on, even though I knew I must sound insane. "It didn't talk. It didn't have a face or a mouth. But I could *feel* it. I could feel its chaos and depravity. It didn't pass through me. I *pulled* it through me. And when it went, I didn't feel its pain. I felt all the pain it had sowed."

Olivia bit her lip. "I didn't know it would be like that for you when I said you should try to feel the magic. I've dealt with these demons for a while. They're instinctual creatures created from a specific feeling, and that feeling is all they live for. It's their entire reason for existence, and they try to inspire it in all who they encounter. I can't imagine feeling everything if it was even a half-successful hitchhiker."

My hand finally began to feel normal. As I massaged the fingers, something else dawned on me. "Michael and Sam seemed disturbed? Do you think…do you think I did anything? I mean, like, God, I mean, not God, damn it! Do you think I performed magic they could see?"

Olivia stood and sat next to me on the bed. Wrapping an arm around my shoulders, she pulled me close. "I'm not sure, but even if you did, they won't believe themselves. Or they'll chalk it up to the exorcism experience. Otherwise, they wouldn't have brought you back here, right?"

I nodded. That made sense. I mean, if they thought they had seen me do magic, I'd already be in a cell. Wouldn't I? I leaned into her embrace. "Thanks, Liv."

She perked up, dragging me with her. "Liv? I like that. I've never had a nickname."

I laughed at her excitement, crawling out from under her arm. "Do you still have Emily's keys? I'd really like to be able to see Luk tonight. I know that you usually only get them in the morning, but..."

She grinned at me mischievously, her eyebrows raised suggestively. "But you don't want to only kiss him through bars this time?"

I blushed but didn't deny it. The energy I now recognized as magic, or whatever I accessed when I used my powers, was building up inside me. Between the passing of the mother and her girls and the exorcism, my entire body buzzed like a live wire. Not to mention learning more about my family, about my real name, and whatever had happened at the altar. I needed to blow off some steam. And I couldn't imagine doing that with anyone but a certain vampire.

She bumped me with her shoulder. "Meet me in the quad in a little bit. It's late enough you shouldn't have to worry about running into anyone. I already did my rounds for the night and turned them in. I'll just tell her I'm getting the keys for tomorrow, that I remembered I have plans in town or something, so I won't be able to get them in the morning. She would have already done her check in."

I bit my lip, feeling guilty. "Won't she wonder why you're asking for them back right after you returned them?"

Olivia's eyes danced. "Honestly, I think she's so terrified of Luk, she's too afraid I'll change my mind and stop doing night rounds to ask any questions."

I hugged her tight and whispered, "Thank you."

Olivia slipped out the door, and I headed into the bathroom to shower and change into a clean habit. It would look too odd walking around the convent not dressed appropriately, though part of me didn't want to go to him like this, dressed like his enemies. I didn't want to be his enemy.

I walked into the night, coming out of the basement quarters to the garden path. Shrubs interspersed with lilac bushes and different kinds of flowers lined the cement walkway. The paths wound around the quad, and the green of the tulips burst forth. It wouldn't be long before their bell-shaped flowers brightened everything up. Spring had just begun begging for a hold against the lingering winter chill. The mud had begun to dry, to everyone's relief. With no clouds in sight, the stars and waxing moon lit the sky so brightly I could find my way by them.

I peered up at the moon. Many Pagans considered the moon a symbol of several goddesses. Hecate herself was a triple moon goddess, representing the maiden, the mother, and the crone. I thought back to the swirling white smoke and wondered if it had been real or just a dream. I wondered if my patronage watched over me even now, if she had tried calling out to me earlier today. As a child, what God wanted had been laid out for me so plainly. Over seven billion people in the world, and I had been raised to believe each one had a predetermined purpose. Everything that would ever happen to them was already known. I shivered in the cool night air, even through my habit and the long sleeves I'd taken to wearing to hide the marks from Luk's fangs.

The idea that I didn't know what would happen, what was coming, was like flinging myself out of a plane with a parachute on my back. I had done it once, solo, with minimal training. I hadn't wanted to be strapped to someone, their body and thoughts intimately behind me while I learned what it was like to fly. I remembered the staccato rhythm of my heart and my irregular breathing as I had tried not to hyperventilate during the longest moment of freefall, after I had pulled my chute, before it had fully snapped and caught me in the air. Then the few seconds I had held my breath, willing the wires to remain untangled on my first jump. The realization that everything had worked how it should, and I had done it. And then the eternity of silence. The way the world slowed down to a crawl, I had time to contemplate every decision I'd ever made.

At the time, I had felt oddly empty. Like I just needed to close my eyes and accept my fate. It wasn't anything I could change—the loss of family, feeling like I was fitting into the wrong shape my entire life. Like I didn't belong, didn't fit, my presence alone a burden on those around me. I looked at the moon again and bit my lip, suppressing that giddy feeling of freefall, this time, excited for the silent moments of contemplation. I had a lot more to think about. And instead of it being a burden on my soul, it was a boon lifting me up.

"Eliza!" Olivia's voice came from somewhere over by the dogwood. I found her pacing under it, its budding leaves soon to bloom and brighten the entire courtyard.

I quickened my steps, stopping short of running. Olivia's expression was tense, and she looked around furtively. She pressed the keys into my hand. "I passed Mary in the halls but put her off. I need to go meet her though. She's feeling neglected."

"Is your friendship with Mary genuine?" I asked as she went to leave. I had been curious. We hadn't really talked about the moment she had interrupted us, when Olivia had skillfully lied to throw off suspicion.

Olivia stopped and turned back to me. She gave me a look like she was uncertain how I'd react. "I like Mary. She's suppressed. She doesn't express a lot of what desires lie under her belief in what is right. Desires that aren't bad but make her feel bad. I was hoping I could help her," Olivia waved a hand in the air as she searched for the words, "let loose a little. Maybe I could if I had more time."

I raised my eyebrows in surprise. I had expected Olivia to say interacting with Mary was a burden. "Oh."

Olivia walked back to me for a second. "Mary isn't so different from you, you know. You're just a little stronger. Before you knew any of this, you still pushed through. You didn't let decades of childhood lessons tell you there was only one way to be or you'd burn forever. Mary, she clings to her teachings. And they aren't all wrong. But at this point, she feels like they're so powerful, so omnipresent, that anything she wants for herself, anything that makes her unique, makes her bad. Makes her wanton. I like spending time with her and teasing out her individuality."

"Teasing how?" Olivia's perspective of Mary was like a sucker punch. I had never given her that much credit. I had never thought about her background, only knowing she hadn't grown up in my orphanage.

Olivia's mischievous smile was back. Sometimes it was so wide you could see her pearly white teeth, and I swear a sparkle flashed in her eye. "Succubae aren't just about sex. We're about teasing out suppressed desire. In Mary, I try to use my power to get her to do anything she wants. Even if it's eating chocolate before bed or walking the garden path after curfew." Olivia laughed at my widened eyes. "Don't worry, I'll skip that last suggestion tonight. Now go! You should still be back as soon as you can."

I nodded. Impulsively, I reached out and squeezed her hand. "Goodnight, Liv."

She squeezed my hand and slipped away.

I walked along the garden paths toward the infirmary at the other end of the compound as if I was headed to the library and not a dungeon. I hurried there, keeping my head down, the excuse of sleeplessness at the ready. We might have a curfew and expectations of politeness, but we weren't children. We could take late-night strolls. I just didn't want to garner any more suspicion than I already had before Olivia and I could prepare to leave.

It was after ten, and I didn't encounter anyone; the guards were long gone for the night, with only a sister on shift to tend to the patients. Tonight, that sister would be me. I swiped the badge to the long hall and took everything in. Soft crying drifted from the patient room where we had performed Mathew's exorcism earlier. My heart hurt for him a little, but the hitchhiker had only teased out his previous behavior and heightened his natural inclinations. I took the time to perform the actions that Olivia had said she'd taken over from Emily. Using the call button, I checked on each patient room to see if they needed refreshments or medical attention. Each room had an adjoining bathroom, and most things they'd need for the night they'd already have, but sometimes Liv said someone would want a cup of tea or a kind word.

Only one patient requested that, and I quickly put on the kettle, tapping my foot impatiently as I waited. I knew Luk would already know someone was here. I wondered if he somehow would know it was me. After dropping off the cup to a middle-aged woman, her blond hair matted and tangled on one side, bags under her eyes making her look haunted, I made sure the hall was secure. Satisfied, I didn't linger any longer and hurried to the small staircase that brought me to the hidden dungeon below.

Part of me still couldn't believe the Church had rooms like this, let alone sanctioned using them. I passed the first rusted iron bars, most likely skipped over because they were so brittle a strong blow could snap them, and kept walking. Luk got up.

"Little witch." His mouth quirked. I knew what he wanted.

"I told you not to call me that." It came out husky rather than annoyed.

His gaze instantly sharpened. He walked so fast he blurred. The bars creaked as he gripped them. "I'll call you whatever I want. You are mine."

I couldn't work up the energy to care about the misogynistic declaration. "Prove it."

Luk's lips curled back, his fangs dropping, and he hissed. Instead of feeling threatened, the show of aggression made me wet. "You know I can't get through these bars. That's very cruel, little witch. Come closer."

The corner of my lip turned up, and I dipped my hand into my pocket, letting the keys fall from my fist, holding them by the ring. I saw his eyes follow the gesture, saw him back up to make room. I knew I should tell him about visiting the temple, about what I'd learned about my family. But right now, that's not what I wanted to think about. "How about I come in?"

Luk didn't say anything. He just watched me intently as I approached to open the door. Nerves finally took over, and my hand fumbled a little at the lock. As soon as the click sounded, Luk was there. He flung the door open, wasting no time.

He picked me up and wrapped my legs around his waist, walking us into the hall and out of the cell. He walked us a little ways from the bars of his cell before he turned, pressing me against the wall, his mouth on mine in seconds.

His tongue licked into my mouth, and my thighs squeezed around his stomach almost involuntary, craving pressure. He brought his hand down to my skirt while he licked and tasted my neck, right under my ear. A long moan pulled from my throat, my eyes going to the ceiling.

With all the boys in all the bars, trying to release the pressure had never felt like this. The medieval surroundings, the stone floor scattered with pebbles and dirt, faded. Luk pulled my skirt up, reaching underneath to find nothing separating us. I had known why I was coming here. When he found it, he growled, the rumble against my throat the sexiest thing I'd ever heard.

Panting, he said, "Tell me."

"Tell you what?"

"Tell me you're mine, Eliza." He pushed two fingers inside me. I cried out something that might have been words. His fingers hooked and sped up, and I grew wetter still as I involuntarily squeezed myself around his fingers. It was too much, but I wanted more. I didn't know how he was holding me up and doing that so perfectly.

"Tell me." His voice, just on the edge of anger and desperation, brought me back down from euphoria for a moment. I brought both hands up to cradle his face. His fangs had descended, and he stared at me, crazed, hungry. So was I. I leaned in and pricked my full bottom lip against one of his fangs. I felt the snag, the sharp sting, and then the coppery taste of my blood filled my mouth. I kissed him, filling his mouth too. Letting him taste me.

I pulled back just enough to whisper against his lips, "I'm yours."

Luk roared, and with the swish of clothes, he was inside me, driving hard and fast. I held on, riding the wave that took me over almost instantly. The sweetness contrasted with the sharpness. My vision blacked for just a second before I realized he'd dropped to the floor and turned me around.

"Stay with me, little witch." He pulled my hips back against him and entered me from behind, grabbing one hand and putting it high on the wall above me. His other hand guided my hips where he wanted them. The slap of our bodies against each other filled the hall.

"I'm with you," I gasped out. His fingers left my hip and came around to touch me exactly where I needed. "Luk, oh, my God, Luk."

He growled in my ear, "You don't call for anyone but me. Do you understand me, Eliza? While I'm inside you, I am your god."

I moaned. All I could say back was, "Yes. Yes. *Yes.*" All thought was taken over by driving waves of pleasure. I fell back against his chest as his hand kept up the firm circular pressure on my clit. That euphoric rush came surging back, and I was pulled under the waves. As wetness spread down my thighs, I knew he hadn't been far behind me. And that answered another question I'd had. Even vampires cum.

Twenty-Two

Luk

I stroked her arm up and down from elbow to wrist. She sat between my legs, my back to the wall, my head thrown back to rest. I couldn't remember ever feeling this content, even in this hallway, with the bars to my cage thrown open but not really free.

"Why don't we just leave right now? Right this second?" Her voice was sleepy, satisfied. I hardened again.

I pulled her closer to my chest, to where one day, when I earned my rebirth, our hearts would beat together forever. "We can't. The second I go missing, the Church will deploy forces you've never seen to hunt us. The exorcism I saw you practice is child's play compared to what the Vatican is capable of. They were a formidable force hundreds of years ago. Who knows what they've come up with since. I imagine they've only become stronger."

Her head fell back against me, and I nuzzled into her hair, smelling the rose in it. I wrapped myself around her a little tighter, terrified to let her leave me. I hadn't told her about the visit from Father Paul yet. "You need to leave tonight, though. I don't know what the supernatural world looks like outside anymore. Who my allies would be. Olivia has given me a small glimpse, and I've learned what I can from people I've heard or interacted with, but I'm going to be a liability, not a strength."

"I'm not leaving without you. Besides, I saw the way you moved earlier. You were so fast I couldn't keep track. How would you be a liability?"

I closed my eyes against her hair. Her faith in me made me feel strong, but I knew I was right. "Eliza, there are forces stronger than even an ancient vampire. And no matter how strong I am, if enough people band against me, they'll still win. The second I leave here, the fact that a Sekhmet vampire from the age of the Crusades is still alive will garner attention. The rest of my kind have most likely either died or earned their rebirth. Any alive would not be something you wanted to encounter."

"Why not?"

"Because any ancient vampires that still lived would be here for this life and this life only. Their only goal would be to satisfy their own desires. Considering the limitations of this life and where our strengths lie, those desires would be nothing good for anyone around them. And the amount of death they would have had to deal to continue to chase those desires today—I'm not sure either of us could fathom. They would be incredibly dangerous."

She shifted, turning to look at me. Her hand came up to cup my cheek, and I leaned into the touch. I could never get enough of her. "Your desires are something very good for me."

I smiled back at her, flashing my teeth. "My desires are good for you and you only."

She shifted to sit in my lap, lining us up, making my attention shift. One side of her mouth tilted in a grin, a dimple appearing on her cheek. "I can live with that."

"We still need to talk," My voice was like gravel, and

with her in my lap, it was hard to remember what we needed to talk about right now.

"Can't we talk after?" she whispered back, and her brazenness was my undoing. I gripped her hair, wrenching her head back gently, letting her feel just a bite of pain. Her gasp was all the encouragement I needed.

I ran my fangs against her pressure point, wanting to claim her for all the world to see, but I couldn't. Not yet. Not until I had a soul to offer back.

Instead, I gripped the habit around her hips and brought it over her head, along with the nightgown she had beneath. Her breasts were heavy with peaked nipples, and her narrow waist sloped into surprisingly wide hips for someone so slight. Her full lips in a heart-shaped face and brilliant almond eyes staring back at me were so beautiful it hurt. Her body was shapely but delicate, like porcelain, though strong enough that I knew she wouldn't break.

Suddenly, she seemed shy, biting her lip and looking down. The change confused me. She must have known she was beautiful. "What is it?"

She shifted, bringing us closer, and the air left me, my eyes sharpening on her. My hand palmed her breast, exploring the fullness of it in my hand, my thumb rubbing over the bud of her nipple. Her head fell back as she reveled in the feeling. "Are you sorry that I'm not more…chaste? You come from a time when women had even stricter expectations. This isn't my first time."

Her words seemed to fall out of her, the nervousness in them distracting me from my current mission. I gave her my full attention, already deciding what part of her I wanted to taste first. What part of her I wanted to mark. "Little witch, do you think I've been chaste? I don't care who you've been with as long as from this point forward, you're mine."

The line between her brows smoothed out. She shifted forward, and the sensation against my head almost made my eyes roll back. "Can I taste you?"

She smiled wickedly. "I'd love for you to taste me."

My mouth watered when I realized what she meant. "That too, little witch. But I meant, can I mark you?" My doubts from earlier pressed in. But the overwhelming urge to make her mine was winning.

She cocked her head, her hips moving in a steady rhythm, threatening to distract me. But this was important. I wanted her to be mine for all the world to see. I wanted to erase any doubt in her mind that she was anything but perfect for me. More than I wanted to be inside her again. "Like before?"

Before, when I had drunk from her for strength. I shook my head. "No, not like before. That was an offering, and one that helped me greatly. This would be for pleasure. This would be to show the entire world that you're mine."

She wrapped both arms around my neck, moving in time with my hips. She swallowed, and my eyes followed the motion, snagging on the beat of her heart. The pulse of it, how willingly she gave herself to me, how openly she trusted me, had even the small friction of the sweatpants I wore almost unbearable against the sensitivity of wanting to be in her. "I already am. You might as well show the world."

A growl rumbled up my throat, but I couldn't stop it. The aggression didn't seem to bother her. I gripped her under her ribs, pulling her far enough away from me that she could pull my pants back down, then she dropped on top of me, and I glided home into her smooth wetness. She moved just slightly, enough to tease, rubbing her clit on my shaft as she went. I groaned, watching her breasts heave with her breath, her cheeks flush with pleasure.

"Eliza," I whispered as my fangs descended, and saliva pooled in my mouth at the thought of her blood. "I need you to understand first. This would connect us." I groaned as she pulled out, so just the head of me sat at her entrance, then she slid forward, fully seating me again. Stars danced behind my eyes, and it was difficult to concentrate on what I was trying to tell her.

"Connect us, like we're connected right now?" she teased, her voice a purr. I wanted to say fuck it and take her, but this was too important.

"This would connect us through the ages, Eliza. Only, I don't have my rebirth yet. I don't have a soul to offer you back."

Eliza pulled back from me, from riding me with her slow, torturous pace. "Is marking like a marriage?" My gut clenched at the uncertainty in her voice. Maybe she wasn't ready. This was fast, even for my time. But I knew what I wanted. I knew it was her.

"It's more than a marriage, Eliza. Your soul will always look for mine; in this life and the next."

Her mouth opened to a small O. She looked at me for a long time, fear in the dent between her brows, uncertainty in the way she chewed her lip. Just when it became almost unbearable, when I began to tell her it was fine and we would wait—we should wait, anyway, until I had a soul for hers to find—she spoke.

"Then mark me. And let's get out of here and figure out how to earn you your rebirth." Her words filled me with a swell of pride. Of devotion. Of love. I kissed her once, gently. The act seemed to surprise her. I traced that kiss down her cheek to her throat. She bent her neck for better access. My hand, so large it covered half her chest, laid over her heart. I thrust up hard once, making her drooping eyelids open wide. Twice.

She looked down at the sudden change of rhythm, and I opened my mouth to expose my fangs. There was no fear in her face, only want. I wanted her so badly. I lowered my mouth to her breast, giving her time to stop me, to call out and say she'd changed her mind. When nothing but a moan and a twist of her hips to meet my thrust met my ears, I bit into her breast. Blood flooded my mouth, and I groaned at the sweet taste. I felt her life. The power of it flooded me as she wrapped her arms around my head and took over the rhythm. I was too overwhelmed to keep it steady.

She rode me, her breaths coming quicker until she collapsed, biting into my shoulder to bury her shout as she came. As she trembled from her own pleasure, I took in the sweet nectar of her essence, marking her chest as mine for the rest of her life. At the sharp sting of her bite, I fell over the edge, and as I came, I swore it would be a life as long as the gods would give her. She lay spent in my arms, not moving to separate us. I felt her in every part of me every time either of us took a breath. I pulled her habit, crumpled next to us, around her shoulders, fearing she trembled from the cold, but the tremors didn't stop. Her lips pressed against my throat, then her teeth scraped before she gave a gentle nip. Even after everything, I twitched inside her. I felt her smile against my throat, realizing that was what she wanted. My own lips tugged at the corner.

I ran my finger over the mark on her breast, the wound still fresh. "Little witch, as much as I don't want you to, you need to leave soon. But first, I have to tell you something."

She shifted, and I fell out of her, eliciting a gasp from her lips. Knowing she was so sensitive made satisfaction thrum inside me. "What is it?" she asked when she'd gotten herself more under control.

She moved to straighten her clothes, preparing to dress,

but I grabbed her wrist, stopping her. Brushing my hand over my mark, over her beautiful naked breast, I contradicted myself and said, "Just one more moment." That dimple appeared, but she didn't argue. Just waited patiently. "Father Paul came to see me after the exorcism you performed."

Her eyes widened, and she sat back on my thighs. I had gotten her full attention, but she was unintentionally distracting mine. Making myself focus, I looked up into her hazel eyes, losing myself in the swirling yellow, green, and brown. "What did he say?" she prompted when I didn't continue.

I gripped her hips on either side, grounding her. "He said you exhibited obvious magic, that he believes, with this new evidence, he can put you in a cell next to me. He plans to bring you in as a patient, Eliza. He thinks he can do it soon."

The color left her face, and she sat frozen at my words. I wasn't sure she even took a breath. My anxiety ratcheted up. I had expected her to be scared, but not this scared. I shook her a little to get her to focus on me. "You need to leave tonight. You need to get away."

Her eyes went from staring into space to concentrating on mine, her hand coming up to cover the mark I had left. Then coming to cup my cheek again. "I'm not leaving without you."

I grunted. "That is not why I marked you. You are mine wherever you go, but for your safety, you need to leave now."

She shook her head. "Why can't we get you out now? Your cage is open."

I cursed under my breath. I was becoming frustrated. "I told you, Eliza, I would be a liability, and their search would be even more fervent if I was with you. I won't bring that kind of danger down on you."

She shook her head again. Her face was still white; her

trembling had stopped, but moisture pooled in her eyes. She was terrified. Still, she leaned closer, kissing me gently. My arm came up to roughly grab her hair, bringing her closer. She kissed back just as hard, just as desperately. When we broke, she said, "I'm not leaving without you."

I grunted in disgust, picking her up to stand beside me, pulling up my pants as I went. She righted her clothes and pulled them over her own head, and despite my annoyance, regret churned in me as she covered herself. I pulled my hand through my hair, pacing back and forth. "When do you go into town next?"

"Tomorrow is our weekend off."

I nodded. That was lucky. "Go into town with Olivia. Ask her to find contacts for anyone who would give you shelter. Tell her to ask gently about me. She'll know what I mean. But if she can't guarantee me sanctuary, if she only finds a way for you to get out, promise me you'll go."

Eliza opened her mouth, and I knew it was to protest before she said a word. I strode quickly to her, gripping her shoulders, and shouted, "Promise me! Do *not* end up here in a cell next to me, Eliza. I will lose my mind."

She stood there, opening and closing her mouth with no words for a few seconds. Finally, she said, her voice small, "Okay."

I took a deep breath of relief. Behind her, my open cell beckoned me, calling me back to my prison. I closed my eyes and prayed to Sekhmet to help tip the balance, to get me out of here. I would fulfill my purpose with renewed vengeance. I swore to her silently—if she could just help me get out. Leaning down, I took Eliza's mouth, hungrily tasting her, wishing we had more time, for her, for everything. She reached up, threading her fingers through my hair and tugging, every bit as hungry as me.

Finally, we broke away, and I walked silently to my cell, pulling the bars closed in front of me so she didn't have to. The resounding click of the lock falling into place echoed around us as we made unspoken promises to each other. Eliza nodded, and with a look of determination, she left. If only one of us were to break out of this prison, I swore it would be her.

Twenty-Three
Eliza

He had ruined me. That was the resounding thought circling my head as I walked back through the night, guided by the goddess moon, back to my room. I hadn't told him about the temple in the end. I worried it would just make him more willing to sacrifice himself, more insistent he couldn't leave his cell. I was so lost in thought, in planning, in praying, not even sure anymore who I was praying to, when abrupt words stopped me in my tracks.

"Eliza? What are you doing out here?"

My eyes flew up, startled. Sam stood in my path, hands casually in his pockets. I cursed. Of course he would pick tonight to be out for his own midnight stroll.

"I was restless, so I decided to take a walk." I prayed he would think my disheveled appearance resulted from earlier, not what I had actually just been doing.

He walked forward, and I made myself stand still, not act suspiciously. He gently rested his hand on my shoulder, rubbing in a comforting gesture, and I forced myself not to recoil. "Are you sure you're okay? By all accounts, the exorcism was successful earlier, but you really had us worried. Is it a thing now that the women of this congregation will pass out whenever we successfully banish a demon to hell?"

I laughed, but it came out a little shrill. I remembered

Olivia's sickness following Luk's attempted exorcism. "I guess we really are the fairer sex."

He smiled, squeezing my shoulder before backing up. "There's nothing fair about you other than your looks, of course." He blushed at the compliment, and I shifted, wanting to end this, not liking the intimacy he was trying to create, especially not after what had just happened.

"I am pretty tired after all that though. I'm going to head to bed."

As I went to pass him, he called out, "Wait! What happened? Is it like Olivia? Have you been sick? You just, you seemed to almost," he swallowed hard, "float, Eliza. I swear, for a second, I thought you were asking the demon to come into you. You really scared me."

I swallowed, remembering reaching, doing exactly what he said, calling the wraith to me, though not for the reason he must think. I hadn't asked the demon into me. I had called it through me. "I'm not sure, Sam. It's all kind of a blur."

He nodded. "Well, I guess I better get back to my rooms. Take care of yourself, and take it easy this weekend, okay?"

I gave him a weak smile and a murmur of thanks as we left each other, and I headed back to my dorm. I felt wrung out. I headed straight for Olivia's room so I could tell her about the coming danger and what we had to do. I wouldn't leave Luk here. It wouldn't take them long to realize he needed to be killed instead of exorcised. And who knew what they would do to him in the meantime.

They were starving him but didn't know I'd been giving him blood and that he was stronger than ever. Eventually, they'd use their cattle prods, they'd overpower him, and they'd kill him. I wouldn't let that happen.

I snuck up to Olivia's door as stealthily as I could and knocked. Waiting impatiently for her to answer, I looked up and down the hall. Finally, she opened the door, hair rumpled. I rushed past her to the chair, identical to mine, while I waited for her to close the door and sit down with me.

"I wasn't expecting you tonight," she said with a yawn. Getting a better look at me, she grinned, "Ooh, but I'm not sorry you came. You certainly look like you had fun."

I rolled my eyes. "That's an understatement. But we have a problem."

She nodded, not catching my tone or how serious this was yet. She waved her hand at me. "Go on."

"Father Paul said that my exorcism today was suspicious. He gloated to Luk after I was carried back here. He thinks he has enough evidence to have me in a cell soon."

Olivia instantly perked up. "What is soon?"

I shrugged. "I'm not sure, but Luk seems to think soon is tomorrow. It's our weekend to get away. I'm not leaving without him. He said we need a place where he can be safe while he gets his bearings. I went to a temple today, and it sounds like the Hecate witches were feared but respected. They still have a temple to the goddess. I think I can find the place he said he needs with the witches."

Olivia began her customary bouncing, chewing her lip while she thought. "I'm not sure. I don't run in the same circles as your kind exactly. Or his, for that matter. There is overlap, of course."

"Olivia!" I caught her attention. "You're rambling. I was thinking about going back to the temple, seeing if I could find the lady who spoke to me today, Emmaline. See if they have, I don't know, safe houses or communities we could go to. If we got out at night, when the guards aren't around, we wouldn't run in to anybody. We could just walk out."

She looked back at me, nodding slowly. "We can try. I had planned for just me and you to escape. I figured Luk would honestly take care of himself and meet us eventually. We may be able to walk out, but there are cameras in the top hall where the patients are. They'll know right away we left with him. That we broke him out."

I couldn't help but feel skeptical at both Olivia's and Luk's confidence he'd so easily be able to join us if we left without him. He was powerful, sure. He moved so fast my eyes couldn't track him, and he could easily rip out a human's throat. But what was that against multiple people? Against guns or powerful witches? How would he even know how to navigate this world without one of us to show him? I couldn't wait years for him to join me. I felt like I'd just found what I'd always wanted; I wasn't ready for it to be ripped away. I said as much to Olivia.

"Then we'll find a way to bring him with us. But Eliza, don't underestimate him. He might need time to find his twenty-first-century legs, but he's more powerful than you can imagine. It wouldn't take him years to find you."

I gave her a stubborn look, my mouth set. "I'm not willing to risk it."

She shook her head. "You don't understand, Eliza. Not everyone is given the kind of time vampires are. Not even vampires are given the kind of time Luk has had. I've only heard of one other. He was a favored child of Sekhmet and was only allowed to remain because he continued fulfilling his purpose after he earned his rebirth. Even witches, even demons, have such a small amount of soul that we are recycled back into a human lifespan unless our creators bless us with more."

"What does that mean, 'A small amount of soul?' What do you mean, 'A small lifespan?'"

Olivia leaned forward, her elbows on her knees. "Energy never ceases to exist, Eliza. The Tree of Life, the mother, the conduit of all. It shares its life force with the gods and goddesses. They had an eternity of soul, but they were lonely. They split that soul for their creations. Humans, trees, animals, demons. They are all offshoots of the gods' and goddesses' souls. Some were more generous than others."

I swallowed. "I'm not sure I really understand. We have borrowed souls?"

She grunted in frustration. "Not borrowed. They transfer it, and when they do, your soul takes on its own characteristics, its own beliefs, its own destiny. But it diminishes the gods' souls. It lessens their immortality. Which is why they don't like to give it away too often."

I nodded like I understood, but I still wasn't sure I did. "What happens if they give away too much soul?"

Her face looked bleak. "It rarely happens, and usually only by lesser gods or goddesses. When that happens, they cease to exist, they live on through their creations, but their soul is dispersed. Energy is transferred, and they are no more."

"Who has it happened to? All humans have a soul. How does God still exist?"

She sat back. "Nymphs, various beings of generosity and love whose names are lost to history. The one you call God has gone by many names, Eliza, and while he gives his energy away, he can also take it. Whenever those who wrong him are smited, whenever he strikes someone down, he can take back the piece of soul. Also, humans, as you've noticed, have short lifespans in relation to us. His creations do not require as much soul by our standards as other beings."

"Olivia, you are turning everything I've ever learned on its head."

She nodded. "I know. But that is why Luk is so powerful. Most vampires do not sustain the longevity he has. To keep that, the amount of soul Sekhmet must have given him is extraordinary. He was able to be kept in that cell because he was weak. I suspect the only reason he stays in that cell now is because he thinks it keeps you safe."

I sat back in the chair, my eyes finding the ceiling. "I never expected this to happen. I never thought this would happen so quickly for me."

She laughed. "I never expected a Sekhmet vampire to be alive this long. I never would have thought his singular focus would have become love, not revenge." I looked back at her in surprise, and she smiled gently at me. "I'm not sure how you found each other across time and space, especially with him not having earned a rebirth. Sekhmet will take back the soul she has gifted him if he dies. She will not transfer it to him for a rebirth. But however it happened, I think you two were supposed to find each other. Your energies and magnetism are beautiful to watch."

I looked at her questioningly. "Aren't you meant to tempt people away from their significant other?"

She laughed, the tinkling bells I sometimes heard when she was purposefully charming ringing with the sound. "No, Eliza. I am meant to punish the unfaithful when it's already in their heart. To expose them to their partner so their partner doesn't waste their life and heart. Lilith was so angry at what happened with Adam, she created a succubus, and later succubae, to prevent anyone from enduring her level of hurt. Or at least that was the idea."

My head was spinning. Determination set in the squareness of my shoulders and the hardness of my jaw. "I know this isn't going to be easy, but I can't leave Luk here when we go. This weekend, we need to find a coven. We need to find a place that makes him feel secure enough to leave that cell, that convinces him he won't be putting me in jeopardy. Can you still come with, without hurting your own purpose?"

She frowned for a moment, filling me with apprehension. When she spoke, though, it eased some of the tension. "I can go. Luk isn't wrong though. The Church has more resources than what you've seen, and if you escape together, they'll hunt you with everything they have."

"If we leave him here, they could kill him."

She shrugged. "It really is unlikely."

I frowned, annoyed at how cavalier she and Luk were with his life. "Is it possible to kill him? Is he immortal?"

She bowed her head. "No, he's not. Yes, they could kill him."

I nodded. "I'm not leaving without him."

Olivia stood, and I stood with her. She wrapped her arm around my shoulder, walking me to the door. "Go to bed. Meet me early in the morning. I have some ideas of where we can go. With the spring equinox and the full moon coming, I have a few haunts I can revisit with you. I know Luk said not to visit other witches, but at this point, I'm not sure what it can hurt, especially with you visiting that temple. Besides, what he doesn't know won't hurt him. I've been hearing some whispers."

"Whispers?" I asked as we reached the door.

"You know that vampire I told you about? The one who might be almost as old as Luk?"

I nodded.

"I heard he was coming to town. A short visit to bucolic New England on his world tour."

I raised my eyebrows at her, making her laugh. "If I can figure out where he will be or find a way to meet him, you'll see what I mean."

I sprang forward and hugged her tight, thankful I had her on my side. "Thanks, Olivia."

"Don't thank me yet."

Twenty-Four

Eliza

We wound our way through the busy bar on Church Street. We had come to town early to find a bed and breakfast and get a room, then we headed out to look for somewhere the witches might gather on a weekend night.

I wasn't unfamiliar with the place Olivia picked, the small, elevated stage placed next to the bar, about halfway through the seating area for patrons. Wobbly high-top tables and chairs were scattered haphazardly in corners for drinks. Some people were sitting, and some would sway or dance to the music behind their tables, but there was no centralized dance floor. Some local alternative rock band played; the female singer dressed in Doc Martins and a short skirt gave a good rendition of Paramore. I had adopted my Eliza-the-modern-woman persona and shed my Catholic guilt. I swung my hips as I walked, my dark hair falling down the middle of my back in gentle waves and framing my face. My blue-black eyeliner brought out the gray-blue color in my hazel eyes. Who needed contacts when your eyes could change color on a whim?

As we neared an area in the corner that hadn't already been taken, I moved ahead and tucked myself in behind a corner table, opting to stand, and asked Olivia, "What are we doing here?" She had snuck out shortly after we had checked in to the hotel. After the explosive energy I'd burned off with Luk the night before, I had been oddly exhausted and opted to stay back and take a nap. None of the dancing or one-night stands had ever given me the kind of contentment I felt after being with Luk. I had never felt that way with anyone before, I was beginning to realize. It helped keep back the hysteria whenever I thought too hard of everything we'd done, of the claiming.

Olivia looked over her shoulder toward the bar, swaying her hips, nudging me with her shoulder to get into the music. I danced with her, loving the thrum of the bass vibrating from the floor to my feet. My entire body moved with the music. My heart beat in my chest along with a tug of someone else, a restlessness. I smiled, knowing it was Luk. I swept my long hair to the side, twirling it into a bun and then dropping it to fall again across my neck. Mud season must be officially over. The unseasonably warm spring day, coupled with the press of bodies, made me just a little too hot.

"We're trying to run into one of the members of the local coven. This is a popular hangout for the goth type."

"Are all witches goth?" I thought of Emmaline. She hadn't been wearing anything that would make me think goth, but Sarah Lee could have fit the description.

Olivia laughed. The tinkling bells had some men at the table across from us looking over with interest. "No, but the energy in here is the type to attract them."

"Alternative emo?"

Olivia gave me a look of almost disappointment, her mouth pulled to the side, and guilt seeped in.

She smoothed her features, pasting the flirty smile back on and rocking her hips in her painted-on jeans and flowery cap-sleeve top that showed a sliver of her waist. "No, the lack of judgment. You know, the whole, I-am-who-I-am vibe."

She gave me a pointed look, properly chastening me. Even though I had only been kidding, she was right. Different personalities mixed in the eclectic spread of fashion before me. A group of people in heavy black pants with chains sat next to a college prep girl with a high ponytail at one table. Everyone intermixed and laughed together without pretense. I relaxed a little more and ran my fingers through my hair, sweeping it over my shoulder this time and giving a conciliatory smile to Olivia. She squeezed my hip in response.

We weren't alone at our table for long. Olivia looked over as a man came up to us, dropping off two whiskeys on ice. "From the gentleman." He tilted his head back to indicate the guys who had noticed us earlier. We saluted them with our drinks, and I took a sip. It wasn't long before they walked over to say hello.

"Hi, I'm Andrew," a tall man with sandy blond hair said, smiling wide. He was attractive in a nondescript way, like he didn't spend hours in the gym but was naturally fit.

I nodded back to him. "Eliza."

Olivia sipped her drink, making a show of her lips on the straw, drawing both men's attention. The other one, short with broad shoulders and a pudgy middle, said, "I'm Eddie."

Finishing her sip, Olivia held out a manicured hand and said in a voice I had never heard her use, "Liv."

I spit out my drink a little when I coughed. She really did like the nickname.

Eddie looked at me askance and concentrated back on Olivia. She continued to flirt, batting her eyelashes and playing with her straw, eventually sidling up to Eddie. He basked in her attention, his face going from interested to enraptured to devoted. Olivia leaned to speak into his ear at one point, and he enthusiastically nodded to whatever she said.

Olivia linked an arm through Eddie's and pulled him toward the side exit. Before she slipped through the side door, she threw me a wink over her shoulder. Eddie didn't bother saying goodbye to his friend. Andrew looked uncomfortable, but I had a feeling it had nothing to do with the fact that his friend had just abandoned him for a quickie.

He turned to me and said, "So, are you a UVM student?"

"No." My lips pressed in a tight line.

He nodded in response, looking around as if trying to find someone in the crowd. His face lit up when he must have recognized someone at the bar.

"I'll be right back. I've got to go check on someone."

I just nodded in response and watched him walk back to the bar to an animated coed who gave him more than one-word responses.

I nursed my drink, not minding. I looked around the place curiously. The energy around me seemed to have picked up. The band had run through a bunch of punk rock classics of the early 2000s and had settled on something a little softer from Death Cab for Cutie.

I tapped my foot, trying to relax to the mournful beat and the singer's soft crooning. She was talented, but I was beginning to feel like I was crawling out of my skin. It hadn't been that long since Olivia left, and I knew she was taking her chance to feed. I knew I should wait for her, but I needed to go, needed to do something.

The club a street down was calling my name. The idea of losing myself in a sea of bodies, dancing to a more erotic beat, sounded better by the minute. In response, I felt a sharp tug in my chest and realized Luk felt my impatience, my growing arousal. I smiled, picturing him growling and threatening. Instead of feeling better, my discomfort increased with another sharp tug. His possession leaked into me and took over.

I needed a distraction, needed to get out of here. Just then, a girl about my height with rusty red hair laid her arms on the table, leaning toward me. She seemed a little tipsy, using the table for support, but smiled wide. Her freckled face and small upturned nose were charming, and intoxication left her face open and guileless. "It's the moon."

My brow wrinkled with my confusion. "Sorry?"

She smiled wider and walked around the table to stand next to me. "The moon!" she said, her voice loud right as the music ended, causing a few chuckles around us.

I laughed nervously with them, putting thoughts of the possessive, angry tug to the side and concentrating on the girl. "What's the moon?"

She hiccuped, falling a little against the table. Leaning her elbow on it, she looked up at me, her head tilted in confusion. "You're a sister, aren't you? I saw you getting overwhelmed. I felt your energy. You feel like a bomb about to go off! The full moon is tomorrow night. It's the waxing moon feeding you energy."

I swallowed. We had found someone. One of the local covens.

"How could you tell?" I asked honestly. Nobody had ever told me I felt like a bomb or identified me as a witch before when I had no knowledge of this hidden world.

She shrugged, accepting that I was who she thought I was. I figured it was true and not true. "Something about your aura just glows, almost white, which is *super* weird. It's not a color or an emotion. It's almost like you *are* the moon. And your restlessness was practically *screaming* at me across the room. I haven't seen you around. Did you come in for the ceremony tomorrow?"

I frowned, wondering how I should handle this. "I'm just passing through. What ceremony?"

The girl's eyes widened, and she caught herself before she fell forward. "You don't have plans to celebrate the equinox? How is that possible, as powerful of a witch as you are?" She hiccupped again on the last word, and I looked to the side, noticing people were beginning to watch us more closely. I wished Olivia was here. I didn't know how to proceed with this.

"Last minute plans I couldn't change," I said finally, talking above the music that started up again.

She nodded seriously. How drunk was she? "Let me give you my number! I'll talk to our high priestess; you shouldn't be alone on an equinox!"

Relief coursed through me, and I smiled gratefully at her. Pulling out my phone, I handed it to the girl to put in her number. As she tapped at the buttons, I asked, "What's your name?"

She looked up at me, eyes a little glassy. I hadn't noticed before. "Annabeth. Text me in the morning so we can get coffee. I'll talk to Cassandra and let you know."

Grateful, I told her I would. Taking back my phone, I decided it was time to find Olivia. I stepped out the side door I had seen her disappear through and pulled up her contact in my phone. Before I could hit the call button, her voice came from the darkness, making me jump.

"Hey, did it work?"

Hand to my heart, I said, "Jesus, Olivia, you scared the hell out of me."

She smiled wickedly. "Really getting comfortable with those blasphemies, aren't you?"

I realized what I'd said. Normally, I would feel so guilty when I'd take the Lord's name in vain, I'd count up the Hail

Marys. I laughed and walked over to her. "Where have you been? I think I met a witch from the coven! She gave me her number. We have a date for coffee tomorrow. I guess there's a ceremony for the moon or maybe the equinox. I don't know."

I got a good look at Olivia. She didn't have a hair out of place, her outfit as immaculate as ever. "That's good. Let's get back to the bed and breakfast and get a good night's sleep."

I frowned and repeated my question. "Where were you? Did you need to feed?"

Olivia looped her arm through mine like she always did and turned us in the direction of our room for the night. "I did, but that's not why I left you. Witches won't approach a demon. Demons, especially a mid-level demon like me, make powerful friends for a witch. They wouldn't impose on you."

My brow puckered in confusion. "But we saw Sarah Lee together."

Olivia barked a laugh. "Sarah Lee is a power-hungry opportunist. She probably invited us in as much to see if she could get an opportunity to entice me away as to take our money for a reading."

I sighed. I still had so much to learn. Luk thought he'd be a liability, but the truth was, even if he knew this world during a different time, at least he still understood the supernatural. When I had been nothing but a novice exorcist, I had thought I knew more of reality, of what happened in this world and the next, than anyone else. Especially since the ghosts gave me an actual glimpse of the other side. I'd thought I had one up on everyone else. But since finding out what Olivia and Luk were, I realized I was still naive.

"So, you left me so they'd approach me?"

Olivia must have heard something in my voice because she looked over with worry in her eyes. "Yes. I'm sorry I didn't warn you. I thought if you expected me to return any second, you'd be less nervous."

I shook my head. She was right. I had been. "It's okay. So, yeah, we're meeting her for coffee tomorrow." I frowned. "Or am just I meeting her?"

Olivia squeezed my arm. "I think we can both go. I saw who approached you. Annabeth is an empath. She would have felt you didn't mean her harm. We can also wait until she's settled and then join her."

"How do you know who she is?"

"We keep tabs."

"We?"

"Demons."

I nodded again. Sometimes, I forgot that Olivia was a demon. Uncertainty and fear suffused me. I felt inward for that soft beat of Luk that tethered me to something. His growly anger had dampened, and he just felt content inside me. With me. With one arm looped through Olivia's and one hand on my chest, we walked to the bed and breakfast to rest for tomorrow. To rest before climbing into the lion's den.

Twenty-Five

Eliza

I sat across the cobblestone street watching the café chewing my lip. Other shops and eateries lined the strip.

"Stop that," Olivia said for the hundredth time.

I smoothed my tongue over the sting. "I can't help it. I'm so nervous."

"Everything is going to work out. She's going to come. We're going to see the witches. They're going to take you in. You're one of them."

"Me and Luk."

Olivia nodded. "You and Luk." She said it absently but didn't meet my eyes. She never did when I talked about Luk coming with me. It irritated me, annoyance building in my chest. Like they were handling me.

I was tired of being handled. It turned out I had been handled my entire life by the Church. I had gone along with what I was told, what was required of me, because I was bad. I never did the right things or wanted the right things. For the sake of my salvation, the sake of the greater good, I was always doing as told like a good little girl. Only to find out I had been meant for something entirely different. The greater good might have looked very different had I been raised by my real family.

I huffed at the thought. Olivia side-eyed me. Before she

could say anything, though, she straightened. "She's here."

I perked up, ready to head to the crosswalk to meet her, when I caught something out of the corner of my eye. An old man, but not an old man. The homeless population here was rampant, and at this point, I recognized the weathered, premature-aging look. Scraggly beard, stiff clothing from soil that dried, lined face, and shining, hopeful eyes.

"Wait."

Olivia was already a few steps in front of me. She turned back to me, expression quizzical. She understood the look on my face. "*Right now?*"

My lips twisted to the side at her impatience. When the dead finally came to me, they couldn't wait. "I'll meet you there."

She shook her head. "She won't meet just me. Just try to hurry up." Olivia winced as she said it. "I'll keep watch to make sure she doesn't leave."

I nodded and walked forward to lean against the brick wall between buildings. I bowed my head, letting my curtain of hair fall forward to block most people from seeing my face, and held my hand palm out. A beckoning. Permission. It didn't take long.

I inhaled a sharp breath as I absorbed this man's pain. A life born of trauma and addiction. His early years had been marked by death and war, which his mind could never quite resolve. Alcohol and heroin numbed the feeling of guilt and sorrow, the yawning emptiness that he could never fill with family and friends. His death was a relief. His hope for peace was a bright light. He wasn't an evil soul, just a lost one.

I sat for a couple seconds recovering after his passing, just breathing in and praying that, wherever he went, he found some solace. Before I raised my head, I realized I wasn't praying to the god I had grown up with anymore, unsure of what he even did with lost souls like that. Who was I praying to? Would Hecate guide the spirits on the other side? Should I be begging her to give them a chance at their next life?

Before that thought took root, Olivia whispered, "Pssst, hurry up. She's getting ready to leave. She just got the check."

My head shot up, dizziness engulfing me from being in such a weird pose for so long. I blinked it away and joined Olivia. Together, we hurried across the crosswalk.

"Annabeth!" I called right as she hit the sidewalk, going in the opposite direction of us.

She looked back and, when she recognized me, smiled uncertainly. Her eyes drifted to Olivia, and her uncertain look turned uncomfortable, her shoulders caving in as if trying to protect herself.

As we joined her, she raised a limp hand in a wave. "Uh, hi, Eliza, was it? I'm sorry for yesterday. I was plastered. My friend was the singer in the band. I'd been there way too long."

I smiled back, trying to reassure the concern evident in her pinched brows. Her eyes kept sliding to Olivia. Remembering what she had said, I decided to just get it out in the open.

"This is Liv, my friend. We work together. She's not. She's," my cheeks heated as I stumbled over my words, "we're just friends."

Olivia snorted beside me as Annabeth's eyes grew wide. Olivia muttered out of the side of her mouth loud enough for all of us to hear, "Smooth."

Annabeth's eyes swung between us. My stomach clenched, and my frustration began to grow. Frustration that I didn't know this world well enough to gracefully navigate it. Thankfully, Olivia saved me once again.

"Hi, Annabeth. I'm helping Eliza. She's a lost witch."

Annabeth licked her lips, shifting her weight. Looking back at me, she said, "You seem awfully powerful for a lost witch."

I swallowed, remembering Olivia telling me they recruited demons for power. "My family was killed. I just found out I'm a witch. I'm looking for some guidance."

Annabeth's brow smoothed, and her eyes softened in sympathy. She stepped forward and placed a hand on my arm. "I'm so sorry."

I nodded. "You had mentioned a gathering today. I was hoping I could take you up on your offer and come along. I'd like to talk to someone in charge. About me, about where I come from."

Annabeth's eyes darted to Olivia again, but she said to me, "I cleared it with our priestess. She said I could bring you. I didn't know about the dem—"

"Me and Cassandra are old friends. She won't mind," Olivia interrupted.

Annabeth looked back at her with wide eyes. "Uh, I should just text her first. Make sure."

Olivia showed her pearly white teeth. "Go ahead."

Annabeth shook her head and turned away, pulling out her phone.

I turned to Olivia and asked quietly, "You know the high priestess? Why didn't you tell me or just ask to see her directly?"

Olivia looked at me, her eyes troubled. "Cassandra used me once to help her with some trouble she was having with a significant other. I exacted a high price. I'm not exactly her favorite."

My eyes widened. "More details later. Do you think she's going to let us come then?"

Olivia nodded yes as she watched Annabeth look at us over her shoulder, her expression guarded. "She'll be curious.

And a little jealous. She'll want to meet you just on principle."

Uneasiness threaded through me at this newest complication. Another layer I hadn't known or understood. I missed Luk. Even though I didn't know his world or understand it, even though I didn't know what my own world was apparently, he made me feel steady, strong. Safe. I reached for that tug now as I waited, and I leaned against it like a solid weight, beating steadfast in my middle.

After we had performed the marking, I had noticed the extra awareness but hadn't thought much of it, figuring that's what sex was when feeling was involved. But over the last couple of days, I realized I could pick out emotions. It wasn't so much an exact knowledge as an impression. Like when he was standing in front of me, and the narrowing of his eyes or tilt of his grin told me what he was thinking. It was comforting, not just because it connected me to him emotionally—it let me know he was alive.

That brought me back down to earth like nothing else, reminding me of what was at stake. Finally, Annabeth approached us. "She says it's okay to bring you both. Let's go. I'm parked around the corner."

We followed Annabeth to a little VW bug decked out in purple with beads hanging from the rearview mirror. Olivia climbed into the back, so I took the front, and we put on our seatbelts.

"Where are we going?" I asked as we settled in.

"Centennial Woods. It's the closest place around here where we can get a little privacy. Burlington is quirky enough that people mostly leave us alone, but it's also religious enough that we like to find places out of the way."

I hummed my understanding. As we drove, Annabeth asked questions. "How did you find out you were a witch?"

I shifted in my seat, unsure how much I should tell her.

I waited for Olivia to chime in, but she sat quietly in the back seat. Of course she chose now to not be helpful.

Swallowing, I thought of what Luk had said about people trying to steal my power. I decided to go with what I saw as the least attractive part of it. "I've always been able to see ghosts. They pass through me to, well, I'm not sure where to. When they pass, I feel their emotions, their pain, their essence."

I looked over to see how Annabeth was receiving this information. Her mouth was gaping, her eyes wide. I shifted my weight again. Perhaps I had shared too much, but it was too late now.

"I met Olivia, and she explained that I was a witch. She encouraged me to find others to explain what was happening to me."

Annabeth shot me a look, her mouth closed but eyes still wide in wonderment. "I wasn't just drunk. Your aura really was white last night."

My brow wrinkled in confusion, wondering what that had to do with what I'd just told her. She saw my expression and clarified, "You're a Hecate witch. A gatekeeper. We thought you were all gone."

I swallowed, looking forward through the windshield. I whispered, but it must have been loud enough for everyone to hear because silence fell over the rest of the car ride. "Not all of us."

We passed through the hodgepodge of townhouses and rambling businesses to the tree-lined streets of the forest pretty quickly. It wasn't long before we pulled off the road on an unmarked trail, the road a little soft still as we passed from Vermont's winter to wet spring. It brought us to a gate, but Annabeth hopped out of the car without pause, messing with a padlock before swinging the gate wide. After pulling through, she went through the motions of resecuring the gate before taking us through the woods to a clearing where several other cars were parked, the ground firmer here.

She led us down another trail, too narrow for anything but foot traffic. We arrived at a small meadow. The trees were beginning to bud, small wildflowers had popped up, and the grass had changed from brown to light green. Ten women stood in front of me, all barefoot in the grass.

Stereotypical long skirts swayed in a slight breeze, and bohemian sweaters hung off shoulders of all shapes and sizes. We got some curious looks. I noticed some women murmuring to each other, but for the most part, everyone's eyes were facing forward. One woman stood tall above the others, a wreath of trillium, bloodroot, and hepatica crowning her afro curls in varying shades of white and purple. Her skin was dark and smooth, and where she moved, the women seemed to move around her, gravitating to her but instantly making way.

"That's our priestess. She will lead today's gathering."

I looked over my shoulder for Olivia, but she had blended in with the crowd. I started picking at my thumb. "What am I supposed to do?"

She watched me as if waiting for something miraculous to happen. "Nothing tonight. Just watch. She'll come talk to you after."

With that, Annabeth left me, her hunched shoulders lifting, going from a solemn young woman to a happy, carefree one. She headed to a tree where a circle of shoes lay and kicked her own off, allowing her feet to sink into the springy meadow.

"Sisters." The woman with the commanding presence walked to the middle of the meadow. Everyone gathered around her in a circle. I walked to the outskirts, looking around surreptitiously for Olivia.

"Welcome. In two short weeks, we'll be welcoming the spring equinox. Today, we come to pay homage to the goddess and to the moon."

Cries of elation and excitement rang out. The woman smiled, exalting in the energy of the crowd. "This equinox, we welcome a full moon. A rare and magic-filled occurrence that hasn't come around for nineteen years!"

Laughter and clapping joined the cheers, murmurs of excitement slowly dying off. I looked down and realized I was still wearing shoes. Feeling oddly guilty, I toed them off and held them in my hand behind my back.

As the chatter quieted, the woman continued, "I will lead you in a prayer to the Mother."

Instead of bowing their heads, everyone raised their hands in elation, and the woman led them in a chant I had never heard:

"The willow bends, and the heart mends
Air winds through budding leaves
The Earth takes a breath as winter breaks
And as seasons turn, life springs wild
Let my spirit grow like a weed
Coming back despite constant picking, prejudice, and greed
Let my heart's roots grow deep like the oak
Steady and strong, marrying the Earth
Eager for the heavens to open and rain to soak
Let the next season come, let the equinox break
My heart is open, let my path make
And I will honor you, Mother and Earth
Away from me all that you need, take."

"Blessed be," the women said in chorus. They then began humming a tune, and the women moved in a circle around their priestess. I was caught up in the motion, the laughter. The women's words soaked into me, sinking into my heart, through my feet, connecting me to the earth. Before long, I found myself with one arm around someone on each side of me, dancing in a circle and calling out thanks to the Mother, calling out thanks to the Earth. And as we came to a breathless stop, everyone heaving oxygen, I found myself laughing along with them. Cassandra, the priestess, ended the ceremony with a grateful, "Blessed be."

Afterward, I held a hand to my chest, looking again for Olivia in the bodies milling around me. I was a little surprised and overwhelmed by the emotion that had filled me. It had been like when I was at the club, dancing in the middle of the floor with twenty people around me, the music pumping in my ears.

As I tried to pinpoint exactly what that feeling was, I was jarred out of my thoughts. "You," said Sarah Lee, the Carmantae witch who had read my cards. It wasn't exactly a happy-to-see-you tone.

My head jerked in surprise, still riding the high of the ceremony. "Hi. Uhm, hi, Sarah Lee."

She looked me over, her lips pursed. "What are you doing here?"

I coughed, searching for a friendly face among the others. "I was invited. By, uhm, by Annabeth."

She looked me up and down. "How did you draw the Hecate card?"

Her delivery was so abrupt I flinched back, despite knowing what she probably wanted from me when I first heard her voice. I smiled painfully. "I'm not even sure what that means. I'm just getting into all this stuff. I thought you were—what did you call it? A Carmantae witch? What are you doing with the Green Sisters?"

"The Sisters of Green," she snapped, and I shifted on my feet. I was supposed to be making friends, not enemies. "I don't have my own coven in the area. They let me join for important events. This coming moon is going to be one of the largest days of power we'll see in two decades. I wanted to be a part of a sisterhood for it." Bitterness laced her voice.

I nodded, my heart going out to her despite myself. I knew what wanting to belong was like. Before I could open my mouth to offer an olive branch, Annabeth found us. "There you are! Cassandra, this is the girl I wanted you to meet."

She rushed up to us with Cassandra in tow behind her. Sarah Lee moved over and lowered her eyes in deference, leaving without another word. I watched her go, not knowing what to make of that. Turning back to give Cassandra my full attention, I found myself looking up.

Cassandra towered over me, and I craned my neck to see her. "Where's the succubus?"

Nerves wound through me, and I cursed Olivia for disappearing on me again without telling me the plan. "I'm not sure. She disappeared when your ceremony began."

Satisfaction stole over Cassandra's face. "It's true then. You don't command her. Or if you do, you aren't very good at it."

Embarrassment heated my cheeks despite not knowing what I should be embarrassed about. Cassandra's tone had been mocking, so whatever her meaning, it wasn't complimentary.

"I guess not."

Cassandra sniffed and then began walking toward the tree line. She called over her shoulder, "Follow me."

Annabeth gave me a sympathetic smile before setting off after Cassandra. I trailed behind them to the tree line.

As I trudged my way through the roots and leaf debris, Cassandra and Annabeth waited for me. Cassandra had taken a seat on a broken-off log, and Annabeth leaned against a tree. I walked wearily into the little circle they'd made.

"Annabeth said you requested to speak to me. What is it you want exactly?"

No niceties, then. "I want shelter. For me and another."

Cassandra's brows slashed. "Shelter from what?"

I took a deep breath, my eyes darting to Annabeth's curious face and back to Cassandra. I wasn't sure how to ask for what I wanted without just plunging in. "I am a nun. And an exorcist." Annabeth gasped, but I kept my eyes trained on Cassandra. Her face had gone expressionless, and she stood.

"I was raised by the Church. I tried to break away once, and it," I wrapped my arms around my middle, trying to ease the anxiety turning in my gut, "it didn't work out. Several years ago, they invited me to a school for exorcism, and I accepted. We received a new subject not too long ago. A man who claimed he was a vampire from the Crusades."

I watched Cassandra's face closely. She tried to keep her expression blank, but her eyes narrowed in on me. I swallowed, not sure what that meant. I pushed forward. "He's telling the truth. He is what he says he is. I want to break away from the Church again, for good. I found out they killed my family and stole me. They raised me so I could be a weapon for them. I want out. I want to get Luk out."

Cassandra began circling me, looking down her nose at me. She still wore no discernible expression, nothing I could read to gauge her mood or how she was receiving this. I shifted my gaze to the forest floor, nerves taking flight in my belly. That tug in my middle felt worried. I wished Luk was with me now.

"Why would they think you were worth stealing? What kind of weapon would you be?"

"She's a gatekeeper!" Annabeth's voice bubbled over with

excitement. Cassandra stopped her circling and looked over at the girl. "She told me on the way over. She sees ghosts and passes them to the other side. Maybe that's why?" Her voice tilted in confusion at the end, trying to work out what the Catholic Church would want with a ghost whisperer.

Cassandra knew though. She now wore a smile, but it wasn't welcoming. Her eyes brightened. I could practically feel the malice and excitement emanate off her. "She's not a gatekeeper. She's a death witch." Her voice rang like a bell. Dread pooled in my stomach. The tug in my middle became a frantic pull as Luk read my energy. How would he ever deal with this connection locked in that cell? That was my last thought before blackness enveloped me.

Twenty-Six

Eliza

Light danced on the ceiling. My blurry eyes made it difficult to work out where I was or how I got here. As they cleared, the soft, warm glow of candlelight spread all around me came into view. I moaned at the stiffness in my shoulders and tried to move my arms to work out the pain, only to realize they were tied. I struggled harder. My legs were tied down, too, to chains that were bolted to the floor.

I started to pant, fear soaking me with sweat. That tug in my middle felt frantic. Panic climbed my throat, and I had to close my eyes tight against the hysteria. I started to count. By the time I got to twenty, I could open my eyes again.

The telltale stone walls and support beams that stretched back and forth told me I was in a basement. Condensation dripped near the breaker box to my right.

"Hello?" I called out. I wanted to smack myself. Who was I calling out for? I tried to concentrate inward to see how well this connection worked. I didn't know what Luk could do or where Olivia was. Maybe he could get word to her? Maybe this would be enough for him to realize he wasn't a liability and I needed him?

I couldn't get anything new though. All I could feel was his panic. And anger. I pulled against the ropes around my wrists again. They chafed my skin, which began to feel wet, but I didn't let up. The squeak of a door opening brought my eyes to a staircase, interrupting my efforts. Looking at it upside down disoriented me further. The entrance was hidden, but it wasn't long before I saw people walking down, black robes obscuring their feet.

White ghost masks covered their faces. I swallowed, and my heart dropped as a total of three figures walked down the stairs. The one in the middle pulled her mask off, but I didn't need that to recognize her. Her height was enough of a giveaway.

"Cassandra."

She looked down at me grimly. The other two took her cue and removed their masks. Sarah Lee and Annabeth. My chest seized. Sarah Lee's eyes glittered with excitement. Annabeth seemed shaken, her face white.

Cassandra spoke. "You are a sister, and what happened to your coven was a travesty. But you are too old to be taught to fully harness it now. You don't even understand your power. The best thing you can do is give it to us."

I tried to swallow, but there was no moisture in my mouth. The dryness in my throat cracked, and I coughed. Once I got myself under control, I spoke, my voice rasping. "What do you mean, give it to you?"

My gaze swung between the three of them. Anger joined my fear. Tears filled Annabeth's eyes. Sarah Lee smirked. Cassandra remained imperious, her emotions kept closer to the vest.

"It's a sacrifice. To steal a witch's power, they must be dispatched. A spell separates them from their power right before their passing."

"You're going to kill me?" The anger was beginning to consume me. First, the Church, and now them, witches, the very people I was supposed to be.

"We are. As soon as the rest of the circle arrives."

"The witches from earlier?" I asked. My wrists strained against the restraints. Blood dripped down my arm, but I didn't care. My anger was becoming all-consuming, fed by the seething anger Luk sent through our connection.

"This kind of spell requires thirteen witches. Some you met, some you didn't. It won't matter. They'll be here shortly."

With that, Cassandra turned away from me, going to a shelf. She took out chalk and began drawing something around me. I lifted myself up to see it was a star, a pentagram. My breath sawed in and out of me.

I tried to talk sense into one of the other women. They were rummaging on the shelves, Annabeth removing crystals, and Sarah Lee doing something with candles.

"Sarah Lee, help me!"

She cackled. "If Cassandra hadn't arranged this, I would have kidnapped you myself. Who is some unknown to harness the power of Hecate? You have no coven anymore. You don't deserve this power. I do."

Cassandra's sharp voice rang across the room, "But it will go to *my* coven. Which you agreed to join."

Sarah Lee cast a hateful look at her before she quickly dropped her gaze down, appearing chastened. "Yes, Priestess." Cassandra narrowed her eyes a moment longer before turning back to her task. She took out candle holders and laid them at the pentagram's points. Sarah Lee followed behind her, placing black taper candles in each holder.

Tears streaked Annabeth's cheeks. She stood frozen with various crystals clenched in her fists. "Annabeth. Please," I whispered.

She opened her mouth to say something, but Cassandra's sharp command stopped her. "Come here, Annabeth. Help me."

Annabeth closed her mouth, then her eyes tight. She nodded, perhaps at some internal battle, then she opened them and went to Cassandra. Despair combated the anger in me as I watched her methodically place the crystals at different points in the pentagram. How was I going to get out of this?

"Sarah Lee, bring me her blood."

Sarah Lee pulled something out of her robe. A long knife. From my research, I remembered it was called an athame. She approached me, her smile wicked, and I thrashed once more against my bindings. The sharp sting of the rope agony against my sores. She took pleasure in this. There wasn't an ounce of remorse in her. "This is going to hurt." She said it with glee.

Annabeth whipped around. "It doesn't have to hurt, just cut her hand. Wait!"

Sarah Lee drove the knife into the left side of my stomach. The air whooshed out of me. Blinding pain took over. Blood rushed in my ears. Anger unlike anything I'd ever known swamped the despair, swamped Luk's feeling, swamped everything. Years of being taught to toe the line, to be quiet, to obey in order to survive, fled my subconscious. I wasn't going to bow to this fate.

I opened my eyes and stared up into Sarah Lee's hate-filled ones. "Hecate curse you," I spat at her, spittle flying across her face.

She jerked back, eyes wide, fear crossing her features for a moment. She looked around as if she expected a lightning bolt to strike her down. When it didn't, her shoulders sagged with the breath she let out. She casually wiped the spit off her face and began to laugh. I growled in frustration, baring my teeth at her as she walked away.

Cassandra walked calmly up to her and took the knife

dripping with my blood from her grip. I could feel it soaking my side. Turning to Annabeth, whose face was stricken, she said, "You see? The insolence with which she calls her goddess. She doesn't even offer her a prayer, just a demand. Why would she ever come to her aid? It is better we take this power. We will make true offerings to Hecate. We will show her the love and devotion she deserves."

Annabeth didn't look moved. She swallowed. "But it isn't us Hecate blessed."

"She will."

Before Annabeth could say anything else, the door opened again. Cassandra raised her chin, her face lit with expectation, satisfaction oozing out of her. Sarah Lee shot me a gleeful look of triumph, and I tried to breathe through the pain as my lifeblood leaked out of me. I was beginning to feel cold.

Familiar black robes began descending the stairs. Cassandra turned, not bothering to see which of her coven had arrived for the sacrifice. It turned out to be a mistake. The slight figure pulled back its hood, and I relaxed against my restraints. Relief consumed me as I saw Olivia's cherubic face. It looked like murder.

Four tall, burly men stood behind her. "Kill them." Her voice dripped menace.

The men rushed forward with a war cry. Formidable witches, the women's shock didn't last long, and they fought back. One man dropped unconscious, seemingly for no reason, just like I had crumpled in the woods. I didn't have time to see how the other three were fairing, though I heard cries of pain.

Olivia had reached my side, and she began cutting through the ropes that bound me. Her face was stricken as she touched my side, her hand coming away painted red.

Before long, my arms and legs were free, the commotion in the back of the basement loud and angry. Spots danced across my vision, but I forced them back. Now wasn't the time.

"Can you walk?" Olivia's commanding voice now sounded frantic.

"I think so." I dug an elbow into the cement, letting the scraping of the cement floor against my skin ground me. Olivia was under my arm in an instant, helping me sit up.

Together, we managed to stand. The pain was blinding, and I kept wanting to collapse, those damn black spots invading from the corners of my vision. I breathed shallowly and concentrated. She couldn't do this alone.

As we reached the first stair, I said, "Should we help them—" Looking over Olivia's shoulder, I saw Annabeth crumpled on the floor, her face bloody. Cassandra's arms were held back, her eyes covered, and she screamed in indignation. I couldn't see Sarah Lee, but I heard smacks, fists against flesh.

"No, they'll be fine. Let's go." Olivia's voice was urgent. I didn't delay any longer. Each step was a lesson in agony. Every time I heaved myself higher, I thought I couldn't go on. But then I did. I couldn't die, not here, not now. Not before I really got to live. Before I figured out who I was, before I got to learn what love was really like with Luk.

I felt a distant tug from him in my middle, but my pain consumed everything, and I couldn't focus on it. By the time Olivia had helped me to the street, most of my strength was gone. My side felt soaked. I coughed and felt wetness on my lips. When Olivia's gaze swung to mine and she noticed, fear made her eyes tight.

"Come on, I'm parked right out front." She went to open the door, but even the slight absence of her support was too much, and I fell against the car. She used one hand to press me against it, and opened the door with another, then helped me in, pulling the seatbelt across me.

Getting into the driver's side, she looked over at me, eyes wide and face white. "I need to get you to Luk, Eliza."

I coughed again. Breathing was becoming impossible. "I think you need to get me to a hospital, Liv."

She shook her head, started the car, and looked forward, determined. "I don't think a hospital can fix you anymore." The engine turned over, and the car rolled backward, then lurched forward as she hit the gas. I didn't argue. I didn't have the energy. It would be a long drive, and this time when the spots threatened, I fell into the blackness, my old friend. Vaguely, as my adrenaline died down and my strength fled, I wondered if Luk would earn his rebirth after I was gone. Would I see him in the next life?

Twenty-Seven

Luk

The bars cracked under my grip. The only thing that had kept me from completely disintegrating them and breaking out of this prison was Olivia's message to me through the fearful little nun, Emily. She was on her way. She had Eliza with her.

I swallowed and went back to pacing. I hadn't expected to feel Eliza. That was only supposed to happen when our souls joined. I didn't have a soul to join with her yet. Regardless, I did feel her. And she had gone from terrified to hurt to distant. I barely felt the tether of her that had wrapped around my heart and, suspecting what that meant, my blood ran cold. I wasn't sure how much longer I could keep myself under control.

Sweet relief swept through me at the sound of the infirmary door opening above. I heard hurried footsteps, erratic and stumbling, sometimes dragging. I couldn't wait any longer. I needed to get to Eliza. I felt her less and less as the moments passed.

Terror swept through me when I realized why. Two people stepped out of the tiny staired hall. Olivia supported Eliza under her arm, trying to move her forward as quickly as possible. Eliza was barely conscious, and I could smell her blood. It darkened her and Olivia's clothes. I raced for the door of my prison and ripped it open, my strength easily breaking the lock. Olivia stood, barely supporting Eliza's weight anymore, breathing heavily. I rushed to her side, lifting Eliza's light body into my arms.

I barely registered Olivia falling to her knees, catching her breath. I could smell Eliza's blood, but it held no temptation. I could barely hear her heartbeat, its thready rhythm interrupted with long pauses that struck fear in me I had never known. I quickly backed up and lowered myself to the dirt-packed floor, my back leaning against the stone wall. Biting ruthlessly into my wrist, I opened Eliza's mouth and dripped blood in. I held her nose closed so she had no choice but to breathe through her mouth, prompting her to swallow.

My wrist healed, and I bit into it again, going for the radial artery, letting as much of my blood as possible flow into her. Even knowing she didn't need this much for the elixir to work, I couldn't make myself stop until I saw her eyes try to open. My heart finally beat again, the vice grip that locked my chest loosening when, a few minutes later, her eyes started to flutter.

As Eliza's heart rate picked up and her breathing evened out, her eyes opening and closing in a sleepy pattern, fighting for wakefulness, the rest of the room came into focus. Olivia had moved to squat next to me, face pensive.

Before I could ask her what happened, Eliza came to enough to talk. I sat her up, resting her back against my chest. Just in time, she began to cough. Her head fell back against me, looking up at me. I smoothed her brown hair back, thanking Sekhmet for getting her here on time. I felt along her side where her clothes gaped and were the most soaked. My fingers met a thin, raised line. The wound had closed. I looked down at her wrists and tried to keep the rage at bay. The anger I felt as I fingered the raised skin at her delicate wrists was nothing compared to even the fury I had carried into battle centuries ago. She bore scars around her wrists like bracelets from where they must have tied her.

Her voice came out broken but beautiful. "What…what happened?"

Olivia fell back on her butt, giving a shaky sigh. "You scared the hell out of me."

My eyes sharpened on her face. "What happened?" My question came out as a demand.

Olivia wiped a hand down her face, but when she answered, she looked at Eliza. "I wandered off to the woods when you joined the witches. I thought Cassandra's jealousy would be more trouble than it was worth if I showed up with you. If it was just you, then she would assume I had been using you, not the other way around. I figured I'd hover on the outskirts until you had an answer one way or another. Then I saw you drop. Cassandra is a powerful mentalist. She somehow gained the favor of Hypnos, and he blessed her with powers of sleep and reading minds. I didn't think it would be a problem, especially with me not there. They needed to know about Luk anyway if they were to give you sanctuary. I didn't expect…I didn't know…

"It's okay," Eliza whispered, closing her eyes and letting her head fall back against my chest.

I looked at Olivia with narrowed eyes. "No, it isn't. What did you not know?"

Olivia swallowed. "It wasn't a matter of if they would give Eliza sanctuary or not. When Cassandra heard what she could do, when she realized what she might yet be capable of, she saw an opening. I heard her say Hecate hasn't blessed a witch since Eliza's family line died. She decided to hold a circle of thirteen to harness the coming full moon's power. To steal Eliza's power."

A growl started up my chest, vibrating against Eliza's back. I would rip their throats out. If they were already dead, I would travel to the underworld and take part in their torture. "Where are they?" My voice was a barely understandable snarl the anger in it was so potent.

Olivia shook her head. "I don't know. When I saw Eliza go down, I ran for the nearest place I could find men to thrall. It took a while, too long. I found as many as I could as fast as I could, and I followed the taste of magic. It was so strong I couldn't miss it."

Eliza licked her lips and looked up at me. "What is that taste?"

I looked down at her and forced my eyes to soften. I didn't want to scare her with the fury behind them.

"My blood, habibi."

Her face grew fearful. She jerked upright, and I helped her, letting her lean into my side so she could see Olivia and me. "What happened? Why did I drink your blood?"

"Shhh, habibi. You were hurt. I needed to heal you."

Her eyes bounced frantically between me and the succubus. "How hurt was I? Will I be a vampire now?"

I shook my head, smoothing her hair down on one side and tucking it behind her ear. "No, Eliza, it doesn't work that way. Sekhmet doesn't just offer death; she is balance. She sends death for the wicked but offers life as well."

"I don't understand. I was in the basement. Sarah Lee stabbed me. Cassandra said they were going to take my power, that I would never know how to use it anyway. That it was owed to the witches. Olivia and I, we barely got out."

I growled again at the witch's audacity. "You will learn to use your powers just fine."

Olivia was shaking her head. "You already use them, Eliza. You have your entire life. Cassandra is a jealous old hag.

They didn't need to kill you to take them. There's an offering spell. If she thought she was doing something just, something right, she could have gone about it in a completely different way. She was taking what she wanted, afraid if she didn't do it fast, someone else would."

Eliza took a shaky breath, and I began to rub her back. She looked up at me. "We can't stay here."

I kissed her forehead and looked at Olivia. "She's right. Where can we go tonight?"

Olivia stood and began bouncing. She paced back and forth on the dirt floor, looking down at a small object she had pulled from her pocket. I watched her, my brow drawn down, wondering if something had taken her over. A soft chuckle from Eliza drew my attention.

"She does this. It's how she thinks."

I looked back at the curvy blond but couldn't find any humor in me as my mate lay scarred in my arms. Instead, I muttered, "Odd little succubus."

While Olivia bounced around, calling out, "Aha!" and then shaking her head and continuing her pacing, I kept stroking my hand up and down Eliza's arm. She looked up at me and asked, "Did you know? That we would feel each other in this way after the marking?"

My mouth pulled to the side. "No. I knew it would happen eventually, but it shouldn't have happened until I earned my rebirth. What you feel, what I feel, is our soul's talking to each other. I don't have a soul to give. I'm not sure why we can feel it."

Before she could respond to that, Olivia gave one last triumphant sound. "I have a place for us tonight. Let's go."

I stood up, bringing Eliza with me. "Is it secure?"

Olivia looked nervous. "Uhm, as secure as it'll get."

Eliza looked at her suspiciously. “Where are we going, Liv?”

Olivia put on her most innocent expression. She had a remarkable ability to appear like a naive cherub when she wanted. Ironic, considering what she was.

“You’ll see.”

Twenty-Eight

Eliza

As we drove away from the Church, an odd sort of apprehension overtook me. It had nothing to do with the danger surrounding us, the fact that I'd just stared death in the face, or that Luk somehow miraculously sat next to me in the car. Not even my amusement at his uncertainty and distrust of the *metal horse* was enough to distract the melancholy threatening to take over. I had just left the only real home I'd ever known. I hadn't even said goodbye. I wasn't sure who I would have said goodbye to.

What a sad thought. I had spent twenty-five years with the Church. I knew people there. I spoke to them every day; some I'd known since childhood. But I couldn't think of one goodbye that was so pivotal I'd need to risk discovery to tell them I'd miss them. Not even Abigail, my surrogate mother through the years. Though she had offered me support and guidance and had some sort of fondness for me, she had never understood me. I had always held myself apart, in a way, to avoid tainting the others.

My breath hitched. Luckily, Luk was too enraptured by the buildings and homes we passed to notice, his bright blue eyes wide in wonder, his neck craning back and forth to get the best view as we passed. Looking over his profile, and Olivia's in front of me through the rearview mirror, I hoped this next home came to mean more. I hoped if I ever had to leave, Olivia and Luk wouldn't let me go without saying goodbye.

Olivia shook me out of my thoughts. "You both look like you're either wearing very realistic Halloween costumes or you've just come out of a fight with Freddy and Jason."

I snorted. Luk asked, "Who's Freddy and Jason?"

My snort turned into a full belly laugh, Olivia's tinkling bells joining in. The tension had needed to be broken, and as the laughter leaked out of me, it was a welcome relief from the anxiety that had thickened the air of the car before.

"We need clothes. We can't stay in Vermont, Liv."

She met my eyes in the rearview mirror. "I know. We aren't."

As if her words conjured it, she turned onto the Eighty-nine South right after she said that. I perked up a little. Luk's face was plastered to the window. "What might these nations must have." He looked over at me fearfully, wrinkles deepening between his brow. "How can I protect you against someone who can build this?"

I didn't laugh at him. Even though I saw humor in his words, I didn't see it in his reaction. I thought back to his time, to what this must look like to him. "Luk, in this day, building a road like this is easy. Well, maybe not easy. It's time- and labor-consuming. But materials are readily available for a price. And nations are large and can afford that price easily."

Luk looked at me gravely, his eyes wrinkling in the corner with his worry. "Eliza, that wealth is what makes them so dangerous. Anyone with money and power will do terrible things to avoid giving it up."

Any mirth I had at his reaction leaked out of me. No matter that I couldn't fathom the US government mobilizing against a vampire. He was right. I kept wondering at my ability to find things he did unusual, at my ability to think I didn't understand his world. I'd spent my adult life learning to be an exorcist. I'd seen and dealt with the passing of ghosts since I was a child. I might not have known everything, but I had been scratching the surface of this world my entire life. It was time to stop thinking woe is me and to start paying attention.

I shook my head. "You're right, Luk. But to get this powerful, they've had to give us power too. We aren't helpless."

Pride smoothed his brow, and his lips tilted. "Hubiy ya muharib."

"What does that mean?" I remembered him saying something similar to me down in the infirmary, but I'd still been so out of it I'd assumed I'd just heard him wrong.

He just took my hand and held it tight, bringing it to his lips and then to rest in his lap. I let the question go. Turning back to Olivia, I asked, "So where are we going?"

"To Salem."

I gaped at her. "Salem, Massachusetts?"

She nodded, her hands tightening on the steering wheel. "Yes."

"What's in Salem?"

She looked back at me in the mirror again. "That person I told you about. Xavier."

My breath hitched as I realized what she was saying. I looked at Luk, but he wasn't paying attention. I remembered two things at that moment: Olivia telling me about the vampire who had been spared, allowed to stay on Earth like a god because he was so adept at performing his duties. And Luk telling me that no vampire from his time must exist because, if they did, they would be powerful beyond measure and care only about their own pleasure.

"Are you sure about this, Liv?"

"It's our best option." With that, she turned on the radio, discouraging conversation. Luk jumped at the sound, but then his eyes were drawn from the road and enraptured by the radio's dials. He chatted about ballads of his time and changed the station to explore the different kinds of music late-night radio had to offer.

At different points, Olivia got annoyed. Luk's body was permanently bent over the middle console, fiddling with the station. I laughed softly, but before long, the lull of the road pulled me to sleep. It had been a long day, a long night, and a lot had happened. My hand brushed the crusty ends of my shirt, dried with my blood from what would have been a mortal wound if Luk hadn't brought me back.

I thought of what he had said. *Sekhmet is balance.* My last thought before I fell asleep was, what is Hecate?

Twenty-Nine
Luk

Wonders, the like of which I hadn't seen during my time, filled this world. Magic seemed to be everywhere, accessible to even the most mundane. Eliza had woken up some time ago and showed me what she called a phone. It was like some kind of portal, though it worked faster and with less ceremony than any portal I'd ever seen before. It gave me instant information on everything, from how the Crusade I had fought in had ended to what wars had been fought since.

There had been many. I was wrong about having lived in a singular time for earning rebirth. I wondered how Sekhmet still had soul with all that she must have had to give away. Or maybe she'd made it harder to earn.

Olivia drove us through a town teeming with buildings, people walking on the street, other things called cars, the iron horses trotting through town. Eliza threaded her fingers through mine, but fear wormed its way and embedded in my heart. The Church had grown with these wonders. It had been powerful in my day, but its power now must be a fearsome thing. How could I ever protect her?

"We're almost there. Luk, we're going to need you to gain entrance."

Olivia's words grabbed my attention. "Entrance to what?"

Olivia shifted, and my eyes narrowed. "I think I know someone who can help us. He's in town. He likes to make a circuit once every couple years, remind people he's around."

"Who is he?" Venom laced my words, but I didn't try to soften my tone.

Olivia's eyes darted to mine in the mirror, then back to the road. So many roads. Wide, accessible roads connecting what would have been a week's journey.

"Xavier. He's a," Olivia worried her lip, "a Sekhmet vampire."

"Why would a Sekhmet vampire stop to help us when he has his own rebirth to worry about?"

Eliza's hand tightened in mine. "Because he already earned his rebirth. A long time ago."

"That's impossible."

Olivia answered. "A lot of what you used to think was impossible is possible today, Luk. What's more, he's from the time of the Crusades."

My eyes widened. "If he has walked this Earth so long, he is not someone we will want to meet."

Olivia shook her head. "He's stable. Ish. As long as you aren't a murderer or rapist. He kinda loved his job too much. And he was *very* good at it. Sekhmet allowed him to stay in return for continuing to do it."

I didn't say anything else, just looked back into Eliza's troubled eyes. I didn't know what to think. I brought our hands up to my mouth and kissed her knuckles, whispering again, "My love," in my language. She was so beautiful it hurt.

Olivia's shoulders stayed tense at my silence, but she continued making turns until we arrived at a large, three-story square box of a house. Windows lined the different levels, and the curtains were pulled tightly closed. We climbed out of the car, and I groaned, stretching out the stiff muscles in my long legs.

"This isn't much better than riding a horse."

Eliza laughed, and I smiled at the sound. I loved saying things to make her laugh, even if they were usually accidental. "Okay, Luk. You lead the way. Just knock on the door."

I nodded sharply and scrutinized the area for escape routes in case it became necessary. "Eliza, you stay behind Olivia."

"Okay."

I looked back and marveled at her ability to see the danger, to listen. As if reading my mind, she smiled and shrugged. "I'm still way out of my depth with all of this. I'll follow your guys' lead."

"Guys?" She just smiled. I shook my head and walked to the door, rapping loudly against the wood.

A voice came shortly from behind it. "Go away!"

Olivia rolled her eyes. "Announce yourself," she prodded me. She looked left and right as she said it, watching for others. Even their walkways were paved. I looked back at the door—red, felicitous for power.

"I am Lukman. I come to speak to the Crusade vampire."

I felt a smack on my back and turned, teeth dropping, hissing. Olivia glared back at me. "I said to announce yourself, not him, you idiot."

"I'll do what I—"

I was interrupted by the door being wrenched open. "Who in the hell are you?"

A man stood before us, dark-skinned and bald-headed, with sharp features. His eyes pinched as he attempted to look down his nose at us. Quite the feat since I stood half a head taller. I squared my shoulders.

"I am Lukman in hell as well. Is your master here?"

The man snorted and advanced on me. I stood my ground and listened. To his heartbeat—hollow, like an empty drum. He had life but not soul.

"Listen, you high asshole, I don't know what you heard in the club, but you need to—"

This time I interrupted him, dropping my fangs, letting the venom collect and drip from them, my face taking on the monstrous hallows and shadows of when we were on a melee, lost to death.

The man's face paled. He may be blessed with Sekhmet's gift, or curse, but he knew an elder when he saw one. He stumbled back from me into the house. I tried to follow but came up against an invisible barrier that pushed me back. I hissed.

The man scooted back on his butt, his imperiousness nowhere to be seen. "Wh-who are you?"

Before I could answer, another man, a pipe in hand, walked to the front door. The scent of strawberries reached me with the smoke floating from the bowl. "Luk, you said your name was?" He wore a dressing gown, a red and gold pattern in the thick material, over soft cotton pants. He didn't even twitch at my face of death. My features slowly relaxed.

"Yes."

"What time are you from, Lukman?"

I cocked my head. "Twelve ninety-two."

The man was good at regulating his emotions. His face stayed carefully unchanged, but his breathing hitched. He looked at his pipe as if in deep thought.

"Xavier thought he was the only child of Sekhmet left from that time."

"He is from the time of the first war?"

The man grunted. "A little after. The second Crusades."

I smiled. "Then I guess politeness dictates he break fast with his elder. Are you the witch who shields this abode?"

The man spat to the side, making the one who opened the door roll his eyes and disappear. "I'm no witch."

"You're not a vampire." The man smiled as the one who had opened the door reappeared with a rag and wiped the floor. A servant then, not nobility. His opinion of himself seemed misplaced. I'd have to disabuse him of his ranking later.

The man cocked his head, studying me. "I'm a human. Descended from Xavier's line."

I narrowed my eyes. "How does Xavier have a line?"

The man smiled. "That's his story." The man walked toward us, and I tensed, but all he did was take out an athame from his robe, prick his finger, and wipe it along the doorway before whispering words of passing. "He'll want to tell you himself." He stepped back, allowing us entrance.

I stepped through, reaching my hand back until I felt Eliza's soft one. The man missed nothing, watching the gesture. My shoulders tightened in anticipation. "I thought you weren't a witch."

The man shook his head, moving his gaze to look down the hall, past the entry table standing in the middle. Flowers I didn't recognize filled a vase. "I'm not, but we do use them to ward the house. Xavier is beginning to get soft. He's lived long enough to earn it. I'm Angus, let me show you to some rooms. I'll let him know you're here."

I narrowed my eyes again, feeling my fangs against my bottom lip, not trusting this situation. Not trusting how casual it was. "He'll already know we're here."

Angus's lips tipped up, no guile in his face at the accusation. "True enough, but I'll still have a chat with him before you meet and allow you to get cleaned up."

I opened my mouth to say I wanted to meet Xavier now when I felt a tug on my hand. Immediately, I looked back at Eliza.

"Getting cleaned up would be a good idea, Luk." She held out the tattered end of her shirt, shredded and crusted in old blood. I took in her face, still pale, with blood staining her. If it wasn't because she'd been harmed, I'd want to ravish her. Olivia at her side was shifting uncomfortably, looking around like a rabbit in a trap. This was not the hunting ground of a succubus. I felt myself soften toward her a little, knowing she was risking her own future to stay with Eliza and ensure hers.

"Show us to our rooms."

The man walked casually, showing me his back without fear. Nothing in this world worked the way it had worked in mine, and uncertainty wormed its way into my chest. Eliza walked behind me, between me and Olivia, her hand in mine. I needed to catch up. I needed to learn all I could as quickly as I could if I was going to protect her.

Not for the first time, I wondered at the wisdom of falling in love, of taking a mate after such a long stasis, before I even knew how I'd go about earning my rebirth in this time. Letting something, or someone, distract me from that goal in the first place. Just as the thought flitted across my mind, I felt the squeeze of Eliza's hand, heard her steady heartbeat, and I knew. I knew why. There had been many times in that cell I had felt the impossibility of what I faced. There was a real possibility the Church would learn how to end me, and my fate, my time, would end in a dank, dark cell in rags.

The despair of that had threatened to take me under, stripping me of my identity, my sense of self. My curiosity about Eliza and her situation had given me something else to concentrate on, something that helped keep the despair at bay. Then, getting to know her, having her see something in me, that had done something altogether different. It had given me hope. And in this time or mine, hope would always be the strength that carried entities through. So, I had clung to it, embraced it. And once again, I vowed I'd never let it go.

"One of you here."

Olivia strode forward from the back of our little group, her hand raised, "That'll be me."

I huffed a breath, "Demons."

She smiled at me sweetly as she passed, twitching her hips in an enticing movement. I rolled my eyes and looked at Angus. He watched her hips, shaking his head as if to clear it. Looking back at me, he said, as if a little lost, "The rest of you this way." As we passed by, Olivia stood in her doorway, a mischievous smile on her face, and winked. I heard the beautiful sound of Eliza's chuckle behind me, and I felt myself soften even more toward the succubus, not entirely forgiving her for her mistake but wanting to kill her less.

Angus stopped at the next door and held a hand out in a grand gesture. "One of you can stay here." He let the words hang as if it was a test. He already knew what I was going to say, so instead of saying it, I bared my teeth. I wasn't sure what game he was playing, but I wasn't in the mood.

Eliza stepped around me. "We'll be staying together, Angus. Thank you." Without waiting for his response, she stepped into the room, dragging me behind her when I tried to stay rooted, threatening Angus with my eyes. The sound of the door resounded as Eliza closed it with finality. She looked up at me, amused. "Get that out of your system?"

"Not even close," I said, still looking at the closed door, shooting daggers at it with my eyes.

Eliza stepped close, her proximity garnering all my attention as she walked close enough for our hips to align and looked up at me with a smile. But there was sadness behind her eyes.

I brushed her hair back, cupping her cheek. She leaned against me and closed her eyes, breathing in. "What's wrong?"

She opened her eyes reluctantly and straightened. "Everything is changing so fast. Over these last weeks, everything has been changing so fast. Everything I knew is wrong. I spent my entire life with this church, and I just left. And nobody will miss me. Nobody will even notice I'm gone until they decide to use me for something, and I'm not there."

I reached up to cradle her face in my hands. Leaning down, I brushed my lips lightly over hers, not wanting to take, only to give, but even the small sensation, the slight taste of her, breathing her same air, gave me comfort. Gave me hope. "I would miss you."

Thirty
Eliza

It was the perfect thing to say. Validation of my insecurity right when I needed it. I marveled at Luk's ability to see me. To see the real me. In twenty-five years, I had never felt like anybody understood. My heart, my needs, my darkness. But Luk did, and he embraced it. Sometimes I felt crazy for leaving everything so fast, for not going to Mother Superior and asking her point blank if what I was being told was true.

But then I remembered the way Father Paul used to trap me in corners, telling me I was bad. To not play with the other children, or I would taint them. The way the other nuns would rap me on my knuckles, my bottom, my back, trying to get the sin out. The way I would hide from some of the more lascivious priests, who told me not to listen to the meanness of others, I looked like an angel, all while their hands tried to move to places they shouldn't. Abigail had known about all of it, but it hadn't been a big deal. It was the way of the Church. I just needed to pray and forgive and let it all go.

Luk had threatened to crush a building, to burn the world because Father Paul breathed at me funny. To feel that kind of protection, that kind of possession, was new. It wasn't something I thought I'd like. I valued my sense of self. I had learned to keep myself apart, an island, to survive. But I was coming to value the fact that I could hate the evil things around me. I could hate them freely. And Luk would hate them with me.

"Eliza." His hand brushed my hair back, then fell from my face to my shoulders. "Is there anything I can do?"

The question, devoid of telling me what I needed to do, devoid of asking me to *understand*, lit a fire in me. I reached up, wrapping my arm around his head to bring it down to me. Just before his lips crashed to mine, his eyes holding all the feeling and heat I needed to banish my cold emptiness, I said, "Yes."

And then he was on me. His lips, his teeth, drawing out a long moan. I should feel disgusting, crusted in blood and filth, but Luk put his hands around my ass and lifted, allowing me to wrap my legs around him as he feasted on my mouth before trailing kisses across my face, behind my ear in that spot that made my breath hitch and heat pool low in my belly, and down my neck to my collarbone.

He nipped, and I groaned, wanting more, wanting it all. I felt him moving, but I had no idea where until my back pressed against a wall. I heard a rip, and then cold air caressed my chest. I opened my eyes to see Luk, his teeth descended, looking at me like he wanted to conquer me. Like I was his next meal. I smiled wickedly and squirmed until he let me down. Unbuttoning my jeans, I dropped them down with my underwear until I stood bare in front of him.

He moved to come back to me, a growl in his throat, but I shook my head, my eyebrows raised playfully. He cocked his head, his growl becoming deeper, more dangerous. His hand shot out, gripping me around my throat. "Give yourself to me, little witch."

I tutted. "I told you not to call me that." I gripped his forearm. "Come with me."

He dropped his hand, baring his teeth, but followed. I

had noticed the door to the bathroom when we walked in. I started the shower and thanked whatever god I was praying to these days that the water turned hot quickly. It was always a gamble in these old New England homes.

Luk was momentarily distracted, and I used the opportunity to lead him into the shower. "What kind of witch do they have working for them?"

I snorted at his wonder. "It's called indoor plumbing, and us lowly humans are the ones who invented it. Not witches."

He looked back down at me, taking in my naked form, water sluicing down, darkening my brown hair. I imagined I looked like a melting painting with all the grit and blood that had been on me. "You aren't a human, habibi."

Once again, I wondered what that meant but decided I'd find out later. "Fair enough. In that case, let me show you more sorcery."

I picked up the bar of soap in the holder on the side. A basic shower, but a spa as far as Luk was concerned. I started on myself, getting the soap wet and lathering it through my hair. Moving it over my face and arms, I watched Luk's face. He stared back, mesmerized. His eyes were slightly glazed, unblinking as he watched me wash the rest of my body. He held his hand out reverently, just short of touching. I took his hand, washing it as I brought it closer to my breast.

He cupped it gently, inhaling sharply as his thumb brushed over my nipple, making it harden and peak. I felt myself growing wetter, and I moved him so he stood under the water instead of me. He was distracted again, looking up at the warm water, then closing his eyes, letting it cascade over him. His beard had thickened, and next to his stark blue eyes, olive skin, and dark hair, he was striking in his handsomeness. While he kept those brilliant blue eyes shielded with his eyes closed, I encouraged his hand lower until it was right over that bundle of nerves that was crying for release.

His head snapped back, looking at me intently as his fingers found their home, brushing around my opening teasingly, taking on their own rhythm, owning me the way he wanted to. I bit my lip because that's exactly what I wanted. I began brushing the soap over the rest of his body, letting him work, letting him play. I tried to stay focused as his fingers sped up, as he brought me to the precipice quicker than I could ever remember doing myself.

I washed the grime of his imprisonment off him as he made me cum, screaming his name. After he brushed his fingers across my clit, teasing out aftershocks, I bent over his arm, which put me at the perfect level.

"That was amazing. But it's your turn."

"My turn for what, habibi?"

"What does that mean, Luk?"

"I'll tell you later."

"Well, let me show you what I mean now." I continued my ministrations, washing him along his length, his powerful hips, that beautiful V that the muscles of his abs created, forming a beacon. As I continued down his thighs, I got to my knees, reached forward, and took him in my mouth, not stopping until his dick was hitting the back of my throat, gagging me, and my lips rested against the root. His hiss above me filled me with satisfaction.

I ran my tongue along the base of him and let my teeth scrape gently along the top. His hand gripped my hair until it was almost painful, then he quickly loosened it.

"Is this what my turn means?"

I glided back to his tip, letting him go with a pop. I looked up at him with big, mock-innocent eyes. "It is."

He was breathless, his face slack. He groaned when I

flicked my tongue against the soft part of his tip. He gurgled, "I like my turn."

I looked up at him, my eyes innocent but my smile wicked. "You're really going to like this." And he did. I pumped him with my hand, tongue, and mouth until he was coming down my throat, screaming my name.

Thirty-One

Eliza

Luk and I found clothes in a walk-in closet after we climbed out of the shower. The sweatpants I found were far too big for me, so I tied and double-knotted them, then found socks for my bare feet instead of shoes and a sweater that dwarfed me. I'd gone from feeling like a sex goddess to a child in my too-big clothes.

On Luk, though, it was something else. I'd seen him as an emaciated victim and a god-like prisoner in his tattered linen pants. But I'd never tire of seeing him in modern clothes. With his hair combed back and his dark black beard wild, it was even more attractive, and my mouth watered. He wore a black T-shirt that complemented his complexion and hugged his muscular shoulders and gray sweatpants that hung low on his hips, skimming the line of his ass. Such basic clothes, but he moved in them like he was a model.

He was gazing at himself in the mirror as if in wonder. I walked up behind him, skimming my hand over his arm, feeling the power in his forearm as it trailed off, and my arm fell at my side. "You keep trying to take care of me. But are you okay, Luk?"

He gazed at me through the mirror. "I'm fine, Eliza. It's just all so different. I don't know how I'll ever protect you if I can't learn fast."

I smiled at him. Despite everything happening around us, smiles seemed to come easier these days. "How about we protect each other?"

He turned at those words, leaning down to kiss me. In between breathless swipes of his tongue, his fingers threaded into my hair, and my blood heated again.

"That sounds like a lovely promise," he whispered against my lips, not stopping long enough to break away from me.

I started to reply, but before I could, before his clever fingers could slip lower to where I suddenly wanted them again, there was a knock on the door.

Angus called, "Xavier will see you now."

My eyes swung from the door to Luk's thunderous expression, and I laughed. "There's time enough for that later."

"There's time for it now," he muttered but took my hand, and we walked together to the door. In the hall, we found Olivia already waiting, leaning against the wall with her head back and her eyes closed.

"Liv?" I asked, a little concerned.

At my voice, her head rolled back, and she yawned as she took us in. "You are like the sweetest feast I've ever tasted."

I snorted, realizing what she meant and that her room was next to ours. Luk had a different reaction when her words hit him. "Find another meal, succubus. Eliza is mine."

Her eyes widened innocently. "Sharing is caring, Luk."

He hissed, lunging for her. I grabbed him by his shirt, hauling him back. He wrenched around, his arm out, before seeing it was me. Standing there frozen, short of attacking back, he took a deep breath, huffed it out, and let the tension leak from his muscles. "Fucking succubus."

"Fucking is right."

This time, I let them at it, laughing as Olivia skipped down the hallway, just out of Luk's reach. Angus looked at me in amusement as Olivia tripped. Instead of leaping on her, Luk simply brushed by with a scowl in her direction. "Are they always like this?"

I grinned at him. "No. They're just finding their rhythm. We all are."

He looked at me quizzically. "Your group carries a lot of power for people who seem to be in a state of helplessness."

I thought about what he said. Thought about the power everyone kept telling me I possessed, what Luk was capable of. Who Olivia really was, besides my best friend. "What good is power without a purpose?"

Angus raised an eyebrow. "So that's what you lack? Purpose?"

My eyes traveled to my friend's back, walking ahead of me down the carpeted hall. The days ahead would be filled with needs. Luk's need for a rebirth to have more than this life constantly seemed fleeting, considering the danger we were in. Of Olivia's same need. Of my desire to find out who my family was and why they died. What they died for. "Not anymore."

Angus's lips quirked on one side, and he muttered, "This should be interesting." He gestured me forward, and I walked ahead of him, following behind Luk and Olivia, who waited for us at the top of the stairs. I looked down into the foyer, the stairs curving with a pie-shaped turn, the banister a deep brown oak polished to shine. We had a purpose. We were each other's purpose now. The truth of that soaked into me with every step down the stairs, past the entry table with a vase full of snowdrops and snapdragons, until we were in the library where Xavier, the man, the vampire of the house, waited.

He sat, dressed innocuously in jeans and a white crew neck shirt. He had curly red hair and a bushy beard, a beak of a nose that somehow suited him perfectly. His eyes, small enough to be called beady, made him look like he straddled the line between madness and sanity. Uncertainty made my steps falter, but Luk, who had fallen behind me, pressed a hand into my back. The click of the door behind us was like the bolt of Luk's prison falling into place.

"Please, take a seat," Xavier's brogue invited us. I looked around the room as we went to the couch. Olivia moved to the other armchair that sat in front of a fireplace. It was a grand library with two walls boasting floor-to-ceiling shelves filled with old tombs. The third wall had a curtained window with a desk in front of it, and the fourth, a fireplace with a Persian rug in front of it. The old leather seating spread comfortably in front of the crackling flames.

Luk sat, surprising me by sprawling comfortably, welcoming me into his side. "*As Salaam Alaikum*, Xavier."

Xavier's gaze was pulled from taking us all in to Luk. I couldn't really discern his expression. His eyes were small and gray-blue, and his face, taken over by the mass of his bushy red beard, hid any expression. "*Wa Alaykum assalam*, Lukman."

Luk stared back steadily, breathing easily, saying nothing else. Anxiety curled around me, and from the corner of my eye, I saw that Olivia had begun to bounce.

"I thought I was the only vampire left alive this long."

"I didn't realize I still lived until not too long ago."

"Should we kill each other?" I blanched at Xavier's casual question. My eyes darted to where Angus leaned indifferently against the door we'd come through, to Olivia's legs bouncing so fast, you'd think she was about to lose her bladder, to Luk, who only leaned back into the couch, more relaxed.

"I'm older than you. I'd probably win."

Xavier flicked his fingers at that. "I've lived more days than you awake. I think I could take you."

Luk tsked, one side of his mouth curling in a lazy smile that looked sinister. "True enough. Ready to find out?"

Xavier guffawed. "Soon. Whiskey first?"

Luk inclined his head, casually letting his arm fall against the back of the couch we sat on, cradling me in. "Scotch?"

Xavier raised a bushy eyebrow. "Don't insult me."

Luk's smile widened in response as he watched Xavier walk to a liquor cart by his desk.

Olivia's mouth hung open in shock. Her eyes were narrowed on Xavier, but her bouncing had slowed.

"What in the hell is—" I started to whisper to Luk, but his hand tightened on my shoulder, silencing me.

"Hell doesn't have as nice of whiskey as I do, darling," Xavier said as he came back to us and handed me and Luk a rocks glass with light brown liquid.

Xavier walked casually back to the cart, poured another glass, and walked it to Angus, who took it with thanks. Olivia looked positively livid at that point. "What about me, vampire?"

His bushy beard rustled, and I realized that it was a smile. He was amused by her reprimand. "You need alcohol to make your powers more potent now, succubus?"

She sniffed. "When dealing with you, I might, you ogre."

Xavier barked a laugh but poured her a glass with his own, handing it to her before retaking his seat. "So, tell me, Lukman. If you didn't come here to duel, what did you come here for? And why didn't I know you live?"

Luk took a sip, taking his time setting it on the table in front of us before leaning back into the couch and pulling me back into the crook of his arm. I went, liking the comfort. "I was caught. One night, on a hunt in Damascus, sentries of the Church surrounded me. I thought it was my end. I had been separated from my hunting party. We fought, and they sliced at my thighs, my forearms, severing my brachial and femoral arteries. But they didn't take my head. They didn't light me. I surrendered to the nothingness. But then I woke. In cement and dirt, I woke with the taste of blood on my lips. Enough for me to break through."

I realized that Xavier had been, to a point, joking up until now. His demeanor had been enough to put Luk at ease. Because what Xavier had looked like before was very different from what he looked like now. His back was ramrod straight. His small beady eyes, which had looked half-mad, were suddenly sharp. And his hand gripped his whiskey glass so tight, I wondered at the fact it hadn't shattered.

He gulped the two fingers back in one swallow and then stood, walking back to his desk to pour himself more.

"They bled you?" His voice was rough.

The expression was foreign. I frowned, looking at Luk. He looked back at Xavier steadily. "Yes."

Tired of taking a back seat, I scooted away from Luk's embrace. "What does that mean, 'They bled you?'"

Luk started to answer, but it was Xavier's roughened brogue that spoke into the silence first. "It means they wanted to torture him. Study him. And so, they bled his strength, his vitality. They left him as a husk and had intended to prod him, to see how long he'd exist."

"Is that how they kill you?" I asked, fearful that Luk had almost been taken from me before I'd ever had a chance to meet him.

He shook his head. "No, that's how they desiccate us."

"How did your brothers not find you? Take you back?" Xavier still stood by his desk, knocking back another sip.

"I do not know. I just escaped the Church's prison."

Olivia broke into the silence. "They've created an infirmary there. It's only about a decade old."

Xavier studied her. "I heard. It's part of why I've come to the region."

Olivia sat back, her legs still now and crossed, cradling her whiskey in one hand. When she spoke, she sounded bored. "And here I was, thinking you were just holding court on one of your world tours."

He smiled, his entire face lifting with it, making me realize the man did have an expression behind that beard. "That too."

Olivia rolled her eyes, and my brows drew together, confused. She wasn't usually so instantly antagonistic. She huffed and turned her head away, suddenly intent on the bookshelves. Xavier looked back at Luk, and his expression grew serious. "I am sorry nobody came for you, Lukman. To either end your suffering or to help you escape. I am surprised Sekhmet blessed you with soul this long."

Luk held his hand out, palm up. "You and me both."

I looked between them, feeling irritated as I tried to catch up again. "Why would you not still have your soul if your life wasn't ended? I thought you had until your death to earn your rebirth?"

Luk likely heard the annoyance in my tone. He dropped his hand to my thigh and squeezed. "I do. But typically, the centuries of desiccation would have counted as a death, albeit a bad one. Sekhmet would have taken back my soul to bestow it on another, to complete her mission of Ma'at. Of balance."

My eyes widened. "And you don't know why she didn't."

"Aye. Or why she's let me live."

I swung back to Xavier. "Olivia said that Sekhmet let you keep your soul, this life, because you were good at your job. Because you kept doing it."

"An admirer, wee lass." Xavier's brogue deepened with the tease.

"In your dreams," Olivia hissed at him, swinging her head back, her eyes narrowed.

It only made Xavier laugh. "It's true enough, but it's an assumption. Mine as well as others. And while I continue to punish those who need it, it's more when they annoy me. Out of boredom. I am not some altruistic vigilante, witch."

Luk hissed, suddenly rigid. "Her name is Eliza."

Xavier looked at him steadily before breaking the tension, a wide grin on his face, though still not quite as wide as Olivia had evoked. He poured himself a last drought and walked back to his chair, taking his seat. "Eliza, then. So, it's true?"

"What's true?" I shifted, suddenly uncomfortable. With how intent he stared at me, I wondered if it was possible he could know. About Luk and I, about the marking.

"That he's spent all these years underground. Our kind thirst for revenge, but he laid it aside long enough to put you first. To have some kind of connection to you."

My eyes narrowed. "That surprises you?"

Xavier cocked his head. "Aye. Honestly, it surprises me he's anything but a madman casually ripping out every throat he sees. I don't think you understand the thirst. The raw pain of being desiccated for that long, lass."

"Eliza," Luk growled.

I laid my hand over the one covering my thigh and squeezed. "Luk said he had surrendered to the nothingness." I turned to him. "I assumed you were just...passed out during the time between when they buried you and when you were put in that cell."

Luk's lips flattened like he wanted to smile for me but couldn't quite. "No, Eliza. The nothingness is just," Luk scrubbed a hand down his face, "the lack of options. The torture. We are supernatural. Though we breathe, we don't stop living because we don't breathe. We just feel the burn in our lungs, the want of oxygen, the absence of it every moment it's gone. When we can't get blood or any other substance, we don't die, but we feel the hunger, the need, every second of every day that we exist. It is why when we are taken, our brothers will do anything to get us out or end our suffering. We were not taken often."

I swallowed, horror consuming me as the reality of what Luk must have suffered sunk in. "How are you not insane?"

He curled my hair behind my ear. "Because you are my sanity." Warmth filled me, and I suddenly wished we were alone.

Xavier's voice brought us out of our intense stare. "I think I'm beginning to understand."

Olivia broke in. "That's a surprise."

I frowned at her, but she just shrugged. Luk looked back to Xavier. "Good, because I bring double the danger of having broken away from a church that has held on to me very closely all these years. They've also held on to Eliza. Do you know what she is?"

Xavier looked at me and cocked an eyebrow. "Is this a pop quiz? What about your witch, Lukman?"

Luk glared at Xavier.

"Concentrate," I muttered.

Xavier continued to study me intently. He sniffed the air, and my stomach squeezed at the odd gesture. His eyes widened in understanding. "How did I miss it?"

"Because you're an idiot?"

"Olivia!" I exclaimed, surprised and exacerbated by her.

"Well," she muttered.

Xavier stood abruptly, walking over to Angus. I had

almost forgotten he was there; he stood so quietly at the door. He left after whatever Xavier muttered to him.

"What was that about?" I asked as Xavier strode back to his seat, jaw tight, his entire demeanor changed.

"You brought a death witch to my door." Turning to me, he said harshly, "You were all supposed to be dead."

"So I've heard."

"You don't understand." Xavier's voice had grown rough. "Everyone will be hunting you both. Not just the Church. The witches, the vampires, the gods themselves. I don't know how such a pairing came together or what the Mother, the Tree, is threading together, but the fabric of fate is changing, and I should have been preparing protections long before now."

It was like Xavier had suddenly begun speaking another language. "What are you talking about?"

Luk squeezed my hand, but he spoke to Xavier. "There's more. We took each other as mates. I have not earned my rebirth, but I can still feel her. And her, me."

I squeezed his hand back, not understanding why his voice held such gravity. "Do you know how that could be?"

Xavier's eyes widened as he sat back. "No. But I do know you are breaking all the rules, Lukman. Somehow you live. You still have soul. Borrowed soul. But apparently, our little death witch here has decided that is not enough. The only way you could feel each other is if she gave you a little of hers. Your soul is not yours to share. It shouldn't be possible. She shouldn't be able to do that. But if you share a connection, you also share soul."

Luk hung his head. "I was afraid of that."

Thirty-Two

Eliza

Frustration suffused me. I was getting more than tired of always feeling like I was playing catch up. "What does that mean, we share soul? And why is it so bad?"

Xavier raised a brow, but Olivia broke in. Surprise and a little fear were evident on her face too. "It means your soul is broken, Eliza. If Luk were to die before he earns his rebirth, his own soul, when you die, yours will forever be looking for its missing piece. But it won't be enough for Luk to come back. At least, I don't think."

Xavier confirmed. "It won't be enough. And you, Eliza, will always be looking for that missing part of you."

I still didn't see the problem. "Luk is going to earn his rebirth. If that's the only problem, I don't see why we're all getting so excited about—"

I was cut off by a crash, like wood splintering. Luk and Xavier hissed in unison. Something about the sound, the gesture, their descended fangs, instantly told me something was very wrong.

"What was that?" Olivia asked, fear leaking into her voice. Luk and Xavier moved as if one, Xavier taking the lead to the door. Olivia crept over to me and took my arm.

Luk looked back, his face a stark mask, almost like the first time I saw him, the planes and angles shadowed, *wrong* somehow. A child's nightmare come to life. "Stay here. The Church has found us."

My eyes widened. "What do you mean, 'Stay here?'" He didn't wait to explain or for me to disagree. Luke and Xavier slipped out the door soundlessly like death walking.

"Olivia, what is happening?"

She shook her head at me, tears gathering in her eyes. "I don't have vampire hearing, Eliza. If they said stay here, we should stay here."

I pulled my arm from hers, my forehead wrinkling. "If it's the Church, they've come to exorcise them, Liv. They might not be able to push Luk across the threshold, but it weakened him last time. What if it weakens him enough that they can kill him?"

I stood to go, my own words injecting fear into my heart, but Olivia grabbed my arm, pulling me back. I turned to her, and surprise shot through me. A tear leaked down her cheek, and she was visibly shaking. "Eliza, my powers are in seduction. I can enthrall a human with enough time, and he can help me with his strength, but I'm no more powerful than any other woman like this. And if they see me, they'll push me across. I won't survive an attack by the Church."

I realized what she was saying. Somehow, knowing that Olivia was a demon had made her seem indestructible to me. Like one of those beings in the movies that, if shot down, just kept coming back. I had felt like the weakest link of my friends, not knowing who I was or how to use the powers I supposedly had. But I wasn't. And the chink in her armor didn't make her weak either. It just meant she needed a shield; for now.

"Get under the desk, Liv. Go, hurry!"

She swallowed back her tears, rising, gratefulness holding back the hysteria. She looked at the desk and back to me. "Are you sure?"

I shooed her toward the desk, "Liv. Go. We need you. If you aren't able to fight them, we'll get hurt trying to protect you. Hide. You might not have a gun in this fight, but I do."

She held fast to my hand, and I tried to stave off the impatience as another crash, this time like glass, sounded from the other room, followed by shouts. "What are you going to do?" Her voice trembled with her hand.

I looked at her solemnly, fear for Luk, fear of what I was going to see when I walked out of the library, thrilling through me. I buried it down, letting determination take hold. "I'm going to exorcise."

Another crash erased any patience I had, and I tugged my hand out of her grip and raced for the door. Before turning the knob, I looked back one time to see her rushing under the desk. Satisfied, I opened the door and walked into pandemonium.

A chandelier sat broken in the middle of the floor, and men in ski masks were fighting Luk and Xavier at separate ends of the hall, three at the back of the house on Luk and two on Xavier in the foyer. The bald man who had answered the door when we'd first come lay with his head and body on opposite ends of the front doorway. The men in masks seemed to be human, but despite the disadvantage that should bring, they kept up with the blur of fists and kicks that Luk and Xavier aimed at them with weapons that looked like swords but held a visible current of electricity.

Luk had knives he must have won off someone during the fight and was using them to parry away the swords while he dislocated arms and fought back ferociously. My head swung to the front, where Xavier danced in between a sea of broken glass and flowers, and I stood with wide eyes as I saw him rip a man's throat out with his bare hands.

Angus sat close to the library door, huddled with his

hands over his head. I called to him, his head snapping up, and I motioned for him to come to me. He got to his feet, rushing toward me, and I pushed him into the library. "Find Olivia," I said quickly before closing the door behind him.

I started to turn, to move toward Luk, when the appearance of three shadows in the front door snagged my attention, stopping me. They were hard to make out until the light and floating debris cleared enough that I could see their faces. Skirting around the fighting trio at the front, walking through a river of blood were Father Paul, Sam, and Michael. My blood ran cold at the look of satisfaction on Father Paul's face.

"I've got you now."

I looked back at Luk just as someone caught him from behind, the pain of the blow bringing him to his knees. He managed to swing out from under what looked like would have been a killing blow just in time, getting back to his feet and straight back into the melee. I huffed, deciding I was done with this. I wasn't a helpless girl. I wasn't that child who had tried to earn the Church's approval, who had tried to fit a mold that was never made for me my entire life. The derisiveness that this man carried for me wasn't mine to bear. It was something that grew in his own hateful heart. I wasn't going to be a liability out here. Everyone kept telling me I had power. Mother Superior in the Church, Olivia and Luk, and even the coven witches because of my heritage. It was time I used it.

"We'll see," I said as I moved toward them with purpose. With a shout from Father Paul, they stopped abruptly, and Father Paul held a crucifix in front of him. Sam, his face laced with disgust, burned frankincense and myrrh and stared at me with hateful eyes. Michael's jaw set, always the good disciple. His hero had told him there was a monster and had invited him to slay it. He stood with bells and a book of Psalms. They began chanting together.

I laughed, but as I advanced to slap the tools of our trade out of their hands, something tugged in my middle, and I was compelled to a stop. I tried to shake it off, to keep moving toward the three men, but it was like something tied around my middle and jerked me back. My eyes flew up, widened, and fear made my chest tight.

"Begone, *demon*!" Father Paul shouted, and then they fell into another chant from the Romanum.

Michael called on his favorite patron. "Archangel Michael, carry this beast away from the innocent. Remove her wicked stain!"

Sam remained silent, keeping the smoke of the incense moving toward me and shielding the others with it. I narrowed my eyes. I knew the rites of exorcism too. I could play this game, I reminded myself, and began the Lord's Prayer. They weren't the only exorcists in this house. I called on the God I'd grown up with to help me. To shield me from their attack.

But Michael's call rang again, and I felt another tug. Then a *shove.* I grunted, winded as if someone had punched me in the stomach. I kept chanting, the rest of the room falling into the background as my focus became consumed by the men in front of me. I was determined to win this, to take back control.

I opened my mouth and began one of the psalms. Suddenly, it was like cotton had been stuffed in my mouth. And then I felt it. The other side. That line that hummed to me whenever a spirit crossed over. The room seemed to fade into mist. Father Paul's eyes went wild, and his face flushed in triumph. Behind him, I could just make out more men crowding Xavier. I heard a war cry, and from somewhere, he'd procured an ax that dripped with blood. I tried to look back for Luk, but I couldn't, the force that held me around my middle keeping me facing front. Whoever their chants and prayers were to seemed to be listening, but mine weren't being answered. Xavier swung his ax, but a blow to his back stopped him short, his arms hanging as if frozen in time before he dropped to his knees. I watched as the figures with ski masks converged on him, desperately trying to see what happened, to see Xavier get up, fight back.

With one more shove and pain, like spikes being stabbed into my eyes, I was pulled away before I could see what happened and was brought fully into the mist. I stumbled to my hands and knees, dizziness disorienting me and fear trying to overwhelm me. For a moment, I was frozen, but I knew I needed to move. I started to flick my thumb, letting the pain center me. My head down, my eyes closed while I tried to get my bearings, I started to pray again, but it didn't feel right. Where before I had felt something, a strength, a watching when I'd pray, now I felt empty. Almost enmity. Like whatever I called on was offended for it.

My words faded on the Lord's Prayer, and I took a deep breath, concentrating, trying to come up with a plan. Before I could grasp a thought, a spike, like a dagger, pierced my stomach, and the familiar pain made it all the more potent. I cried out, falling back to my knees. I opened my eyes and shouted at the sky and cursed, feeling spittle fall across my chin. Tears soaked my cheeks, and I raged at this misty, mysterious sky and the God who had abandoned me. But how could I blame him? Didn't I abandon him first?

Before I could really fathom that, I heard a voice. "Daughter. At long last."

I opened my eyes on a sob, ready to face whatever this new enemy was. But it wasn't. It was a woman. She wore a long black dress, with sleeves that covered her hands except when she moved, flowing down a shapely body with a lovely face. But she kept changing. Suddenly, the dress hugged a fuller frame, the face lined kindly, with wisdom to spare. As one leg found purchase, and I began to rise from my knees, she flitted in and out again, this time to an old lady, the dress dripping off skinny shoulders that were bent, her face knarled, the wrinkles obscuring the beauty that was just there.

"Who…who are you?" I asked, tears in my voice.

"I am the maiden. The mother. And the crone."

My breath hitched. I had done research when this all started. I knew what that represented. This was Hecate.

"Where? How? What is this?" I shouted. The idea of being before a god and not bowing, not showing my reverence, would have been abhorrent before, but right now, all I cared about was the fact that my family, the family I'd made, was back at that house being killed. Being exorcised.

Hecate didn't seem to be offended. She kept skipping in and out between beauty, grace, and age. "You are at the line, daughter. The priest is strong, and he brings the might of a church that has gained strength through fear."

I cried, nearly falling again, but shored myself up with strength I didn't even realize I had. Holding my hands out beseechingly, I found my humility. "How do I help them, Hecate? I don't know who I am, who I should pray to anymore. I don't know what the gods are anymore or what I am. But I do know I want them to live. How do I help them?"

I was sobbing, every part of me aching for the fact I was here. But here wasn't where my friends, my lover, needed me. "You will learn, daughter. And I need you to learn fast. But for now, you are right. You need them to realize your potential. To do what I sent you here for."

Before I could really ruminate on those mysterious

words, she was before me and suddenly beside me. She whispered mystical words in my ears that felt like home. Then she backed up until we were squared in front of each other. She in her diaphanous gown, the maiden, and me in my over-large sweats. She looked at me kindly, the mother. She stooped before me, the crone, and with a yell, she pushed me back. I fell. And I fell. Through the blackness, once again, I fell.

Thirty-Three
Eliza

I opened my eyes to the sounds of shouts and clang of weapons. The priest and his followers, people I once counted as friends, stood with their backs to me. Xavier was on his knees with Luk beside him, Xavier clutching his chest, Luk's hand on his head, blood seeping between his fingers. The men stood before them with swords poised over their necks.

I knew what to do. Hecate had told me. I scrambled to my hands and knees, not bothering to take the time to stand, and pulled the men closest to Xavier and Luk to the line. It was like with the wraith, where it wasn't their physical bodies I pulled, but that thing in them, their essence. They came out like light—one muddy brown, one yellow. They went across the line, their souls screaming, their bodies crumpling to the ground. Nothing but satisfaction reigned in me. Suddenly, the entire room's attention was on me. The soldiers, I imagined that's what they were, stood behind the priest, whose face screwed up in confusion.

"It seems you take more than one exorcism to go down, witch. No matter. I thought it was a little too easy the first time anyway."

He immediately launched into a psalm, not even bothering with the introduction. His words weren't meaningless. I felt that telltale pull. I wasn't so sure of myself that I gave him any time. I launched into a prayer of my own.

"Hecate
Mother of gates
Mother of my line
Lend me your knowledge
Lend me your courage
Lend me your power
Teach me your ways!"

It was laughably simple. Such basic words, such an uncomplicated ask. But it was all it took. I was thrown back on my butt, my hair blowing behind me, and all the men in front of me were thrown to their knees. The time that they'd been focused on me had been enough for Xavier and Luk to recover, and they began to dispatch the soldiers who'd been about to execute them, wrenching their arms back to take their swords and running them through. The gurgle of blood in their throats was the only last words they were given before they fell forward with their dying breaths.

The exorcists, the men who had orchestrated this, who had stood there proud and powerful, looked around fearfully. Michael's head whipped side to side, his eyes tight, and Sam stood, staring at me, mouth screwed up in anger but face ashen. All but Father Paul. He seethed with hatred. His voice rose, and he brandished that crucifix like it was God's scepter. "BEGONE, DEMON."

The tug I expected to feel instead was a lasso. But it wasn't around me. It was thrown from me. And with a *pop*, the air around the father changed, shimmered like asphalt on a hot day. Through that hazy portal walked two vicious dogs, their likenesses reminding me of the ropy muscle I'd seen on the hounds at Hecate's temple that flanked her. Their teeth dripped yellow fluid and blood, and their skin looked like the muscle that should lie beneath like they'd been flayed. Michael cried out when he saw what was happening and ran for the door. The hounds let him go, concentrating on Father Paul and Sam.

The soldiers that remained and the vampires, locked neck and neck, didn't notice him, and he escaped. Sam didn't even try to run. I wondered at the hatred in his eyes after he had been my closest confidant for years. When I had left, saying goodbye to no one, I had questioned, just for a moment, if he'd be sad. He banished that thought with his words.

"You stupid bitch. We all saw the videos. I was going to take you, did you know that? I would have married you, helped you out of your sinful life. Mother Superior was going to let me when you failed, as we all knew you would. And you chose that demon instead. You deserve to burn."

His words shocked me, the vitriol, the hate. And it was like oil ran over me, realizing they'd had cameras even down in Luk's dungeon, had watched what we'd done together, the violation of it leaving me sick. But it also only made me more determined. Father Paul called on the saints, and the tug returned, but I wouldn't waste Hecate's gift. Looking at Sam, I said, "Good luck in the next life." He looked at me in disgusted confusion before I pushed. Like the other men, his soul was thrown across the line. Though I wanted no part of him through me, I'd give him a merciful crossing. His sins in life could be dealt with by whatever god waited for him in death. His eyes widened in surprise before his body crumbled, and the screams of his soul vibrated through me before they were silenced.

Father Paul only intensified his prayers, determined to take me down with him. I didn't bother pushing his soul. I watched like I was looking at an exhibit at the Louvre as the skeletal hounds, their bodies nothing but sinew and muscle, circled him. Finally seeing something other than me, he shouted in surprise, holding the cross to his chest, to his heart. Finally, he started the Lord's Prayer.

As he said the words, "On Earth as it was," one hound lunged for his leg, the other his scalp. He screamed, and in his desperation, he even asked me for help. "Eliza, Eliza, please, have mercy!"

I watched them drag him to the same nothingness they came from, the hound around his ankle and part of his body disappearing, the other hound holding tight to his scalp. I answered his screams. "My name is Lilah. And don't worry, Father. I'll pray for you. After all, even the devil deserves prayers."

Thirty-Four

Luk: Epilogue

I had known when she'd come into her power, it would be terrifying, but even I wasn't prepared. After all my years, I had never seen Hecate imbue someone with so much strength. Foes me and Xavier had fought with all our strength had melted before her. I had stood in awe after the priest had been dragged to the underworld. A part of me even pitied him.

Eliza had been exhausted after, nearly collapsing. I had carried her to our room and put her to bed. By the time I pulled the covers, she had been asleep. Olivia had come out of the library, crying, Angus close behind her, face expressionless, looking shell-shocked. I was surprised to see Xavier at her side, looking her over almost frantically to make sure she was alright. The second he was assured she was, he turned away like she was a nuisance. Interesting.

Now I stood on the stoop of his broken house. We planned to leave for New Orleans in the morning. Apparently, it was Xavier's second home. While he spent much of his time in his homeland, he loved the depravity this city had to offer. I shuddered to think what I'd find.

Hearing Eliza's latest nightmare abate and her breathing return to its rhythmic sound, I kicked off the stoop, ready to finish one last mission before we left for New Orleans tomorrow.

I intended to find her—the witch who had dressed Eliza's wrists in scars, who had tried to take what was mine. As I began up the street, determined to walk them until I felt the presence of magic, something that would lead me to the woman, I heard steps behind me. I stopped, moving with vampiric speed to challenge the lurker. Instead, I came face to face with Xavier.

He held his hands up in front of him in a placating gesture, his red hair and jovial personality grating on my current mood. "Where are you off to on this lovely night?" His accent from the fair country faded in and out, I'd noticed.

"I'm finding the witch who touched Eliza."

Xavier's smiled wide. "What a coincidence. I had planned to do the same."

I lowered my brow, looking at him with suspicion. "Why would you care enough to hunt her?"

Xavier's smile took on a dangerous edge. "Because I failed you once. And when Olivia told me what caused those scars, I decided this might be a way I could repay you. How we all could repay you for abandoning you to centuries of desiccation."

I stood straighter. "We have no debt."

"We both know that's not true."

I inclined my head. "So, the Church still uses witches to make their guards a match for us?" I asked, changing the subject. I was uncomfortable with his guilt.

He looked out to the street, standing beside me. "They do, the hypocrites. They tell their people it is done with prayers to the one God."

I grunted. "We were amazed at the power Zeus had managed to amass then. It seems he guards his legend with fervor."

"You have no idea. A lot has changed, but one thing hasn't. Revenge tonight will taste sweet."

"We're up for a run. We'll be tired tomorrow."

Xavier laughed, sharpening my gaze and drawing down my brow.

"If you're here to mock me."

Not put off at my indignation, he just nodded toward another steel horse, sitting on the street we'd been gazing at. Its lines were more angular and less boxy than the ones we drove in to get here. "We don't need to run, Lukman. We've picked up a few things in the centuries you've been asleep."

I stared at the steel horse skeptically. "You had something else in mind?"

Xavier barked a laugh at my doubt. "This is a Porsche GT3 911. It's faster than even a vampire."

I scoffed but followed him to the steel horse. "We'll see. I don't intend to leave until the witch is dead."

"You'll see," he said, striding comfortably down the walk.

I turned serious, stopping him with a hand on his arm. I eyed him and wondered if I could trust him, if time had twisted him into an evil trickster like so many, or if he was of as sound character as he seemed. "Then we hunt together?"

He clapped a hand on my shoulder. "Tonight, brother, we kill together."

Thank You!

Thank you for reading, and I hope you enjoyed Eliza and Luk's journey! As always, please let me know what you think in the reviews!

You can find me at:
Facebook: **https://www.facebook.com/maxfield.maggie**
Goodreads: **www.goodreads.com/user/show/154136083-maggie-maxfield**
Instagram: **www.instagram.com/maggie_maxfield/**
Website: **www.maggiemaxfield.com**

Read on for a preview of the first book in my Stepuli Chronicles Duet, a dystopian alien romance. The final book in the duet is releasing October 2023. It's a dual POV slow burn that catches on fire.

The Tracks We Leave - Preview

CHAPTER 1

STASIA

Two stone guard shacks stood like sentinels. I drove up to the base gate on the narrow lane between them with my registration, insurance, and state ID in hand. Nostalgia hit me, the whole scene reminiscent of my military days. My foot tapped restlessly against the floorboard while bittersweet memories played through my mind.

I don't know why a weight dropped in my gut. I had mostly enjoyed my time in the service. I was coming back as a contractor and wouldn't have the same restrictions as when I was enlisted. This was a great opportunity, the pay was outrageous, and so far, everything I saw of Washington I loved. I hadn't even started work, so it's not like I could blame the hospital for this feeling. Regardless, something triggered my fight or flight response.

Before I could dwell on that, traffic moved forward. I

took a deep breath and rolled my window down. As I pulled up to the gate, a large black man, broad-shouldered and decked out in camouflage with an M4 slung lazily across his front, leaned down to take my information.

"Morning," he said jovially. Jesus, he looked like GI Joe and sounded like Mr. Rogers.

I smiled, his energy putting me at ease. Holding my paperwork in easy reach for him, I said, "Hi, I'm here for my first day at the hospital. Christopher Shaw is my liaison. He's supposed to be meeting me here."

The man, Jacob, I read on his nametag, said, "Ah, you were supposed to go to the Passing ID Office." He pointed toward a building I could now see just through the trees. I bit my lip but offered him a tense smile. I was going to be late. I hated being late.

"Thanks so much, I must have missed the turnoff. Do I just turn around or…?"

Jacob waved away my words. "Nah, I know Chris, I'll just radio him to come to the gate. Pull into the turnoff up there," he pointed, "I'll let you know when he comes through, and you can follow him out."

Giving him a more genuine smile, I said, "Thank you." He winked, already talking into his radio. I moved forward to where he indicated, putting my car in park to wait for Mr. Shaw.

He drove through in a black Impala sedan. He lowered his passenger window and waved at me. Nodding back, I put the car in drive and threw a thumbs up back to Jacob.

Shaw led me to a four-story building set in boring angular lines. It was designed like a typical hospital with a straightforward layout. That impression continued inside with plain white floors and walls, low hanging ceilings, and a musty odor that gave away the building's age. It didn't turn me off. It wouldn't be the first old low-budget hospital I'd worked in.

"I'll introduce you to the charge nurse," Chris said as I followed along. "They're very short today, and we heard you'd done some travel nursing in the past and would be comfortable with no clinical orientation."

I nodded because it was true, but I was still surprised. Usually, permanent jobs loved to show you the difference between staff and travel work. They insisted on orientation I wouldn't need as a new grad.

Chris made quick introductions to a woman named Ava. Her brown hair varied shades, and she was a little heavy in the waist. She smiled at me, her pretty, made-up face looking harried. I smiled back because her expression told me exactly what kind of day she was having.

"Where do you want me?" I asked.

She looked at Chris and said, "Thanks I've got it from here," dismissing him without another look. "What are you comfortable with?"

"Anything." I shrugged, watching curiously as Chris walked away grumbling.

"I have no psych nurses today, and we have more boarders than usual. Our regular staff really aren't great with them. We normally ship them so quickly. Can you go to that hall?"

Psych was where I excelled. My ability to sense people, or my good intuition, helped me de-escalate sticky situations. I could pivot between a schizophrenic and a borderline patient like a pro. "Sure thing. What room numbers? I'll head over."

She waved that away. "I'm not going to let you drown completely. Let's do a quick tour of the ER. I'll show you the stock rooms, your closest med cart, and introduce you to

Shelly. You can shadow her for the last hour of her shift just to get the ropes. Then you can take over her assignment. Sound good?"

"Yeah, that's perfect."

Her stressed face relaxed the more we spoke, and her energy lightened from the frenetic quality it had been when I'd first walked up to her.

"Fantastic. I'm so sorry you're getting no more introduction than this your first day."

I shrugged, not bothered. Answering truthfully, I said, "I prefer it this way. Lead on."

As promised, she showed me around the Emergency Room and introduced me to Shelly. We made short work of catching up with her patients' orders. Eleven came by in a blink, then I was taking care of a four-room psych assignment. An easy day, really.

As I thought this, the alarm sounded for an incoming ambulance. I finished off my charting and got up from the desk to go prepare the room. On my way I read the page. *Violent patient, in restraints with military police, recent history of schizophrenia.*

I had just finished clearing the room of sharps and projectiles when the EMTs rolled the patient in. Police hovered at the door. The room filled with people: security, patient care technicians, another RN, and the physician. The EMTs gave a patient report as everyone moved the man to the ER stretcher.

They went about the typical duties involved in triaging a psychiatric patient. Vital signs, change the clothes, take the belongings. The process stopped abruptly when the patient shouted, "I don't wanna be here! This is bullshit! Stop, get the FUCK away from me you BITCH. Fuck you!"

The doctor attempted to interrupt the patient's tirade,

aimed at the patient care tech, who backed away fearfully. I stayed at my computer, feeling bombarded by the patient's panicked and confused energy. There were already too many people in the room. This man didn't need anyone closer to him. Emily, the RN who had come in to help, didn't seem to realize that though.

When the doctor's attempts to explain the process didn't work, Emily stepped up next to the patient and said, "You need to stop yelling. You aren't the only one in this hospital. Security, get the restraints. Listen, if you don't stop yelling, I'm going to put you in restraints."

My mind boggled. She hadn't even given the patient time to respond. Not to mention, he wasn't currently being aggressive. Sure, he had screamed profanities, and no, it wasn't acceptable. But she was making it worse. And she was actively threatening the patient. She was aggressively handling a paranoid schizophrenic in psychosis.

The doctor shrugged, looking bored. "Emily when you get it handled come and get me. Anxiety medications if you need it." Then he walked out. He hadn't even spoken to me, the primary nurse.

"All right, let's get the locked restraints," Emily said to a heavyset older man. The type of security guard who was ten years retired from the force. She walked out with him to retrieve the restraints, confusing me even more. If she was so worried about this patient's aggression, why would she leave the room? With one of the security guards?

I looked at the door, hoping I had time. "Let's clear the room. You and you stay," I indicated to the scared patient care technician and one of the three security guards, "everyone else, mind stepping out the door?"

There were a lot of grumbles, and plenty of incredulous

stares, but my confidant tone encouraged them to obey. Sensing the patient's panic and distrust, I stayed out of his space. Instead, I leaned against the back counter, keeping my body language relaxed. The raised side rails provided a barrier and time to get out of the room if he erupted.

"Hi, I'm Stasia, what's your name?"

He ignored me, not making eye contact. Typical, but it was important to know he was concentrating on me, not the voices speaking in his head. "Hey bud," I said, using my usual moniker. "Bud, look at me. Can you look at me?"

Finally, he did. I smiled warmly. I didn't stare him down, briefly keeping my gaze on his eyes then shifting to his chin. "Hey, I'm Stasia. I'm going to be one of your nurses. Do you know why you're here?"

He yelled again. "Yeah, it's bullshit. My dad called. I wasn't doin' nothin'! I was just fuckin' chillin'!"

I nodded as if this was perfectly understandable.

"I get it." I used a calm voice in low tones, purposefully designed to put him at ease. "Are you having thoughts of hurting yourself or anyone else today?"

"NO. Fuck! This isn't fair. I want to go!" His eyes were wide, panicked to even the casual observer. The feeling I got from him was terrifying. Not violence or meanness, but soul-deep fear.

I smiled slightly. "It's not. I'm sorry. That's good you aren't having those thoughts. You've been here before for stuff like this right?" I hadn't had a chance to look up his chart, but I didn't have a lot of time before Emily got back with restraints.

He nodded. He teared up, his aggression making way to his underlying emotions. Perfect. That meant I was making progress. The fear rolling off him lessened in intensity, corroborating my assessment.

I continued. "So you know the drill bud. Just let us get all the necessary stuff done. The sooner we do, the sooner you can talk to psych and get out of here. How about we get your vitals, your lab work. Let you get changed. I'll bring a turkey sandwich and some apple juice. You can chill and watch TV or whatever you want to do in the room."

I worded it carefully so he understood he had boundaries but also options. It would make him feel more in control and help prevent him from pushing his limits.

"I'm hungry," he said instantly.

This was typical, and I used it as a bargaining chip. "I'll get you the food as soon as we get your blood pressure, blood work, and clothes."

He thought about that. From my vantage point, I saw Emily coming from up the hall and moved to intercept her at the doorway. I leaned against the door jam, standing as if I had all the time in the world for his decision. In the meantime, my position blocked Emily from getting in the room.

Just in time, he said, "Okay."

I looked over at the patient care tech as I felt Emily at my back. The tech looked at me like I was a voodoo priestess. I forced back a laugh. I smiled at her and said to the patient, "This young lady will help you get started. Just a second."

I felt comfortable leaving the tech with the security guard in the room. I turned to Emily, who barely left me any personal space. She had locked restraints in her hand and a pinched face.

"He's good now," I said. "Consenting to care."

Her pinched face became derisive. The portly guard stood at her back. She said, "Bullshit, I don't trust him. Not the way he was yelling. I'm going to tie him down for a while."

The guard at her back looked bored, like he didn't mind

either way. I began to feel a little violent myself at her misuse of care.

"Excuse me?" I said, moving so she had to back further from the door.

"That guy was just yelling like a lunatic." Her own voice rose. "I'm putting him in restraints!"

I breathed in through my nose and out through my mouth. The irony of her shouting his need for restraints wasn't lost on me. I had seen this all too often in healthcare. It wasn't that she didn't know how to handle psych patients, she got off on the power. Violating someone's body, someone's autonomy, was as simple as her convenience, and not actually about safety at all.

"This is my patient. You are going to back away. You are going to stay away from the room if he begins to escalate." I didn't say anything else. I didn't trust myself to. I hated that tears burned at the back of my eyes because of the anger burning up my chest.

Emily's eyes bugged out. "I'm going to get the charge nurse. You're new here, maybe you didn't handle psych patients where you came from but—"

"Get the charge nurse." My flat tone cut her off without room for argument. She stormed off.

On my way home, exhaustion weighed down my shoulders. This must have been what the stone in my stomach had been about. The charge nurse had been underselling it when she said her typical ER staff weren't good with psych patients. They were one of the most vulnerable and misunderstood populations. They were also one of the largest any ER saw, and the small military hospital treated them with borderline abuse.

Ava, after hearing our argument, had sided with me. It helped my case that for the rest of the shift he was an easy patient, sweet even. Emily was going to hate me for life. Considering this was a permanent position, that could prove to be a problem.

Pulling into the driveway of my oceanfront home, I looked to the right. I hadn't met the neighbor yet. I had gotten in late last night with an early morning today and hadn't had much time to explore.

I started up the walk, my head hung from exhaustion. My lower back and calves ached from being on my feet for twelve hours. I looked up as I hit the walkway to the front door and investigated the front windows out of habit. Stopping short, I dropped my bag and laughed. Flynn panted excitedly in the window, the blinds down around his neck like a coat.

This dog could test the patience of a saint. I adopted Flynn from a couple on Craigslist on a particularly lonely night at one of my lowest points. I blame the wine for thinking I could tame a nine-week-old wolfdog. His first two months he tore up my entire carpet, ate my couch, and ripped down my blinds. At first, I had told myself the kind thing would be to give him back to the couple I'd adopted him from, to a shelter, to anyone but my own very unprepared hands. In the end though, I couldn't. I knew from experience there was no worse feeling than being given back.

He had gotten better, but the abrupt change from Florida must have triggered his anxiety. After freeing him from the blinds, we headed to the back yard so he could burn off some of his nervous energy. He danced next to me, rushing out when I opened the back slider. I smiled and followed him.

Flynn took his time smelling around the yard, getting to

know his new home. I took a deep breath. My exhaustion melted away with the crisp air. This view was the reason I'd parted with the lion's share of my savings. Scattered Douglas fir trees offered shade. Lush green grass covered the yard with a small pond set back before the land dropped off to the ocean below.

I went to sit on the deck steps, but Flynn's head shot up, pointing to the yard next door. He took off. I cursed under my breath and called, "Flynnstone!"

He didn't even look back. I groaned, rushing after him. He ran to the neighbor's deck where a man had walked out. I tried calling his name a couple more times as I walked over, but Flynn continued ignoring me.

"I'm so sorry," I called as I got closer.

The man had an easy smile on his face, a beer on the wide arm of his Adirondack chair, and his hands buried in Flynn's thick gray mane. Dark eyes, dark hair, lightly tanned skin. His smile brightened his face, and his eyes crinkled at the corners. I rubbed my hand across the back of my neck, my cheeks warming. I was nearing thirty, but a handsome man could still turn my cheeks red.

"It's not a problem, he's adorable," the man said as I climbed the steps to his deck. Stubble shaded his defined jaw. His large hands found a particular spot that made Flynn's back leg kick. I smiled at the picture of the two of them, his words putting me at ease.

"Thanks, he normally doesn't wander. I think he's just restless from the move. I'm Stasia, your new neighbor. I'm so sorry he barged over here." The smooth lines of the man's defined shoulders tightened, and the corners of his lips turned down.

"It's okay," he said slowly, giving me a searching look. "He made my evening much more exciting. I'm Jack." His polite words were incongruous to the tense energy coming off him. The sudden change confused me.

My smile strained as I wondered what I'd missed. I tried finding something to do with my hands, embarrassment and uncertainty suffusing me. My hand landed on Flynn's backside, absently scratching him. He panted happily, soaking up the attention, oblivious to the growing awkwardness between me and Jack.

"You just moved in last night, right?" Jack peered up at me. He furrowed his brow like someone trying to solve a puzzle.

"Yeah, I got in kind of late, right before dark." Jack's change in demeanor and questions made anxiety curl in my chest. I started to extract myself from the situation when I heard a young voice calling.

"Jack!"

He turned his head and sighed. The slider to his house opened, and a young girl, probably in her midteens, popped out. Her red hair, freckled skin, and brown eyes were adorable. She brightened when she saw me but was quickly distracted by Flynn.

"Who's this cutie?" she squealed.

Flynn immediately abandoned Jack and ran for her, as excited as her for the attention. Jack chuckled softly and straightened. He rubbed the back of his head. "What is it Lill?"

She looked up at me and asked, "Who's this?"

Jack gave her a meaningful look. "This is Stasia, our new neighbor." I wondered if Jack took care of his sister or if he lived with his parents.

Lilly knelt, scratching her way around Flynn's ears. She looked up at me, smiling so wide dimples creased her right cheek. "Hey Stasia, I'm Lilly. Can I dog sit for you?"

I laughed at her abruptness as Jack gazed skyward. "Anytime Lilly, but he's a handful. He busted up your poor brother's peaceful night."

Lilly baby-talked to Flynn. "You can bust up our night anytime. Yes, you can. Aren't you a pretty boy?"

Flynn's tail went wild as he rubbed his head against her hip.

Lilly looked over at Jack. "Sooooooo, I was going to see if I could talk you into starting dinner."

Jack stood, beer bottle in hand. "Figured as much when I heard you hollering. Is Brandon home yet?"

Lilly nodded, still absorbed by Flynn.

"Right. Well, it was nice to meet you, Stasia. Let's go, Lilly."

Lilly, oblivious to his shepherding, continued scratching Flynn's ears. "Do you want to come to dinner, big guy?" She turned to me. "And you too Stasia."

Jack shifted his weight at her question, looking uncomfortable.

"Thank you so much, but I had a long day. Another time."

Jack's hand landed on Lilly's shoulder, steering her inside. "Have a good night," he said. I felt his need to usher her in.

I called Flynn, this time he followed, and was walking off the porch stairs as they reached the slider. I turned back to wave, but Jack never looked back.

CHAPTER 2

Jack

The new neighbor was beautiful, with big green eyes, blonde hair, and a short, athletic body. At first, I had been excited. Finally, another Stepuli family came to Whidbey. One that lived independently and not under the government's thumb. At least not directly under it. It helped that one look from her had set my blood on fire. Her dog, energetic and free with his love, also charmed me. I'd been eager to welcome her. And then she'd stepped onto my porch. Human.

A human living next door to my sister. My sister who was going through puberty with unpredictable powers we were trying desperately to hide. Living next door to my brother who had a chip on his shoulder the size of Mount Vesuvius, and whose mood swings similarly erupted. Brandon had already slipped up and got himself on the Stepuli Eugenics Project's radar. I was barely keeping him together, and the SEP warned if I couldn't keep him together, they would take him permanently.

I went through the motions, mindlessly making dinner, when Lilly pulled me from my thoughts. "The new neighbor is pretty, and oh, my God, Jack, that dog!" She chattered away as usual with too much energy. I had to wake up before dawn just to caffeinate enough to keep up with her.

"It's weird, she didn't feel like a Stepuli. And I kind of expected you to be more excited," Lilly said.

Nervousness churned my gut. She should be able to tell immediately if someone was human, or one of our kind. We could tell another Stepuli by feeling an elemental affinity. Even if their element differed from our own, we all vibrated to an inherent energy. Though Lilly had only ever been around me and Brandon, she could recognize the affinity from us.

I said slowly, "Lilly, she isn't Stepuli."

Lilly scrunched her small, upturned nose. "You said this part of the island was reserved for Stepuli families. That's why we've never had neighbors."

I rubbed my forehead, relieved she had only assumed. Sometimes I forgot she was young and didn't always listen to her instincts before diving into a situation. I set the pasta to boil and turned around to face her, leaning against the counter.

"I know. And I don't know what happened. But Stasia is human Lills."

She considered this. My chest ached as her face dropped. I knew Lilly was lonely, I just didn't know how to fix it. "Oh," she said, unnaturally subdued.

I reached across to ruffle her hair. Her eyes were glassy, but she didn't cry. Not my tough girl. She coughed to clear her throat, but she wasn't fooling me.

"It would have been nice to have another girl around." Her voice slowly got stronger. "Ugh, and I would have loved to play with that dog."

Trying to lighten the mood, I teased, "I can't believe you burst out asking her to watch her dog like that."

Lilly shrugged. "He was adorable, and the goodest boy."

I rolled my eyes and turned back to the stove to finish dinner.

As I was plating the food, Brandon came into the kitchen

looking like hell, his face drawn and a little pale. He practically threw himself onto the barstool next to Lilly. She wordlessly pushed him her lemonade. I did the same with his plate of dinner. He dug in, determinedly not looking at either of us.

I didn't know what to do with him. He had always seemed lost. The water in him was like an ocean constantly beating him with waves of his loss and fear. No matter how strict I'd been, how hard I'd come down on him, I still hadn't been able to keep him safe. I had backed off last fall when it had stopped mattering. One idiotic moment at a Stepuli event and he'd given himself away to the SEP.

The silence stretched uncomfortably. In typical Lilly fashion, she brought Brandon around without effort. "Bet you couldn't channel a stream with that hangover."

Brandon's head snapped up, and he winced. I glanced at the sliding doors, but I had already drawn the blinds. I'd have to talk with Brandon later about the neighbor, but for now, I could let him do the one thing that made him happy. Commune with water.

Smirking at him, I said, "I'll double that," and moved to the sink, turning it on to a slow stream. His dull eyes came to life. His slack face, though still pale, lit with anticipation. Taking one drop from the sink, he inhaled slowly.

He used his hands to focus himself, a bad habit left over from his early days at the Stepul School. I was trying to reteach him to not depend on hand and arm motions, but now wasn't the time. With his first three fingers pinched, he beckoned the drop closer, and then to his right, as if to lay a soft kiss to Lilly's cheek, making her giggle.

Then, with a smirk, he moved the drop toward me. As I watched the small drop warily, a bucket worth of water dumped over my head. Lilly dissolved into laughter, and even Brandon joined in.

I tried to look stern, but I smiled too. I was soaked and cold, but his playfulness made me happy. "You're cleaning that up asshole," I called over my shoulder, heading upstairs to dry off and change. I walked away to the musical sound of Brandon and Lilly laughing.

As I walked out of my room after drying off, I ran into Brandon in the hall. I looked over his shoulder, but Lilly hadn't made it upstairs yet. I heard the distant sound of the TV in the living room.

I reached out and grabbed his arm as he tried to move past me, head down. "B, we need to talk."

His shoulders hitched, and when he turned toward me, his jaw tightened. His wariness ate at me. Since our parents died, I had taken on the parental role. But becoming a father at nineteen hadn't given me the perspective I needed to raise well-adjusted kids. Instead, I'd driven a wedge between us that never healed.

"Yeah?"

"You've got to stop," I said without preamble.

He didn't pretend to not know what I was talking about. He took a deep breath and his shoulders dropped, all the defensiveness leaking out of him.

"I know. I just don't know what else to do."

"I get it B. But you aren't even living anymore. You're even starting to scare Lill."

Brandon dragged a hand down his face, looking ashamed. Lilly was the one thing that always united us. "Maybe I should take a break from the bar."

Relief washed through me. If I had suggested it, he'd resist. He'd managed the family bar after he turned twenty-one. When Brandon was discovered, he at least managed to hide the strength of his powers, and the SEP kept his involvement minimal so far. I had hoped putting him in charge of the business would give him a feeling of normalcy. But instead, he'd buried all his anger and disappointment in the free booze, withdrawing until I hardly recognized him.

"Let's switch jobs. I'll take over the bar, you keep Lilly on a schedule."

"Okay."

Brandon started to move past me to his room. I called out, stopping him. "Oh, and B, we're going to need to stop her training for a while." He looked at me quizzically. Keeping Lilly on a strict schedule was important. My neck ached from the tension as I told him about the new human neighbor.

I rubbed my forehead, a headache starting at my temples. I stared at the books. Walker's Place, the bar I had bought with reparations from my mother's death, was a mess. It had been a couple days since Brandon and I changed places, and I had started going through everything. Supply orders were behind, and we were edging into the red.

I sat back and sighed. Looking up at the corkboard over my desk, I took a break to stare at the family pictures. Mostly pictures of Lilly growing up, carefree and laughing. Sprinkled in were images of Brandon brooding. To the right, almost hidden under other photos, was one of mom and dad.

I ran a hand down my face and rolled the chair back from the desk, standing up to stretch my legs. I intended to go do inventory, something active to alleviate the cramp in my thighs from sitting so long. I wasn't made to be in a closeted office.

I walked out of the office, positioned at the furthest end of a dimly lit hall, and stepped past the bathrooms to my left, the walk-in cooler and liquor closet to my right. Rays of light beckoned me toward the main room of the bar, and already I felt a little less claustrophobic. An open concept room, booths lined the far wall with high tops scattered in between. A green felt pool table stood directly in front of me, a box stage to the back right for open mic nights or bands. To my left was the live oak bar.

I had spent so much on the live oak I couldn't afford to renovate behind the bar. The original mirrored backsplash sat behind rows of liquor bottles. We only had a few beer taps, the classics, and a rotating supply of local microbreweries. As much as I intrinsically hated this place, bought with blood money, it was hard to fail at a bar in a military town. When my parents had died, I'd needed to secure income. It provided Lilly with a better future, and Brandon an inheritance. Until he started drinking it.

Ian, my main bartender, gave me a nod but kept at his task. We were opening soon. On a Saturday, it would be filled with a mixture of sailors from base wanting to get trashed early and hikers looking for an afternoon beer. Wordlessly, I walked along the bar, polishing the oak. Then I helped put away the dishes Ian had cleaned and dusted off the liquor bottles.

We opened at two in the afternoon, and as usual, customers came in as soon as the doors were unlocked. Ian had it in hand, so I grabbed myself a Wicked Teuton IPA and sat in the booth closest to the stage. Putting both hands around the pint, I let the coolness seep into my palms and listened to the chatter.

"Hey, fuck face," Ian called to one of the younger junior sailors. I hid a grin in a sip.

"Yo, what's up Ian? Can I get two Jack and Cokes?"

"Jack and Coke. Bit early for the hard juice, don't you think, Liam?"

Liam laughed. "Never too early for me, Ian."

Ian smiled contemptuously, but Liam didn't pick it up. He poured the drinks and offered them over the bar, taking the young sailor's cash.

"The rest is a tip, right?" he called in the same sardonic voice.

Liam's brows lowered, but he said, his voice a little less sure, "Yeah…you got it Ian." They did a hand slap thing I always found idiotic, and Liam went to sit with his friends.

After the customers vacated the bar, my eyes met Ian's. He winked, and I shook my head with a rueful smile. Ian was an abrasive bartender. In fact, he was downright insulting. But he had a big personality, and he pulled it off. The customers all thought they were in on some kind of joke when he spewed profanities at them or called them names. They liked the inclusiveness and tipped him more. He meant every word.

The afternoon progressed as it normally did. It was too early for the usual bar bunnies to be sloshed, but it was getting to that hour, so I prepared to make my escape. I was still seated at the rear booth, now with the ledgers in front of me and a coffee in my hand. Even with the noise and distractions, it was better than being trapped in the office.

Just as I was getting ready to stand up, my new neighbor walked through the door in a group of people. I recognized Angela, the real estate agent who took care of our mortgage, but didn't recognize the other male with them. Tall and painfully thin, he had a wide smile on his long face. I stayed put for a moment, curious to observe.

I'd managed to avoid Stasia for the last couple days. After a long conversation with Brandon and more stern warnings for the ever-curious Lilly, I made sure the rest of my family stayed away too. I missed my early mornings on the deck, but Stasia seemed to be an early riser as well. She often puttered around the yard with that adorable dog of hers.

The threesome walked to the bar and ordered their drinks. They all ordered a pint and headed to a high top. The sun coming in through the glass window flashed off Stasia's hair, and it struck me again how pretty she was. Her full lips accented her large eyes. Angela said something that made her smile, and the burn in my chest told me that might be her most attractive feature. I still wasn't sure what she did, but she worked long hours. I guessed she was a DOD employee of some kind. Shaking my head at my stalker tendencies, I pushed myself up to put away the ledger.

I had been in the office longer than I meant to be. Lately I'd been dodging calls from Dr. Galton's direct line. This time, he'd left a message informing me he was considering bringing Lilly in to test for latent abilities. He had informed me my medical appointment was moved up and we could talk about it then. The bottom dropped out from under me at the news. I sat in my office questioning his reasons and lost track of time.

When I made it back out to the bar, I looked for Ian. He gazed intently over at Stasia's table. I reflexively turned that way. Ian might be abrasive, but part of what made him a great bartender was his ability to read people. We rarely had fights or police presence despite being generous with the booze, primarily because Ian was so good at de-escalating situations before they got out of hand. The way he was staring told me something needed de-escalating.

A mousy girl with brown hair and a mean face stood next to Stasia's table holding a mixed drink. Stasia's shoulders were drawn up and tense. Around the table, Angela was about to go off. The tall skinny man had his hand on the table. He leaned toward the mousy girl, his eyes narrowed. I moved closer to listen.

"—who you think you are. You're going to get us all hurt one day."

Stasia had her hands around a pint glass, no condensation on it. I wondered if she was still nursing the first beer she'd ordered when she came in. Stasia didn't respond for a moment, so I took a seat at the bar and looked toward Ian. He got the message and came to stand near me. I faced him like we were talking but watched the table in the mirror. Stasia's voice picked up.

"I'm not going to argue with you, Emily. Not in a public place like this. Besides, it's already been resolved. Why don't you go enjoy your day?"

I waited to find out what they were talking about. Stasia's body language screamed discomfort, but her tones were soothing, almost melodic. I felt myself relaxing even from a distance. The mousy-haired girl simmered down as well, but not enough for her to take Stasia's suggestion.

"Listen. You're a new nurse in this area. I'm not going to be a bitch. But just know not to do that again. I've been at that hospital for four years, and I know how Dr. Ferris likes things done. I know how to handle those psycho patients."

I jerked my head around at the girl's words. Doctor? Nurse? Cold washed over me. I stared openly at Stasia, my shock destroying my discretion. A red flush rose from her neck to her cheeks. I realized it wasn't embarrassment I had seen earlier, but barely contained rage. I almost stood to intervene, before her next words stopped me.

She looked at the girl dead on, whereas before she'd been slightly averting her eyes. With a steel undertone, she said, "You obviously don't know what you're doing because what you said to that man was tantamount to assault. The charge didn't agree with me because I'm new. She agreed with me because I saved the hospital from getting in trouble. Now get away from me."

Next to Stasia, Angela smiled like the cat who ate the canary. The skinny man was still leaning forward, but now he was laughing softly. When the mousy brown-haired girl opened her mouth to say something, murder on her face, the man interrupted her.

"Run along Emily. Or it'll be me who talks with Ava. And I've been at the hospital longer than *four* years."

The brown-haired girl, Emily, I corrected myself, went red. She walked away without another word, a petulant stomp to her foot. Stasia looked at the skinny man and said, "Thanks Pat." Her voice had gone back to its soft tenor.

He smiled at her. "Emily's always been a bitch. Ignore her. I can tell you Ava's been doing nothing but singing your praises. I heard she even put you in to be one of the charges."

Stasia's eyes widened, and she said, "I thought she liked me," which caused abrupt laughter all around the table.

I turned back toward Ian and realized he had already moved on down the bar, serving customers, satisfied there wasn't going to be a cat fight. I looked back over and caught Stasia's eye. She stared at me intently, but when our eyes met, they softened, and she gave me a small smile with a slight wave. I nodded politely in her direction. Quickly standing, I loudly called goodbye to Ian.

He waved back, and I smiled tightly at Stasia as I headed to the door. First a human neighbor. Then Galton tries to tell me he's bringing Lilly in for testing despite her never exhibiting any abilities. At least not in public. Now I find out the human next door is a nurse. Was she a spy? Did Galton plant an attractive member of the SEP next door? A temptress for a guy who spent almost all his time burdened down as a dad to his sister and brother? My face set in grim lines, and I climbed onto my bike parked out front of the bar. Taking the helmet off the handlebars, I strapped it on and let the motor drown out my thoughts as I headed home.

Made in the USA
Coppell, TX
23 July 2024

35109006R00157